Hi K

Thanks very much for showing an interest in my book. I hope you gain some value from reading it.

All my best,
Fred

For my wife Carol, whose love has provided meaning and a foundation upon which to build a life during our many years together.

I would also like to thank my editor, Kate Quimby. I did not believe this book needed more than a quick brush-up. She showed me I was wrong and her insights have taught me valuable lessons.

Chapter 1

Jen liked to have a good time, too, when the gang came over. But there was always so much work to do. Sure, Mike would make his meatloaf sometimes which was a big help, but then he'd be off talking, drinking, and carrying on. He had no idea of the effort involved in throwing one of these parties. It seemed that no one did.

The London Broil was almost done and Mike was in the kitchen sharpening a knife. The sharpening utensil consisted of two small grinding wheels secured to a metal base that nearly touched when set in motion. One hand held the utensil's handle, that jutted out at about 45 degrees, while the other pressed the knife between the metal cylinders and drew it through with a strong, quick, steady motion several times. Too much pressure and the knife would get stuck in the rotating spheres, too little and it would not bite, would not get any sharper.

Jen liked to hear the grinding noise of the knives being sharpened, that accompanied most large meals like this, but she wasn't sure why. Maybe it gave her the feeling that things were being taken care of. But no, more likely it suggested the meal would soon be served and she could soon get off her feet and enjoy herself for a while.

They really did not need a reason for getting together but usually found one: a card game, the running of the Kentucky Derby or, as now, a football game featuring the hometown team, New York Giants. The common space of Jen and Mike's house was laid out in a straight line, with small archways separating kitchen, dining room and living room. Somehow they found a way to squeeze in whoever needed to be squeezed in, and no one ever complained of being cramped. In fact, within these rooms, in these days, was felt a general sense of abundance.

Jen busied herself with clearing a space on a counter top for Mike while her older sister, Rose, scoured the cabinets looking for serving bowls for the dishes that were nearly ready. Rose knew the whereabouts of just about everything in Jen's kitchen and the reverse of this was equally true. Both households threw their share of parties with maybe a few more occurring at Jen's house. She'd like to not have to do the work but the food prepared in other houses just didn't taste the same. The key to a successful meal was having all the dishes be ready at the same time, next to that little else mattered. Rose particularly lacked the skill to accomplish this and preferred to not have this responsibility anyway.

At about this time Rose began another task, that of marshaling the kids together to set the table. This was something that invariably expended more energy than it saved, but was persevered through none the less.

"Right in the middle of the exam Dr. Holmes starts talking to me about the high cost of taking care of his big, expensive home and cars. Can you imagine?...The nerve of him!"

Tim, Jen's son, knew this type of nerve was always a bad thing. But many times, such as this one, he was unsure why that was the case. Tim, was getting the knives out of the drawer and listening to his mother's and aunt's conversation about his mother's recent doctor's visit. He finished counting the knives and started towards the dining room table. Before leaving the kitchen, he looked back at his mother and saw her face still reflecting the anger she felt. He had seen this emotion before and was always surprised when it rose up so suddenly. What horrible thing had the doctor done, he wondered, as he walked into the dining room.

Tim had been called from the living room along with Rose's son Don to help set the table. They had been watching the football game with the adults who were not engaged in the food preparations. Dinner was always served during half time and as the minutes and seconds ticked down to that eventuality, their thoughts could not deflect the anticipated call to help in the kitchen. They tried every act of invisibility and stillness they could conceive of but the inevitable call from Rose occurred as surely as the hand movements of any mechanical time piece. They used the old, "there's only two minutes left" stall tactic, but even Ruth, who knew least about the intricacies of football time management, understood the actual duration of the last two minutes of a half of a football game could be exceedingly longer.

Both boys were 11 years old but Don was almost a full year older and a grade ahead of Tim. They were close, practically like brothers, but different in fundamental ways. Tim thought about this as he counted out the knives while Don remained unmoved in front of the TV, determined to have his way.

His younger sister Anne and Don's sister Sara had been upstairs playing with their dolls but were now joined into the task of setting the table. The girls were also a year apart in age and Sara was a year younger than Tim. Anne was placing the forks down on the table and Sara was following up with the spoons. Don, who had been prodded sufficiently and had joined them in the dining room, was supposed to place the plates in the middle of the silverware but Tim was pretty sure he would not do so. And right as the last spoon was put in place, Don went tearing around the table messing up the things they had just placed down on it. He kept right on going without looking back, running up the stairs to barricade himself in one of the rooms up there.

Tim and Sara remained motionless as they took stock of the damage. The simple tasks binding them together had been torn apart, making them infinitely more complex. As they contemplated whether to redo their work, demand reparation from Don, or expose his misdeeds to the elders and violate some tenet of childhood illogic, these considerations were made moot by Anne's actions. Anne ran into the kitchen and declared to anyone in ear shot the injustice that had just befallen them. At some point Don would exact a price from Anne for this action, and Tim and Sara looked at each other now, knowing this would be the case, knowing they would allow this to happen, knowing their inaction when it occurred would amount to an affirmation of Don's right to do so.

Mike had started his work on the meat. He was several drinks into a solid buzz and the mood the booze would put him in was usually a coin toss. Right now things were not going well for him in the kitchen. The big problem was that the meat, itself, was proving less than agreeable as he carved it, and he was also unhappy because Jen had overcooked it.

"Donald just messed up everything on the table after we had set it. He's always doing stuff like this," Anne shrieked.

Mike threw down the carving knife and fork. "Why don't you cuff that kid across the back of the head a few times. Maybe it would knock a little sense into him."

"Oh Mike," came the chorus from both women; for Rose, because she wished it was only that simple and for Jen because she wanted Mike to mind his business.

Rose put down the dish rag she'd been using and walked to the stairs leading to the 2nd floor of the house. She was a large woman, but moved effortlessly, powered by an energy that was uniquely her own and apparent almost immediately to anyone with whom she came in contact. Don had been her challenge almost from the time he was born. He was never one for being touched and would rather argue than listen, and do the contrary of what he was told to do. She had mounted these steps before and even her calm, which was considerable, was broken by not knowing how this would play out.

These seemingly random acts of bad behavior were an all too frequent occurrence. Dr. Holmes tried to provide guidance as did family members like Mike, whose words banged around in her head. Most of the advice had been tried, to varying degrees, and the results of these attempts could only be described as failures. The engine that pumped in young Don's body ran its own course and even though her family blamed her and her husband Ben, she knew that nature was at the controls in Don and her job more than anything was to love him, even more than discipline him.

She found the door to the bathroom closed and then determined it was locked. She instinctively slid her hand across the top ledge of the door frame and found the small screw driver she thought might be there.

"Donny, are you in there?"

There was silence for a short span and then he admitted he was. Don's legs, the floor and the door drew a triangle, as the rest of his body pressed against the door. *Why not do what he had done? Why do what he was told?* were his thoughts if he could be focused enough to define them.

"Why did you mess up the table, Donny?"

There was another pause before he responded and then he said, "I told you I did not want to put out the plates." Rose had not heard Don say this and was certain he had not. But to engage this comment was to get mired down in a "did, too", "did not" controversy in which Don was well adept and was pointless anyway.

"You know that things need to get done and that we expect you to help out. Now you've made a mess downstairs and someone needs to clean it up."

"Aunt Jen can do it in a second."

"But she should not have to." And then after a pause Rose continued, "Do you remember when we baked the cake last week. You liked working in the kitchen with me. You sifted the flour, and lots of it flew around the counter. You helped clean it up and were a big help then."

He thought about baking the cake, his mother's arms around him as they sifted the flour together, and her trying, at first anyway, to control the motions so the flour poured through the sifter as it was supposed to. The smell of his mother and the sweet cake baking also returned and merged with these other memories, and he felt his body relax.

They were now both leaning against the door but in a way totally differently than just moments before. There would be more to say later, but they would get through this incident and, for a while anyway, hope would exist that incidents of this kind would not need to happen again.

As Rose was leaving the kitchen to find Don, Frank was making his way in. His glass was nearly empty, which was what had roused him from his chair. Frank was Jen's older brother and his wife's name was Jessie. Jen had always admired Frank for his job at the bank, and his conservative ways. Jessie was sweet and quiet although a little removed, Jen thought. Why they never had kids of their own was a question no one ever asked but once. In jest, someone from outside the family asked what they were waiting for and Frank turned away with a cloud of sorrow covering his face.

Frank had internalized his role of eldest sibling and assumed the patriarchal role that age had bestowed upon him. Although he was only 47, having been born in 1911, his actions and thought process had slowed to a rate that others might associate with the onset of dementia. The waiting for his pronouncements invariably disappointed, or so Mike thought. Unfortunately for Mike, he stood alone in this regard. The worst of all his theories, nay certainties, had to do with how to raise perfect children and pets; as one might expect, he had not lived with a pet since his teenage years. Regardless, the rest of the family listened dutifully, never questioning a single pronouncement.

Mike drank a lot without needing a reason. But long harangues from Frank led him on to greater drunks, ones that he had little trouble justifying to himself.

"What's got you all hepped up, Mike?" Frank asked and surveyed the scene. He'd heard the knife and fork slam against the plate and now saw Mike cleaning up the small mess he'd made. This made Frank grin from ear to ear and emit short laughing noises like what you might hear a donkey make. He had seen it all before: Mike losing his cool usually over something of no consequence. Whatever mental acuity Frank possessed was drawn out in his attempts to raise the heat of Mike's anger.

"Donald's gone and messed up the dining room table, after the other kids had set it." Mike explained. He hadn't minded making his little scene in front of Rose and Jen, but would have held back a little had he known Frank was on his way into the kitchen. He'd learned to tread cautiously when Frank was in close proximity.

But this was a topic that they basically agreed upon, and Mike knew this. They were certain that Don's acting up was something neither of them would have tolerated. As with his own children, Mike would have "cut Don off at the ankles" if he'd tried any of his shenanigans with him. And Frank lived in the blissful certainty that his children, had he had any, would never behave in any but the controlled, conservative manner perfected by their parents. If his heirs would falter, simple reminders from him of their place in the world would reattach them to the truth that he embodied, and that defied analysis. Analysis of any kind actually exhibited bad taste and was discouraged in a quiet, vehement sort of way. If you were of white, working class American stock you should understand this lifestyle intuitively; and if you were not, it did not matter.

The London Broil Mike was trying to coax dinner out of continued to prove itself to be of the non-agreeable variety. He was always willing to argue with anyone that the taste of a London Broil was as good as or better than a cut of meat two or three times its cost. The trick was the way you cut this type of meat, which needed to be against the grain. Only then would you avoid the stringiness for which it was notorious. But sometimes, as with this piece, the grain would start in one direction and then shift wildly, reminding one of a house frame caved in on itself, the wooden supports going this way for a while and then reversing their course or finding another all together different path. There was nothing left to do at this point but to follow the grain and separate, by cutting from the whole, each individual portion that leaned in the same direction.

Mike slapped the big piece of meat this way and that, searching out its logic. Amid false starts and reversals, Mike labored through this task, aware that there were few things in life that focused him so completely as this. But the alcohol conspired against him, complicating his task of unraveling this confused bovine.

"What in God's name are you doing?" Frank finally asked with incredulity.

"The grain's all messed up. You need to cut against it but its all over the place in this meat." Mike pointed to a few different areas containing the criss-crossing pattern with the tip of his knife, assuming the role of teacher, still committed to the task.

"You still trying to push that blarney on us? Why don't you just spend the few extra dollars and let us eat something that won't make our jaws ache?" Frank said and resumed the grinning and jackass guffawing. He took a long draw from his cigar and emitted the smoke into the small kitchen, setting up storm clouds above the counter where Mike was sweating over his work.

Mike reconnoitered. Again, he had allowed himself to be taken off-guard against this on-again, off-again foe. Oh, he was just kidding... No, he was not. Yes, he was. *NO, HE WASN'T!!!*

"How many times do I need to make this for you before you admit that this is as good as a New York sirloin or strip steak."

"Do you hear this Jennif?" Frank called out to his sister, using the name only her brothers called her, usually when invoking a conspiratorial, sibling attitude. And then loud enough so that his words echoed through the hallways and into the adjoining rooms for everyone to hear, "Mike thinks that London Broil is as good as strip steaks or a good sirloin." The enormity of this blunder was staggering to all in ear shot. Peals of laughter rang through the house. Even Mike felt like he'd blasphemed, which was followed by a sense that he'd been rocked by several short, crisp body blows.

The world around him seemed to conspire against him in ways such as this. A slight, usually innocent comment went across the bow and the return volley came back at him as if from Captain Black himself. And the storm of cannon balls continued until the ship has been boarded, all the men killed and the women abused.

Mike returned to his work, slapping and turning the meat,

immersing himself deep and deeper.

Rose returned downstairs with Don and saw that the mess on the table had been cleaned. She tried to make eye contact with her sister Jennifer, to thank her, but Jen whisked past her and pretended to have moved on to the next set of preparations for dinner. There had been a time when they could discuss matters like this, but those days seemed to be gone, maybe forever.

Even though Rose was four years older than Jen, placing her midway between the ages of Jen and Frank, they had begun having children at about the same time due to Rose's difficulty getting pregnant. Rose was not aware of an unusual amount of competition between them but it was at this time that their distance became more evident. Having life growing inside her affected her in ways she was not expecting, nor prepared for. At first she tried to describe the experience to Jen but she could tell that Jen had no better idea of what she was trying to express than the men in her life had. And this increased their distance from one another that continued even after Jen had her children. The miracle of this life growing totally a part of you and also complete unto itself was something she found wondrous and unavoidably life-changing. But when she looked at Jen, she saw someone who continued through her daily routine as if the children represented just another set of tasks that needed to be attended to between the family functions and get-togethers with friends.

That was the problem. Rose saw herself growing in what seemed important ways and nobody else was growing in any way. No one from her set ever changed. It was as if they swore an oath not to. And when Donald acted up she knew about all the looks that passed between her family members, as if she should have a switch to turn on and off to correct him; not realizing, in any way, that whatever was stirring inside Donald was almost completely his own and what he would carry within him and hopefully learn to love some day. Unless it was crushed, causing spirit to bleed out of him like what she feared was happening to Jen's kids when they misbehaved, in the way that kids do.

The table was nearly set and people were starting to move about in preparation. Mike extracted himself incrementally from his detached state and became horrified with what his conscious mind brought forth. The meat had taken him deeper in than any he had ever encountered. At every slice the grain detoured wildly, and he followed with abandon. But now, as he returned from this challenge, he saw strewn about the cutting board little shards of meat, almost like splinters whittled down from a block of wood. At that moment Frank returned to the kitchen again and gazed intently over Mike's shoulder, silent, at least for now.

Seated, they began passing the food. Jen sat in the seat closest to the kitchen doorway and Mike at the head of the table next to her. The four kids crowded around the other end of the table. Rose and Ben sat closest to them while Frank and Jessie stayed most removed from the children. The remaining seats were taken by Jen's younger brother Dan, the "baby" of the family, and his wife Kelly. They'd been going out for years and finally tied the knot. Still no kids, but Jen hoped that when they had some they'd have more in common, more to talk about, than they seemed to have now.

The plates of food were passed. Attention narrowed to the task at hand and for some it was a time for gentle musings of things not entirely of the moment. Rose gave voice to one of these thoughts, saying, "I read an article about Gandhi's life and I just keep thinking about the people there and what life must be like in India. He seems to have been a great leader and the people did love him even though he was killed by one of his own. I'd love to visit there some day." There was a look of calm on her face, as she recalled the brightly colored sarongs the women were wearing in the pictures she had seen.

The few large pieces of meat were whisked away quickly. Mike made sure that he got some of these, and maneuvered some of them onto Frank's plate as well. The meat plate now was in Ben's hands and Mike saw him tipping it to one side and using his fork to gently roll the meat onto his plate. Ben could be counted on to keep his thoughts to himself and his mouth shut. He was quieter than the rest and that put some people off. But once he got a few drinks in him he loosened up and could be counted on for a good time.

Frank did not take kindly to this talk of India and Gandhi. What did he think he was doing, wearing those silly clothes and not eating all the time. It didn't prove anything. "Why would you want to leave our country, anyway?" The war had been over for 13 years, and now the thought of leaving this country voluntarily seemed almost un-American to him. "That place is nothing but filth and war."

The meat plate made its way to Jen and she was appalled at what she saw. She had been so caught up in the other preparations that she was not aware of the condition of the meat. All she wanted was to sit down, have a couple of drinks, a nice meal and some fun. She deserved it with all she'd done and been through. But now she felt humiliated. What others were merely thinking she gave voice to.

"You expect me to eat this? Why, I wouldn't even make a stew with this meat. And here we are serving it to our guests, our family. It's not like we're poor, compared to lots of people. At least we can afford to feed our company properly."

"It's not that bad and the flavor's good," Mike responded.

Sure, he'd wanted to save a buck or two but he didn't realize what all he had invested in this cut of meat. It was a way for him to show them a thing or two, that he was smarter than them in some way. But now he was deflated, his argument destroyed. He tried to place a couple of complete slices of meat from his plate onto Jen's but this infuriated her even more and she met his hands in mid air and forced them back to his plate.

There was plenty of food, most of it very good and unadorned. The adults needed a break from all the disturbance and took the occasion to recharge their bodies and ward off the numbing effects of the alcohol. Even the children seemed content to fill their bellies quietly.

They were all piled into the small dining room while the football game remained on the TV in the adjoining living room. Occasionally the roar of the fans coaxed one or more of the men from their seats and they would report back on what they surmised. In these days that pre-dated "instant replay" you had one shot, and one shot only, to catch the action.

The New York Giants were dominating their opponents. They only led by a score of 10 - 0 but these were the days of a slower, hard-nosed style of play and 10 points could represent an unvanquishable challenge in this type of game.

The roar came up again and Dan, who was already standing in front of the TV, was able to provide a first hand account of the action.

"Huff did it again. He stuffed them right at the line of scrimmage on a 3rd and 1." Sam Huff was the middle linebacker, the brace of the defense and its captain. Even though they were too late to see the play, all the men left their seats and offered some type of congratulation to one another as the teams on the field huddled in preparation for the next play.

Jen enjoyed football almost as much as the men and thought of joining them but held back from doing so. Sam Huff was one of her favorite players as well. She had been heard remarking on his sheer power as he seemed to absorb the charge of a whole row of men and turn them back on themselves single-handedly.

Usually Rose would have been stifled by Frank's comments. Being the oldest fit him perfectly. For as long as she could remember, his demeanor was exactly as it was now. She thought again about the time she let it be known that she was thinking of trying out for the leading role in the High School musical, years ago. This was different than anything any family member had ever considered. Frank, when he heard this, flinched at the news,

"Why are you doing that? Maureen always gets those parts because she's the best singer in your grade."

Rose, at the time, became confused. "That wasn't true, was it?" she wondered to herself. And how could Frank, who was out of high school and seemed to have no interest in these things, have an opinion on this? How did he know about Maureen, a girl who did not even live in their neighborhood? There was no sense of "give it a try", "nothing wagered, nothing lost", no conception of how a person could gain from trying to do something special, win or lose. Rose was too unformed to struggle against her brother and simply never went to the audition. She shut her mind off from this possibility and sensed that Frank was glad not to have to endure the attention and embarrassment he thought might come. She reflected now on the pain of her disappointment and the rawness of it she felt, even now.

"How can you say that, Frank? All Gandhi wanted to do was to bring peace and justice to his people and make sure they were properly fed."

Frank, who assuredly had never held a conversation, or a

thought, on the topic of any part of Indian culture nonetheless had no problem providing final dispensation regarding it. More than anything he was annoyed and a little shocked, as were the others at the table, that this topic was being discussed and wanted to put an end to it.

"What do you know about it, Rose? They don't live or think like we do and would kill you or me if we were walking on the same street as them. They're not Christians or speak English. I don't know why you even care about them."

The ethical response to these questions was uncharted ground for Rose and words failed her. But what she felt was, *How do you give voice to longing?* Finally she said, "There is a peace that I sense in him and the people there, that's all. I don't know about the violence you speak of. It's hard to make sense of it if it's true... But it just seems that we have so much and they have so little. And that we could help them," her words trailing off with uncertainty.

"I've worked hard for everything I have and see no reason to give anything away. Let them figure out how to make their world work. WE did! You know what I say, 'Let the Blue Jays fly with the Blue Jays.' "

His words had the desired effect. Rose was stifled, quieted. Maybe he was right, she thought. But how could he be?

Soon the talk settled back to the game and Sam Huff's exploits.

Rose looked over at one corner of the dining room where a light was sitting on a small table creating a separate, warmly lit area. She remarked to the ladies, "I've been trying to get Bennie to put one of those outlets in so we didn't always have to use the overhead."

Mike, at the other end of the table, heard the comment and replied, "You know that's a lot of work."

"Come on, Mike. That should be an easy change to make." Rose said lightly, half mockingly.

"How do you figure? You have to run some wire and fish it down through the wall to where you want the outlet to be. You may even have to run it back to the box if there is no line to connect up with."

Rose was looking perplexed now and proceeded cautiously. "But all I'm asking for is to be able to put a light in the corner of the room. So all you need is to screw one of those little plastic outlets into the wall."

Mike looked confused for a short while until the light went on in his own head, and then he smiled. "So you think that just because the wall plate is there, you should be able to plug a light into it."

"I thought so," Rose responded sheepishly.

The attention of the whole table had been drawn into this conversation and now the men laughed heartily at the idea that Rose was proposing.

"Did you think the whole wall was wired somehow?"

"I guess I did, or maybe I never thought about it that much."

The room erupted. Everyone, including Rose, was able to share in what even she realized now was an utter impossibility, even if the actual process itself still escaped her. The men felt a sense of superiority, but not in an obscene, overbearing way.

The remains of the meal sat on the table untouched. The glasses, mostly emptied, were raised less frequently.

Dan, ever the showman, began what all looked forward to: the singing, started this time with a chorus of "I've Got a Crush on You". He stood up and tapped the first few beats with slight head and body bobs and then intoned the opening melody. This was quickly picked up by the rest of the group sitting around the table.

The dishes would remain on the table, the drinks would be refilled only occasionally from this point forward. They would be like this for a long time, beyond the football game, and for years collectively in memory singing song after innumerable song.

It was not long before Donny nestled up next to Rose. This was the refuge that the children sought as well, more than the adults had any sense of. He would stay this way a long time, his mind receptive to the call of the music, the fleeting smiles passing between the adults that united past, present and future. Quietly, quietly, he descended into the world defined by the adults; there was no wisdom beyond this wisdom, no feelings deeper than these feelings.

One song followed another, with the better voices taking the lead for the most part. But everyone had their favorite and was given the chance to start and have the others follow through the melodies that were known so well to all.

Chapter 2

The morning after the party at Jen and Mike's house Frank woke at 6:10 AM, the same as always. He remained lying down, looking out the window for 10 minutes after the initial ringing of the alarm. He had a clear view of the sun as it passed completely behind a thick mound of clouds. There were no electric lights on in the room but he noticed the light within the room did not lessen when the sun became obscured.

Jessie was already up. Having finished her shower he could hear her moving about the bathroom, drying herself. When she was done, he would follow her into the bathroom and from there to the other stations of their morning routine. Hearing her movements for some reason caused his thoughts to drift to the meeting in the doctor's office many years before when he and Jessie were given the news they had expected: that Jessie would not be able to bear children, that she was barren, as the doctor had stated it. A strange sensation took hold of him then; he became disembodied, watching himself and the others in the room from a corner of the doctor's office, high up. It was the first time anything like this ever happened to him, but it did not startle him and, in fact, felt quite natural.

"Are you alright?" Jesse had asked him in the office, even as she tried to manage her own shattering emotions.

"Yeah, sure, I'm fine," he said and, in fact, he was. His immediate concern was wondering when he would again be looking through only one set of eyes, living and sensing the world from a single elevation. "I am tired though," he told her. And she agreed, saying that she was too. They left when their few remaining questions were answered. But his world was never the same after that day and, in fact, he grew fond of the second perspective that he used to shield himself from the immediacy and unpleasantness that characterized much of his interaction with others.

The drinking the night before made it difficult to raise himself from the bed but he willed himself to do so, forcing one leg to follow another until they stopped at the threshold of the doorway to the bathroom. Here he met Jessie, whose hair was now turbaned in a towel and whose body was covered in a heavy terry cloth robe. She was a good looking woman and the steam emitting from the bathroom moistened their lips as he gave her the customary kiss that marked this passage, this daily ritual.

The shower water warmed him as thoughts of the upcoming work day encroached upon him. Frank worked in a bank in the financial area of Manhattan. This was a job he applied for after the war ended and had not moved from since. Others had come and gone but he felt content to do what he'd always done, which was work at the window, fulfilling customer transactions half the day, and then balancing ledgers the second half.

Frank liked the regularity of this work. He enjoyed dressing in his suit every day and the orderliness of his work space. He tried to get along with his coworkers, although generally he chose to not socialize with them. There were always one or two problems in the office and right now that came in the form of the other head clerk, whose name was Myrtle.

From the moment he laid eyes on Myrtle he did not like her and things only got worse from there. Within a month of her moving over into his department, she was trying to change all the procedures that he had carefully assembled. Everything about her bundle of energy annoyed him. He had argued against her coming in the first place because he alone had always been in charge of the bookkeeping. But the boss, Walter Jones, said the workload had grown and they had no other choice but to make this change. In the past when the work increased they had hired another junior clerk and he wondered why they had not done that this time as well.

"Just can't leave well-enough alone," he would often mutter to himself. He had no grand illusions about himself, his role, his options, his potential. All he asked was to be able to do the things he did the way he had always done them.

One morning a few weeks ago she appeared standing next to him. Her hair was pulled back and parted perfectly down the middle, as always. She was as sprightly and cheerful as ever and then she handed him a manual. The first page contained the title, "Suggestions for Improving the Financial Month End Close Process".

Myrtle explained, "I've been thinking about how we can process the books faster and came up with these ideas. I thought we could improve the way we gather expenses from the departments downstairs and also improve the way we allocate them, so I wrote my thoughts down and here they are." She couldn't contain her pride and was even beaming a little. " I'd like to show them to Walt but thought maybe you could look them over first."

His head barely moved but his eyes raised up above his bifocals to meet her gaze.

It would have been much more difficult to maintain his composure if he was not instantly viewing this hostile act alternately from his seat and from an elevated spot in the corner of the room. He saw the faint head turns and tightened neck muscles of the other co-workers in the room without having to turn his gaze on them. They would have much to say to each other and the wordless conversations occurring on this topic at this moment were almost deafening for him. "Sure" he said, and pointed to an empty spot on the side of his desk.

As far as he was concerned, this confirmed his suspicions. She was another one who thought she was so high and mighty, a climber whose ambitions would ultimately conspire to make his life miserable. He vowed to have as little to with her as possible and took pride in his remarkable ability to create absences in his field of vision. He would set himself to this, and because he sat directly across from her the ability to see this through would require the full force of his conviction.

The manual sat there and he ignored it, as he did her. Slowly Myrtle came to understand what was happening and instead of folding her cards as Frank hoped would happen, she chose to meet what had become Frank's a priori mission with similar, but opposing determination. Neither spoke nor acknowledged the other; it was amazing how they could function in the office, and at the same time be no more than apparitions to the other.

On this morning he was scheduled to meet with Walt, his boss, and Myrtle to go over Myrtle's ideas, which Myrtle had seen fit to bring directly to Walt's attention. The whole office would be brimming with expectation. The battle was at hand.

His pants were laid out for him on the bed as was his shirt, which had been stiffly starched. He ran his fingers over the shirt and gained a measure of comfort from the sensation.

Jessie got the paper off the front steps along with the milk that had been delivered that morning. She brought them both to the kitchen and placed the paper beside Frank's knife and spoon. The cream from the milk had separated and condensed at the top of the bottle. Instead of shaking the bottle to dissolve it, she reached in and gathered the top layer onto her index finger and brought it to her mouth. The rich taste filled her with its freshness. Not a heavy woman, she felt her sides and sensed her weight. Staring out the kitchen window she wondered at what might have been, and felt a sadness that was all too familiar, but one that she had long since stopped trying to describe to anyone.

He sat and she served him. This morning she made the usual breakfast of two eggs and toast, a glass of orange juice, milk and coffee. All of these were arranged around him along with the paper which laid unopened. He proceeded to read the newspaper, the Daily News, carefully, slowly. He would read the global and national news now but save the local news, sports, and editorials for the train into work. The unknown, the random agent, was the center page that folded open and contained mostly pictures with captions that spanned the two pages. This was the paper's most lurid part, containing graphic images of crimes and accidents. Sometimes there were suggestive pictures of women, both celebrity and ordinary. He could never control whether this would be breakfast reading or train reading, and he could not even anticipate when he would first turn to this page; this bothered and perplexed him.

No matter how he tried, he could not purge Rose's comments the night before from his thoughts. The fact that it was his own sister who was spouting off about things so foreign to their lives left him with an unimaginably strong feeling of betrayal. And the fact that he could not expel these memories and the feelings associated with them left him with a sense that he had been trespassed upon.

"That Rose sure thinks she knows it all," he said finally. He thought again about those little men with their dark skin in their turbaned outfits. "How could she think we have anything in common with them?"

After some moments Jessie replied, "She's probably just trying to find something to keep her mind off of that boy of her's."

"Maybe, but does she think that's what we were overseas fighting for?" His thoughts shifted to his years in Europe and the horrible things he had seen and taken part in. And after they had won and defeated that devil Hitler, he wanted to be left alone among his family and set of friends who were like him in every way: appearance, the things they enjoyed, lifestyle; and when confronted with variations from this, his intolerance grew in direct proportion to the degree of difference these things represented. That is, if he were ever forced to think of these others at all, which he resisted with all the force he could gather; as he resisted now being forced to consider those dark men from the other side of the world.

As he left the house, which was one in a block of connected row houses, he descended the stairs at the same time his neighbor was departing her home. Her name was Mimi Fleischman and she had come from Europe after the war. She had numbers tattooed on her arm and he knew what their significance was, had seen them on the hands and wrists of the wraiths set free from the camps at the end of the war. They had lived side by side for many years with little more than pleasantries passed between them. She had few visitors but Frank sensed she could be a talker if given the chance; it was something in her eyes that gave him this impression, something like laughter in them as they danced lightly over the images before her.

"Pleasant day," Mimi said to her neighbor.

"Yes, isn't it," he responded demurely, lowering his gaze and moving off at a quickened pace to the train that would transport him to the bank where he would spend his day. But he was also flying above himself, deflecting in every way possible the world and its contagions from contacting him.

Chapter 3

Mike sat in his seat next to the fan that filled the only window in the kitchen and which protruded several inches into the room. Normally the fan would have been removed months before but this year Mike simply closed shut the window behind the fan. It had remained there through fall and into the first days of winter and now wouldn't be moved at least until the end of next summer, at which time he would have another opportunity to remove it. He sat there nursing a beer, trying not to think about the fan that was only inches from his head and instead enjoy this time, his last day off work before starting a week of 4 to 12's as a policeman for the New York City Police Department.

Jen was peeling the potatoes. The long strands of the cuttings fell onto old newspapers that were laid out on the counter. When she was done she would roll the paper up into a semi-tight bundle and deposit it in the paper bag inside the garbage can.

The kitchen was serviceable and only felt cramped when it was time to sit down to eat, at which time they moved the table into the center of the narrow room to allow Anne to slide into the seat at the back side of the table. Then, if someone needed to get from one side of the room to the other, chairs would be moved this way and that to allow this passage to occur. There was a no nonsense quality to the table with its metal legs, a wide, corrugated chrome apron running around it and a formica top that contained a random, densely packed pattern of various shades of black, gray and white. The chairs were clunky-heavy too and had rubberized seat cushions that were tightly bound to the frame. This set was designed to withstand all that a family of 4 could throw at it and still provide service long after the children had set off on their own. The only decoration in the room was a single wooden plate with a simple pastoral setting and high gloss finish. It was attached to the wall above where Anne sat and just above her head the words, "God Bless This Home," were printed like a bead around the lower half of the plate.

Mike sat there in one of his threadbare undershirts. The frayed material gave way beneath his under arms first, and flesh peaked out between the still existing strands of material. He was at home and saw no reason to dress differently if no one was visiting. He looked to his side at Jen and the high ball glass she was drinking from, to see if she was ready for a refill. This was the time of day he reasoned when they should be kicking back, enjoying their drinks and relaxing.

Jen looked at Mike and wondered at how the weight had overtaken him. Not that he was ever slim but at least when he was younger, before the war, he was active and that kept his weight from getting out of control. But even now he was still powerful and quick when he needed to be, qualities she admired in him and hoped he would never lose altogether.

"Why don't you wear something decent? You have plenty of nice shirts you could be wearing," She asked without looking at him, keeping her attention on the potatoes she was preparing.

"You know why. What difference does it make? If we were going somewhere I wouldn't dress like this. But it's just us so why should I bother?" He took a long drink from his beer. This was a familiar topic but even after all the battles fought over it, it was hard to know if either of them was aware of what the other was saying when they argued about it.

She thought of slender, muscular William Holden, the actor she most admired, standing in his swimming trunks in the movie Sunset Boulevard, Gloria Swanson spreading oil on his back and shoulders.

"You look like hell, that's why."

" I look comfortable, and that's how I feel," he responded. But he really hadn't been comfortable, hardly ever was. He looked to the booze and the tiff that was starting between them to warm him, to allow him to feel his blood surge within his body.

"Being comfortable and looking like a slob are two different things. But you wouldn't know that because you're usually half in the bag."

"Whether I'm straight or feeling good, I always dress the same."

"That's the truth, I have to admit it. But isn't that a shame?"

"Why should I dress up? Why should I do anything other than what I damn well feel like doing when I'm in my own damn house?"

"That's what you're always say, 'Your damn this, your damn that'. Did it ever occur to you that you're not the only one living in this damn house?"

He looked around him. There wasn't much, but everything he saw was paid for with his paycheck. He provided, put food on the table, had recently bought Jen a new vacuum cleaner. And this did not come easy - working double shifts when he could and a second job painting houses. What else did she want? And when he asked himself the same question, the answer his mind returned wordlessly and vaguely was, "to relax, to feel good". But these were only words and he was suspicious of them and the feelings behind them, wondering if what he knew was what they were. So he kept these thoughts to himself and returned to what he knew would approximate the satisfaction of these needs, which was to have a drink close at hand and entrust his well being to the effect the alcohol had on his experience of the world. These effects could be a variety of things, all of which, when viewed together, were better than anything else that he could call upon.

They went about their business, an unspoken truce recognized between them. And then, not really meaning to start another round in the melee, he said, "Can you believe those kids? Just Don really. He's a bad one and deserves the back of his father's hand a few times. The way he was going, I thought he was going to turn the whole house upside down."

What drives a person to say one thing over another when there is no existing conversation to build upon, when the world of options is wide open? How we handle quiet, pauses from life's directed actions and distractions, expresses who we are better than almost anything else.

"She's doing the best she can." Jen said forcefully, expressing a sisterly affection that felt somewhat foreign to her.

"Those kids should be sat on and hog-tied. The way he tears through the house, you'd think there was something wrong with him." The last sentence was said without sincerity, a throw away thought that he did not believe deserved any consideration. "I'll tell you one thing, my kids would never act that way."

His kids were sitting in the living room, within ear shot of the conversation. They were used to hearing this, not necessarily the content which could proceed along a few preset pathways, but more importantly, the presentation and manner of discourse, which were part of the fabric of the pre-dinner, meal-making ritual. Sometimes they would listen carefully to the back-and-forth banter to see how far it would escalate. But more often these squabbles passed outside of their conscious realm, like other fixed points in the surroundings. If either of them displayed some reaction to their parents' behavior, it would usually be Anne. She could be seen directing her emotion outward, demanding attention, reassurance, and approval, sometimes foolishly and in a way that may leave her embarrassed, grasping. But regardless of her demonstrations, her demands would not be met. It was as if responding to her would be a sign of weakness and falseness for all those involved in the emotional exchange.

But this time it was Tim who listened to the argument. The subject of Don, a common one, inevitably drew him in. The boys were almost identical in body type and yet Tim felt enormously less capable, weaker when he compared himself to his cousin. He agreed with his father; he, Tim, would never do the things that Don would do. And these things were wrong, he knew that too. But he marveled at Don, wondering what it must feel like to whip through a room and upset everything in his path. It thrilled Tim to even think about it.

Tim thought about the encounter they all had a few days before, that centered around Don in the dining room. He again saw Don moving in a wild rampage and reliving these moments now left Tim shaking inside. Then he looked towards Anne, laying on her stomach watching TV. It was she who ratted Don out and caused him to battle and, as always, lose to the adults. And it was she who was responsible, too, for the argument his parents were having right now. He despised her at this moment but would hold that emotion in, which was a skill he was learning unconsciously.

"What do you mean you're thinking of going to the dance Friday night? You're working a 4 to 12 that night. How can you go to the dance if you're working a 4 to 12?" the conversation between Mike and Jen had shifted from Donald's escapades to something that Mike was hatching for himself.

"Maybe I'll be able to slip out for a few hours and meet you there," Mike answered. "It wouldn't be the first time," he added mischievously.

"You think you can just come and go like nobody's business, don't you." she exploded. The next time she referred to Mike's sense of daring it may be with an ambivalent smirk and shake of the head and a sense of bemusement. And then again, some other time, with conspiratorial glee. But not this time. This time her response was shot-through with righteous indignation.

"You know the squad car can make a few wrong turns, get lost for a few hours, and no one will be any the wiser," again, a little triumph showing in his voice.

"Frank said to me that you better mind your Ps and Qs or they'll be getting on to you. Then what'll you do? He said they could move you to another part of the city, or suspend you, even fire you from the squad."

"You don't know what you're talking about. And neither does your brother Frank."

"Listen to you, all big and mighty."

"Have I ever not brought home a paycheck?"

"Maybe not, but you've drunk enough of them away."

"You've got a roof over you head and food on the table. So what are you complaining about?"

Instead of answering the question, which she was incapable of doing because of the rage she felt, she remained silent. But her hands, scouring the pots with which she had used to make dinner, exploded in rapid fire movements. She wondered how much fury her mind and body could endure before she let loose what she was feeling. Jen was small in stature but would never be taken for weak, demure, even feminine. She was hot tempered and never stopped to ask herself where that side of her came from and was not even aware of how frequently she experienced the world through the prism of feelings that coalesced in this way.

Jen turned towards Mike who was looking away from her, flipping the hamburgers in the frying pan. She hooked 2 fingers within one of the holes of his undershirt and tore it clear across his body. She found another hole and did it again. The shirt was now formless shreds and his body sagged down around them.

Mike looked down, stunned by what he saw, as did Jen.

Their eyes locked on each other fiercely, as if they had never before advanced to this precipice. Then their expressions turned warm and they smiled broadly, sardonically, at each other. They laughed til they cried, and hugged each other as they had not hugged in a long, long time. And then they laughed some more.

Chapter 4

It was Friday, 7 PM, an hour before the dance was going to begin at the VFW Hall and Mike was sitting in the cruiser with his partner Mel. They were working the 4 to 12 shift. They'd work that for a month and then a month of 12 to 8's following a month of 8 to 4's just in time to start it over again. Working round the clock produced a fatigue you never got rid of but got used to, like what long-distance runners complain about.

"Come on. Let's go see Bert and Marie. They'll be good for a belt or two." Mike said, swinging the car into motion before Mel was able to answer.

Bert answered the door, "Well, well, well. Since when did two of New York's finest start making house calls?" He remained blocking the door, eyes set back in his head, face dead panned, feigning annoyance.

"Since when did we need an invitation from his highness, signor Umberto. We're getting a little dry and thought we'd see what you were up to," Mike said, reflecting Bert's mock annoyance back at him. "No need to be a gracious host. We'll just let ourselves in and make ourselves comfortable." And with this he grabbed hold of Bert's arm and gently brushed him aside, at which point Bert broke into a smile and welcomed his guests.

Bert would always let them in but wondered what might be in store each time one of the gang came calling unexpectedly, especially Mike. He tried to keep the upper hand, with his cool reserve, but then noticed that they were in his living room while he was still standing in the doorway. "You expect me to feed you and give you drink while the scoundrels prowl the streets?"

"Certainly not. Just need some fortification before venturing out again to keep the streets safe from the criminal element."

Bert left Mike and Mel standing in the living room while he went to the kitchen.

The house inside was immaculate. Greco-Roman statues and pictures of Venice were on display throughout the living room. Not a place to feel comfortable in, in Mike's opinion, until you got a little tight and then it didn't matter.

"Well, look what trouble you've let blow in." Marie said, swooping down from the bedroom upstairs. She had not lived in Alabama since she was six or seven but the South had left its mark. Her voice contained a song-like quality which matched her mischievous nature. She was Italian, and dark skinned. But her personality allowed her entry into areas she might not have had access to during her early teen years that occurred during The Depression. And now, even after the war, it was likely Bert and Marie would not be in the same crowd with Mike and Jen if Marie and Jen had not cemented their friendship during the early years of their lives.

"You going to be able to make it to the dance, Mike?" Marie asked, knowing Mike was working but also knowing he was capable of showing up in a lot of places he wasn't supposed to be.

"We'll see. Not sure if I'll be able to swing it tonight. They're actually expecting us to work a full shift these days, the bastards." He said, while settling into his first rye and ginger.

"Well it won't be as exciting as the last one. " Marie said. She was referring to the costume party this past Halloween. "Did Mike tell you about that crazy affair, Mel?

Mel was also making his way through his drink and had been sitting quietly, listening to the conversation but choosing not to enter into the fray. He had been Mike's partner for about two years and was known to the group as a regular guy, even if he was a Jew. There weren't many Jews on the force that they knew of, not regular cops anyway.

"No, I don't think I heard that one. Although it's hard to keep them all straight. Mike did tell me about how he just put the cinnamon in the meatloaf instead of paprika, which ruined his run of perfect meatloaves."

They downed their first drinks and advanced onward.

"Well you never saw anything like it, Mel. The party was at the VFW for Halloween. Some of Mike's buddies from the war were there. Mike, tell Mel about Mr. Fat Ass."

Mike was watching, waiting, expecting the conversation to come around this way. He didn't mind. His drink was having the desired effect and he enjoyed telling this story and delivering the punch line. He'd told it plenty of times and always got big laughs.

"You remember that I got a battlefield commission, Mel, right? Well I've always been a big man, heavier in some parts than I probably should be. So I picked up a nickname in the army which wasn't very complimentary: Fat Ass."

"That makes sense," Mel said. "There's nothing small about your ass, especially now that you're sitting on it all the time."

Mike was unfazed by Mel's comments and continued telling the story. "So the day after I got my stripes I march the guys out in a line. You know how it is when someone from the ranks moves up and is all high and mighty. So I get them in a line and walk up and down and look them up and down. And I bark out at them,' I know and you know that among most of you I have developed a certain uncomplimentary nickname.' And I pause letting it sink in."

Bert and Marie are leaning over onto the bar, close, barely

touching, sipping their drinks, laughing quietly, emitting almost a purring sound.

Mike narrowed in, "You know," he motioned to Mel. "The guys aren't sure what to make of me. I'm trying to look like every jackass sergeant we've all seen walk the line hundreds of times. Then I turned to the guys and said, 'Well, we'll have no more insubordination of that kind. From now on it will be Fat Ass, Sir!"

"Most of the guys got it right away but some did not let go until I busted a gut." Even after the umpteenth time, for all but Mel, they laughed so hard they almost wet themselves.

Now cruising through the 2nd drink the party is underway, and Marie picks up the story.

"So for the Halloween party Mike gets some oversized pants and fills it up with paper in the middle. He gets a tee shirt and writes on it 'Sir Fat Ass'. The guys he served with, all of them, one by one come up to him. Some wrap their arms around him, some fall down laughing.

"Near the end of the party somehow the underpants are on the outside of the pants and the paper is gone. Jen's slipped herself through one leg of the underpants and Mike is in the other. They're pulling in opposite directions and twirling each other around like whirling dervishes."

"Just another crazy night with the Eatons." It was the first words uttered by Bert during this retelling but he had enjoyed every bit of it.

"Oh, Mike. Look how late its gotten. You've gone and made us late for the dance."

Bert and Marie went upstairs to finished getting ready, leaving Mike and Mel alone with their thoughts. Mike was left remembering the war. Of course it was good to be back. It was all that everyone had wanted, dreamed about constantly. But dreams are funny things...

He ended the war a 2nd Lieutenant, in charge of feeding a battalion of men. They'd be up close to the front ranks, setting up and breaking down camp in a hurry. It was his job to get the guys fed, as well as was possible. He made friends with the locals moving through Normandy scouring the countryside for fresh vegetables, meat and eggs. He'd done his share of fighting too, which was how he got his first promotion. The next thing he knew they needed someone to keep the food lines flowing and he stepped into a position of responsibility he never thought would be his.

He'd never been much good at anything and had never really tried to be. No one from his poor, Irish neighborhood in Queens thought much beyond the next meal, or the other borders of their lives. But cook-up a batch of bacon and eggs for a bunch of guys who hadn't eaten anything but k-rations for a week and you knew you had accomplished something. You were a God to them whether they made a big flap about it or not. And nobody cared where you came from; what state or which side of the tracks.

The locals liked the big, smiling Yank who learned to turn a phase or two of the local dialects he traveled into. Along with the food was the large need for liquor, booze of any kind. Many, if not most of the guys, stayed loaded the majority of the time. The interminable waiting with the constant threat of air strikes, the enemy usually not far away, hunkered down the same as you were. All this punctuated by frequent periods of inhuman battle. What else could you do to not lose your mind but anesthetize yourself. So Mike would scour the towns to barter for barrels of wine and hard liquor.

He did his job efficiently and, without realizing it, professionally.

"So Mike, what do you think? Will I turn some heads tonight?" Marie said, letting the fox wrap fly from her uncovered shoulders as she spun herself around. The crepe dress held closely above her waist and flowed freely to just below her knees.

"I'll say you will," Mike answered appreciatively. Though the thought had not crossed his mind until this moment, she did look wonderful. "If I do get there tonight, make sure you save a dance for me."

Mike and Mel got up and the four prepared to leave. "We've still got a little time to kill. Why don't we drive over with you and we'll pop our heads in before heading off to work," Mike said.

"Sure, we can do that," Mel responded. So Bert and Marie entered their car while Mel and Mike got back into their police cruiser.

The cars moved onto the side street, one of the hundreds of streets that make up a grid that allows heavy traffic to disperse from the major arteries. Night had just descended but there was light everywhere. The metronomic passing of street lamps, containing bluish tinged globes of light, provided a coolly lit passage.

They turned off this numbered street onto Hill Side Avenue and sat. Nothing moved, which was very unusual. They crept along one block and then another and then sat again, this time for 10 minutes. The dance was in full swing by now and those in both cars sensed their inescapable predicament; there was no other way to the VFW hall.

Mike rolled up along side Bert and Marie. Both cars opened their windows and Mike said, "Follow me. If anyone asks, you tell them you think you have appendicitis, Marie."

Bert and Marie still have that look of a deer in headlights when Mike swings his cruiser in front of their car. Then the police car siren starts, as does the cherry top rotating light. Mike straddles the left lanes of both directions of traffic that grudgingly make way for the 2 car caravan. Bert hunkers down in his seat, his eyes receding into his head again which never moves to either side. Marie is laughing hysterically but remembers she is the sick one so doubles over to lend some authenticity to their charade.

They see the problem up ahead after traveling for 6 or 7 blocks. A fender bender that involves 3 cars has snarled traffic in one direction. The police are there as are the tow trucks. They enter the accident scene and Mike makes some indecipherable hand motions to the other officers to which they don't respond. And then they are free, in the clear, not another car in sight to impede them.

They get out of their cars at the VFW hall and all now are in spasms of laughter.

"Just another crazy night with the Eatons," Bert offers a second time echoing, like a mantra, the wonder of these experiences.

Chapter 5

Mike was about to be coming off his shift at midnight when he got the call that a bad accident had just occurred. He had been planning to hit a few watering holes, maybe meet up with some holdovers from the VFW dance before heading home, and now wondered if these plans were in jeopardy. He headed the patrol car south on Francis Lewis Blvd to the crash site on Jamaica Avenue.

They were the first police to arrive and he was unprepared for the devastation caused by the wreck, and its utter stillness. The car, traveling east, had apparently flipped over the divider and continued flipping until it was stopped by the front of a row of retail storefronts. Glass and mangled car parts littered the surroundings.

He was not sure at what point a sense of familiarity seeped into his consciousness. The car was a standard issue early 50's Ford model and it was turned on its side facing away from him as he approached. But with each step he experienced a foreboding that was much greater than what ordinarily would accompany a situation such as this.

"I've got a bad feeling about this one," Mike said to Mel as they left the cruiser and walked to the accident scene. The night was steel-gray and lacked even a single star. The air pressed in hard and each step for Mike was like walking through a substance that continued to compress. The passenger side door was busted open and immovable. Mike peered in and saw Rose's husband Ben behind the wheel, bloodied from the impact to his surroundings. Rose should have been there too but wasn't. He turned and followed the trajectory of the car and let his eyes roam the corresponding field of activity. The foreboding was excruciating until his eyes came upon that which he knew he would find but wished would not be there. Rose had been flung from the car and now lay in a heap, some 30 yards from the car's final resting point. Her body, too, was lifeless; he knew immediately that they both were dead.

Mike's revulsion was swift and immediate but somehow he was able to cast these feelings down, place them within some inert container that he would not allow to be opened now, maybe ever. Mel was already back at the cruiser, calling for backup and an ambulance. Mike ran to Rose's body which was badly battered, the limbs and torso tossed around unnaturally. He pressed hard on her wrist and then on the carotid artery, searching for a pulse. The body was still warm but it was already lifeless, her spirit gone; his attempts were futile.

He had performed heroically to save lives during the war, coming to the aid of his comrades in super human ways on a few occasions. But he also knew that there was no effort within his or any of our grasps that could have meaningful consequence once the mechanical processes of the body had ceased. He looked down at her now from an altered perspective. Rose was Rose, but was not and would never be again. She would not get to see her children grow into adults or fulfill any of the wild dreams she was always cooking up for herself. The death itself lacked all dignity: splayed out along a curbside, unattended by friend or family. He had been at the side of someone only one time at the moment when death arrived, as he tried to aid his fellow soldier who had been shot on the battlefield. He cradled him in his arms as he bled out. Hell breaking loose all around him. But the cacophony of war was replaced by stillness during those last moments of life. The breath, gasping just moments before, calmed in the last few repetitions. And then there had been a surprising sound, like a burp or a bursting free, like a tiny champagne bottle being uncorked. The miraculous thing that happened next he is wary of still and has never shared with anyone. He sensed, in the briefest instant, something lifting from this soldier. This thing, whatever it was, had force, power. It rocketed out of him. Not in a straight trajectory either, but zigzagging, careening wildly until it was simply not there. Mike himself was calmed by this, perplexed and oddly elated. He knew right then that despite everything else, when people die they should be surrounded by their family and loved ones. And Rose, the sweetest of all spirits, was not allowed this basic honor.

The ambulance and backup police car arrived in minutes. Mike stayed with Rose while Mel gave an update to the others who had arrived on the scene. He could hear them occasionally and knew that Mel was telling them of Mike's relation to the victims of this accident. Then the two cops went about their business in a quiet, efficient manner. Mike watched as they cordoned off the accident scene, knowing every step they were taking to restore order and allow safe passage. Mike knew the effects would be devastating to his family and Jen's extended family, because even he knew that Rose was the heart of that family, no matter how much abuse was heaped upon her for her crazy ideas. And he knew that the prospect of restoring normalcy any time soon was remote.

One of the ambulance workers came up to Mike who sat on the curb next to Rose's body.

"My sister-in-law." Mike said, straining unsuccessfully for a normal tone of voice.

"Yeah, I know."

There was no way to make the situation any better than it was but the accident area needed to be cleared, traffic needed to be controlled, order restored. The tech went over to Rose and checked for signs of life while Mike sat, overwhelmed with his feelings. He felt paralyzed and in free fall, the lynch pin of his world now broken.

He got up and surveyed the scene. People were coming up onto the avenue from their houses on the adjoining streets. He could not blame them for their gawking, hungry stares, their hand motions describing attempts to recreate what happened. These people were better than most he came in contact with while on the job. But they were not to be taken seriously, and could easily be discounted. Normally he would set up the barriers, and make sure they were respected. Normally, looking over the top of the idle onlookers with their thirst for titillation, he would be the source of calm, assertive energy they all sought after. It was easy when he was whole, but in this shattered state, it would have been impossible for him to assume this role.

Mel and the other policemen were in motion now, doing their jobs. They set up an alternating flow of traffic, and kept the onlookers at a safe distance. The EMTs were maneuvering the bodies onto stretchers and placing them in the ambulance for the eventual trip to the morgue. Mike stood there in a daze unable to help out, but hyper aware of every movement and sound, overwhelmed by the smell left over from the screeching tires that still lingered in the air and the gray cloud of smoke that would not disperse, because time itself crept along microscopically and would not allow it. The tow truck, bounding onto the sidewalk, pulled Mike from his reverie. It did not belong there, up on the sidewalk where people should be walking; its engine continued to sputter and hiss even after the driver jumped from the cab. He set to work on the pulleys and levers that would fasten and eventually remove the carcass of the vehicle. He remained purposefully unaware of any drama, any story, oblivious to how monstrous his action could appear.

Mike gasped for air and watched these activities occurring around him as if they were uncoordinated sequences in a dream. He knew he had to tell Jen what had happened, but resisted doing so. The conversation would confirm something he still wished to deny. A small voice inside him childishly preserved the idea that if he ignored what he witnessed maybe it would not be so, that the scene played out before him could be undone. He saw himself getting off his shift and meeting up with his cronies at McGrath's, a small gin mill close to home. Nothing fancy but everyone knew everyone else and one night proceeded from the last. He wanted to be there now, far from this horror; there, with them, more even than in his own home and with his family.

Mike walked up to Mel and said, "I need to go."

"Of course," Mel replied. "You take the cruiser and I'll get a ride back to the station with these guys."

They looked deeply into each others eyes. They were friends, had worked through their differences to reach a place most patrol car partners could not claim to have attained.

Mel, searching for words, finally said, "They were a great couple... They knew how to have a good time."

In these days, in this culture, this was high praise indeed, and spoke to a shared identity and ideal that was as foreign to outsiders as bowing to Mecca and offering praise to Allah five times a day was to those not immersed in that tradition. But it was no less real, and posited a defense against an unyielding universe no less defiantly.

Mike sped off in the direction of responsibility, a destination he preferred to avoid but one at which he was often capable of arriving.

Jen had not gone to the dance that night and was deep in sleep when Mike called from the station house. He relayed to her as best he could the horrible event that had just occurred. The news left her stunned silent, slumped over the side of the bed, only her elbows on her knees keeping her from collapsing onto the floor.

"How could this have happened?" she uttered to Mike who could not attempt a response, and then continued to turn the question back on herself over and over again. She sensed the world that she had erected, that they all had erected, was shattered and would never be put back together in the same way again.

"It's not fair. To be cut down so young. To be taken from us just like that."

Jen recovered some part of herself when her thoughts shifted to the care of the children, something that had not even registered for Mike. There was a baby sitter with them now. She would call her brother Frank who she hoped would be able to go to the house and speak to the children. Her mind raced, linking together improbable scenarios. She arrived at the hope that Frank and Jessie would step up and act as guardians, at least until something else was figured out.

She got on the phone at around 1:30 AM and called Frank who, after returning from the dance, had been in bed for around an hour.

"I just got some news from Mike, some very bad news."

Frank, on hearing these words, tried to pull himself from his sleep and finally replied, "Go on Jennif".

"They're gone. Ben and Rose were going home from the

dance and flipped their car on Jamaica Avenue and now... they're gone."

"Are they in the hospital or...? Do you mean...?"

"Yes, that's it. There's no need for a hospital."

Frank sat there quietly, playing the scenarios over in his head, arriving at the same conclusion and then starting again. Rose, upon whom he had so recently heaped such abuse, he saw clearly now. And what he saw was someone of rare beauty and grace. He wanted to see her now, hear her effortless, still youthful laughter flowing easily from within her.

"We need to think about the kids," Jen said.

It was something Frank was more than willing to turn his thoughts to, as most anything would have been. "I suppose we do. What do you think we should do?"

"Can you get over to their house now? I can call the baby sitter and let her know what's happened and I'll meet you over there as soon as Mike gets home from the station house. We can decide how to handle the kids once I get there."

"Sure. That makes sense."

"And I'll call Dan to let him know what's happened."

"Okay." How strange to say "okay" at these times, under these circumstances.

She dialed Dan and let it ring almost 20 times before Dan answered the phone. Jen had noticed this pattern before and wondered what could possibly be taking him this long. You were either there or you weren't. But with Dan there seemed to be a third option that escaped her now, as always.

Dan did answer after crawling over his new bride to get to the phone.

"Hullo," Dan mouthed groggily.

"Dan, it's Jen. I have some bad news." She waited a couple of seconds to allow Dan to prepare himself even though there was no preparation for what was to come.

"Rose and Ben got in an accident on the way home from the VFW... They never made it home."

At this point Jen was seized by the strongest wave of grief she had ever experienced and it came all at once, crashing in upon her, sending forth chaos in every direction. A moment before she was able to think, converse, but now the flood of emotion made such behavior impossible. She gripped at her stomach which spasmed uncontrollably, bending her in two.

Dan could hear Jen wailing and tried to get her to respond to his various entreaties but without success. He feared the worst but hoped for a different outcome. Finally Jen did recover enough to offer more information, "Mike called me. He saw them. Their car flipped over the median and rolled into Frank and Joe's Diner and the dry cleaning place on 210th street before stopping. They were already gone by the time Mike arrived."

Dan wondered what to feel because he felt nothing at that moment and was becoming anxious because of the lack of emotion, the inability to respond in what he believed was an appropriate manner. Finally he asked, "Did you call Frank yet?" An innocent question, and yet he wished it had gone unasked.

"Yes, he is on his way to their house now. We need to decide about Don and Sara. I'll be heading there, too, as soon as Mike gets home and you should come, too."

"I suppose I will." His tone was downright frosty, aloof. They both knew how he felt; that he got little to no respect as the youngest, his thoughts never sought on important matters. Even now he could feel the bitterness rise up in him because Jen had called Frank first and not him. He did not want to be thinking in this way but was incapable of controlling this ingrained pattern.

What can you do, he reasoned, when you feel this disrespect from your own family to the point that you expect it? You expect to not be consulted, and if consulted, never consulted first but only after a course of action has all but been chosen. Worst of all was that this was what his conscious mind was focused on when he knew he should only be thinking about the far greater tragedy of which he had just been made aware.

Jen could sense what was troubling Dan and could not help hating him for it. But if she had been honest with herself, she would have seen that having Dan at Rose's house was not something that she had considered at first and she would have realized the wrongness of not including him in her planning. But this was too much, the wrong time, and she wondered if she would ever be able to forgive him for the conversation they were having right now.

Dan always felt the wrong age. He was too young for WW II and fought the wrong war in Korea which was hardly ever mentioned and never in the same heroic terms as those afforded "The Great War". No iconic pictures or glorious victory awaited him, to propel him back into life's maelstrom. He had joined the Marines to show he was every bit the man the other, older ones were. But he spent almost every moment hating his enlistment and dreamed daily of returning to the nurturing surroundings of his family that now, years later, still conceived of him as the baby. He looked at all three of his siblings as surrogate parents, although he wished he did not, and felt this way especially toward Rose who was now gone. He thought the words, "Rose is dead," but could not feel them and this frightened him.

Frank sat there in his living room, still trying to assimilate all that had happened in the last 72 hours. They had all arrived at Rose's house the night of her death variously and singly. It was the first time spouses were not in tow in years and it felt odd, stripped down and bare, for just the three of them to be sitting down together.

Rose was not a good housekeeper and in order to sit in her cramped living room the three of them had to remove papers and piles of clothing from chairs before they could sit on them. It had been a joke among them, her fruitless attempts to gain an upper hand on the swirling demands put upon her, and now they reflected on this as they surveyed the accumulated bills to be paid, toys, and unfinished projects; and they reflected also on the part these things would play in the legacy that would be hers.

They agreed while sitting in Rose's house the night before last, even Frank had agreed, that if Jesse went along with it, the children should stay with them, at least temporarily. And here they were now in his home, which no longer felt like his home. Everything was different, charged. Even the air, which it seemed had contained an almost solid stillness now swirled.

There was so much going on in their lives right now and he had no mind for these details. All he could think about were the 2 children living with him now and especially the tow-headed boy sitting at his small kitchen table eating his breakfast at this moment. Sara cried herself to sleep both nights since the deaths of her parents and had been lethargic during the days, but Donald showed little emotion. His excessive energy was in evidence and he seemed almost unremorseful. Frank looked at Donald again and wondered how he could be this way, why he refused to see the error of his ways and he wondered how he could make Donald see that the way he was acting was wrong.

Don picked at the French toast his Aunt Jessie had made for him. It seemed dry and crusty, having been cooked in a pan on top of the stove. Egg could be seen streaked between strips of nearly bare bread. He was used to French toast cooked on a special skillet that his mother pulled down from the highest shelf in the kitchen closet which, along with French toast, was reserved for grilled cheese sandwiches. Heavy and imposing, it was something of a luxury item because of its specialized uses and represented a source of unsuspecting power, something holding the household together, protecting it. You would plug it in and keep it closed until the light on its top turned on. Then it was opened clam shell style, heat streaks emanating from it. Eight perfectly saturated pieces of bread were fitted on its two surfaces. Cinnamon was shaken on each which bubbled, coagulated, but at some point in the cooking process would concede and spread uniformly across the surfaces. When the slices of bread were served, they had to them a nearly uniform brown, silken quality almost, but not quite, too perfect to eat. And now even the syrup it was served with was not the right kind, spreading too thinly, tasting foreign.

"Aunt Jessie made this especially for you because you told us this was your favorite breakfast." Frank said to coax Don to eat. But Don, in response, just looked dumbly up from his food at his uncle. Frank continued to watch Don as he extracted the fluffy middle of the bread and occasionally raise a forkful of the mash to his mouth.

Soon Don got up and walked away from his uncle without a word. The majority of the food was not eaten, and looked more like a dissection spread haphazardly around the plate. Frank stared at the plate and the empty seat and felt less sure of how to proceed with his life than ever before.

The meeting with Myrtle and his boss Walter Jones the week before had ended miserably. Without so much as a chance to explain how he felt about Myrtle's ideas he was told that they would be implemented, everyone of them. He saw in her a self indulgent look of satisfaction, an almost manly swagger to her nearly imperceptible movements. Then Walt laid down the crushing blow. Myrtle would be installed above him and the rest of the clerks. It was not a demotion for Frank, he was told. Ha! This new girl who knew nothing of how the business was run was now his boss. He tuned out the rest of what Walt said, something about the business changing and the need for new ideas. Everyone would need to cooperate to implement these changes. We shall see, we shall see, Frank thought.

Then Rose and Ben, dead, just like that. And now two children living in his house with the possibility of a ready made family. It all seemed too improbable and he had trouble flying above the whirlwind that his life had become.

The funerals would be held today. The bodies would be laid to rest alongside Rose's parents; both died within the last few years. They were taken early, his dad from cancer and his mom from heart problems. But they had seen their family grow so it was not so hard to let go as this was certain to be. Neither Don nor Sara attended their parents viewing, one of the many decisions reached by Rose's siblings and Ben's family. Ben's only sibling, Liz, lived in Brooklyn. His parents were also alive and lived close to Liz and her family. The two sides of Rose's and Ben's family had never grown close but were pulling together now to get through this tragedy.

During the discussions about arrangements for the funeral and children, Frank and Jessie sensed the decision-making responsibilities flowing more in their direction. He was used to this, being the oldest among the brothers and sisters. But this was more, he was certain, and was based in large measure on the mostly unspoken desire that Sara and Don would find a home with Frank and Jessie.

Discussions with Sara and Don came haltingly. What do you say? What can you say? Frank was planning to say something to Don during the French toast breakfast, and now he saw how successfully that went. They sat and watched television together, for hours at a time, whatever was on. And during that time only the most trivial comments were made, until the point when they accepted the notion that there really was nothing else needing to be said or that could be said. He would watch them, laying about on the floor during every activity and wonder why they were always on the floor when there were many comfortable chairs all around. He felt his displeasure grow at this preference and it was one they would need to change if they were going to live in this house. But there would be time for this, if they stayed. Once Sara asked him to look at a drawing she was working on, actually expecting him to crawl down beside her. This caused him to let out one of his deafening guffawing noises, a witness to the unlikelihood of this happening and instead he motioned her to his side, drawing in hand, which was something she was willing to comply with.

With needing to get everyone ready for the funeral, there was little time for sitting and watching TV. Most days they went back to Don and Sara's house and collect items that would be needed. Don had no words for the sense of dislocation he felt on these trips. Walking the hallways, bumping into furniture that once felt familiar, he felt the hollowness outside of him flow freely through the hollowness within. On the last trip he collected the clothes he would be wearing to the funeral, clothes reserved for special occasions and that he always took some unexpected pleasure in wearing. His parents had made sure he had at least one suit that fit him well and that would be brought out for special occasions. He, of course, never thought about the expense to constantly outfit his growing body in a suit. The current version included cuffed pants and double breasted buttons on the front of the suit jacket. He felt transformed, completed, when he wore these clothes in a way that escaped him in his everyday life. Only the ties he was forced to wear, the ones already knotted and attached to the shirt with a plastic hook thwarted what he perceived as his grown up image. The horror would be all encompassing if one of the plastic strips that slid beneath the collar jumped the rail and was in full view to those around him. At moments like those he could feel himself disintegrate and it was likely an out-gushing of rage would follow.

Back in their aunt and uncle's house, Don and Sara were in the bathroom brushing their teeth at the same time, jockeying for position in front of the mirror. They dressed with help from their Aunt Jessie and then Don realized that when they were packing the clothes they had forgotten one of his ties.

"I could have sworn we put one in the suit case," Jessie said. But all her inquiries proved fruitless as she rustled through the bags of things that were being relocated into their home.

Frank was in the next room, overhearing the conversation. He went to his tie rack, perfectly assembled in a color scheme from bright to dark. He scanned the selection now with a different idea in mind. Length was the criteria he focused on primarily and the arrangement before him offered no assistance.

He selected a few from his large collection and walked into the room in which Don and Sara were staying. It was the first time he had entered this room since they had begun to occupy it. Jessie was still furtively looking through assorted boxes looking for the missing tie when Frank walked up to Don and began placing individual ties cross-wise over his shirt and jacket, the way a tailor might, to check for the best matching color scheme. He selected a charcoal gray tie that contained small red stripes that ran diagonally across it. Frank proceeded to wordlessly fold up Don's collar, with hand motions that were somewhat rough but necessarily, so that the collar retained the straightened position. Frank placed the tie around Don's shoulders and noticed them as if for the first time, as he looked down at him. Don was certainly not yet a man but there was more strength to his frame than he realized and he sensed the growth that would follow and the sense of *becoming,* as he smoothed the tie over both shoulders in an act of ritual that had no particular value but was regularly adhered to when he made his own tie.

Frank chose the Windsor half knot. It was his favorite anyway but he wanted to use up as much tie in the knot as possible to reduce the length and hoped it would work out. Frank moved behind Don so that his hand could perform the task as if he were tying his own tie. Even in this position his hands move swiftly, confidently. Don quickly gave up trying to remember the array of hand movements, and allowed himself to be jerked this way and that through the process. He trusted his uncle in the process they were engaged in together.

When the knot was complete, and properly aligned between both sides of his collar, Don turned to Frank; he saw in his uncle a look of satisfaction, one he was unused to seeing. Don, himself, felt more emotion than at anytime since the death of his parents. It was like waking up as he returned the look of his satisfied uncle and then went to look in the mirror. The tie was a little long, hanging over his belt about an inch, but it was perfect otherwise and wholly transforming.

"Thanks Uncle Frank. I've always wanted to wear a tie like

this," Don said, still not taking his eyes off his own visage. His uncle stood behind him and from the higher elevation could see the boy's image and the tie: a beacon, a talisman. The air grew still and how, at this moment, the opportunity for joy found a way to make an appearance was unfathomable. Feelings of guilt streaked through, defining and charging these other, unexpected emotions.

The car was immeasurably more plush than any he had ever been in. He sat with his Aunt Jessie and Uncle Frank and sister Sara in the front two seats, and his mother was in a large shiny box behind them. His father lay in another vehicle behind them and it also contained other family members. His uncle had told him to act grown up, to be the older brother for Sara and he had assumed this role to an extraordinary degree on this day. Your mother and father would be proud of you he was told by several family members as they filed past him at the funeral service at the church. During the service he had looked about himself at the small church he knew so well. Usually, when there, he would be engaged in simple games of hangman or connect the dots, and eating penny candy with his cousin Tim. But now he was content to sit like the adults and like the adults expected him to, and garner their compliments.

Only four days had passed since his mother's and father's death and he had not really begun to understand the changes underway in his life. It reminded him of going off to camp, which he did for the first time this past summer. So much was unknown and he required assistance to accomplish the simplest tasks. There were knowing forces holding him up, propelling him in directions he could not even guess at. "You'll be spending some time with us," he and Sara had been told the night before by his uncle Frank. "That will mean getting you enrolled in the local school." Don held this last bit of information away from him. HIS friends were in HIS school and his mind would not consider this change, just as it had not yet considered what the end of his parents lives meant to him.

The hearse turned off the road, which was like many others in this part of Queens, and entered onto a different kind of roadway and a wholly different atmosphere. Don's mind tumbled as the stream of cars plunged and ascended the narrow, winding road. Mature trees rose up along the roadway and many of these were enormous weeping willow trees that swayed gracefully in the wind. Surrounding these sentinels were perfectly manicured, idyllic lawns. They were still in the grip of winter but the air had the quality of a perfect mid spring morning, and felt like a gift to them. Don had never looked at such beauty or knew that such places existed; and that they were so close to his every day world astonished him. The peacefulness was undeniable and the grave stones, lined up in rows, did nothing to diminish this atmosphere.

They walked to the place where the two caskets would be placed into the ground and assembled together with the others who were attending, waiting for the caskets to be carried to the same spot and placed on planks above the holes they would be lowered into.

Peace and sadness reigned, resignation, too. But the insistent desperation and emptiness were forestalled by the serenity of this place. In future years, when Don would reflect on the devastation the deaths of his parents had caused him, he would marvel that he could have felt buoyed by the funeral service, that there could have been any feeling of lightness in his heart. But he stood there, listening to the minister describing his parents in unfamiliar, but pleasing terms, with his uncle Frank behind him and his heavy, manly hand placed upon his shoulder while he, Don, occasionally felt the silk quality of his tie over his stomach or the perfectly tied knot beneath his neck.

After the funeral service they ate dinner at a fancy restaurant that Don had never been to before; an entire back room was reserved for their group. Initially he was placed at a table reserved for the children, but then found himself getting up and walking to his uncle Frank's side.

"Look who we have here?" Frank said. And Don found that the attention of the table drawn to him did not bother him. All of a sudden a seat and place setting was laid for him beside his uncle. He looked over at the other kids and believed he could see envy in the stares they sent back to him before they turned their attention back to each other.

Don was amazed at how much he enjoyed himself during the meal that followed. His ideas were listened to and he laughed when the adults laughed. As the meal moved on, he was aware that he was being allowed to be funny and naughty in ways that he would not normally be allowed to be. He was, in fact, mimicking the behavior of those around him. He realized this was the way he always wanted to behave but that this opportunity was withheld from him in various ways. How freeing, how liberating this was for him. He rested now in his bed at the end of the day, accepting rest and eventual sleep. His parents were dead and he knew an emptiness existed inside him. But he did not know yet that the emptiness would be endless, and boundless, and at times crushing. Right now it was a new sensation to be probed and was, for this reason, endurable.

Frank sat back in his chair in the living room, taking in the day's events. Even the quiet that now pervaded his surroundings was different, containing a charge that was not like what he was accustomed to. Jessie was there next to him wondering, as he was wondering, what the future had in store.

"I thought Pastor Barnes did a nice job of the sermon," Frank said to make conversation, although it was not what he was thinking about and he was quite certain the contents of his wife's thoughts ran parallel to his own. So many years it had just been the two of them and now watching Jessie help the children get ready for bed enlivened feelings in him that seemed fresh and wholly different from anything he was aware of ever feeling.

"That boy was a *buster* during dinner, don't you think? He sure had us all in stitches when he told the story about how he would sometimes sneak down to the refrigerator for an extra piece of pie in the middle of the night. I think we might need to put a lock on the refrigerator door. What do you think?"

Jessie did not answer Frank right away because she was thinking about what had just concluded, her watching over them as they brushed their teeth and then laying out their bed clothes for them to change into. The last thing, right before bed, was when they said their prayers. Sara knelt down beside her bed, placed her elbows on top of the bed, and closed her eyes. The bed was higher than the one she slept on at home so her arms were almost straight up in front of her, but she managed. She spoke her nightly prayer in a measured cadence that suggested some reflection between sentences. *"God watch over the trees and the animals"* "*God watch over* followed by a litany of extended relatives, pets, teachers and anyone else she chose to include and ending, on this night, with *Aunt Jessie and Uncle Frank."* And finally, *"God watch over Don, Mommy and Daddy."*

Don spoke mostly the same words in the same format, but everything else was different. He remained in bed, looking straight up at the ceiling. He had been deciding for some time that he was too old for nightly prayers, but went along with what he considered the charade nonetheless. His goal was to emit the entire contents without taking a single breath and to do so inhaled deeply before breaking forth with a torrent of words. Jessie sensed Don's motivation and was not bothered by what he perceived as his grownup action.

When he was done, Jessie kissed each child on the cheek and walked to the doorway to turned off the light. Before wishing them pleasant dreams one final time, Sara asked, "Aunt Jessie, now that Mommy and Daddy are dead, should we stop praying for God to watch over them?"

This was the first time either of the children had spoken directly about the loss of their parents and what it might mean to them, the first time they asked any of the multitude of questions that must be swirling around them like a tornado of which they were the eye.

Jessie sat down on the bed next to them and put one hand on each of their legs. She was wondering how she would do when this subject came up and now was surprised by her calm, by her confidence. "Honey, just because your parents are with God now there's no reason for you to stop praying for them. They'll always be with you, inside," she said, and patted the palm of her hand on her own chest. "So, if it makes you feel good to ask God to watch over your parents, there is no reason for you to stop asking Him to do that." She sat with them another minute, still touching the meaty portions of their calf muscles until she sensed they were calm. Then she got up and placed kisses on both their foreheads and stroked their hair for a moment before leaving to rejoin her husband.

"It was a nice turnout too. All of the old gang was there." Jessie responded, sensing the unspoken reciprocity in her and her husband's communication.

Chapter 6

Three months had passed since Rose and Ben were buried, and life for their extended family refused to mend. Jessie, on extended leave from her job, tried to create some order in her household, but those efforts met with little success. Sara, after her initial openness towards her aunt on the night of the funeral, had closed down and become listless. Don's adjustment to the new school and teacher was going poorly. He had gotten into several fights and Jessie had to go to school and bring him home on those occasions. They tried to talk to him but he was resistant to whatever they said. They tried minor punishments and now were pursuing a different tactic.

Two days before, on a Thursday night, Frank was talking on the phone to his sister Jen.

"This isn't going so well. I didn't think it would be easy. But," he went silent, searching for words, "everything is so different. The kids running through. Never a moment's peace." When would the pleasure from sharing his home begin, from teaching the kids how to behave, from showing them what in life was important. Instead of satisfaction, he felt a constant sense of irritation; constrained, he was aware of the first seeds of resentment.

"Sure. It's a big change for you," Jen offered, not used to hearing her older brother speak like he was being ground down. She was used to her own husband getting fidgety when things weren't going his way, but Frank, who never broke from his routine, rarely showed the stress and strain of normal life.

"What am I supposed to do, entertain them?" Frank asked not so much to Jen as to the gods inhabiting the lost realm of his cohesive world.

The idea of purposefully entertaining the kids in your charge was such an outlandish idea that they both erupted in a peal of laughter, which broke the gloomy quality of the conversation.

"Look, pretty soon Don and Sara will hook up with the kids in your neighborhood and you'll hardly see them again. Like my two. If they're not in front of the TV they're running around with their friends rough housing and carrying on." It wasn't that easy and rarely ran as smoothly as she was putting on now. But now was not the time for this type of honesty.

"I got an idea. Why don't we head out to Coney Island this Saturday. We'll make a big family day of it." These words escaped before she could withdraw them. It was a great leap that she wished she had not taken just then, but now it was done. "We'll make a day of it." she said as if to correct her thought and the words she had just spoken.

Frank laughed to himself at the sounds of these words, still so strange. Rose and Ben just recently laid in the ground and now he had a family too. He was not made for momentous shifts and challenges. They made him uneasy, weighed him down, as if breathing itself had become a chore. His skin itched almost constantly; the stiff starched quality of his shirts that normally helped him define the image he presented to the world, were now almost more than he could tolerate.

"Sure, why don't we give it a go," Frank offered in reply.

The afternoon of their trip was filled with bustling excitement and energy. They loaded into the two cars, Jen and her family in one, and Frank, Jessie, Don and Sara in the other. They navigated the side roads from Frank's home until they could get to the Belt Parkway which would bring them into Brooklyn and eventually to the Coney Island exit.

They found parking spaces in relative close proximity to the entrance to the amusement area and were pleased by their good fortune. The four kids wanted to race ahead but the adults held them back to within earshot. The mood was buoyant and everything: conversation, groupings, facial expressions, expressed relief. This was the first outing the adults and Sara and Don had allowed themselves since the deaths of Rose and Ben and they found they were able to embrace the carefree quality of the afternoon.

"We've been meaning to get back here for a while but just haven't found the time," Jennifer said to the others. She and her husband had decided to not pinch pennies on this outing, either. No sandwiches in the cooler left in the car for snacks – they'll feast on Coney Island hot dogs and beer, and most anything else people wanted to eat and drink. And they wouldn't hold back on the rides for the kids so much either, and even let loose some change for the games of chance.

Mike was in fine spirits as well. The cool breeze coming off the Atlantic on this day was a welcome relief and the biting salt air was a tonic for any ailment of mind or body, slowing movement, condensing time. Mike put his arm around Jen's waist and gave a mild tug and squeeze, to let her know he was there, and Jen did not rebuke this private exchange and, in fact, welcomed it. The two couples sauntered along the avenue this way, mindful of the children ahead but also allowing separation from them, if only slightly, because even in this large city, on this busy avenue, separation could be managed safely. The uninterrupted row of parked cars created a safe space for those walking on the sidewalks and the children running ahead knew this unconsciously, had assimilated this ally and were using it to their advantage.

Up ahead they could already see the landmarks of their

destination. The first rides you saw even before getting out of the car, towering above all the buildings, and of these the first that came into view was the Parachute Drop. The children in both cars knew this landmark, already indelibly etched into them, infusing in them an understanding of where they lived. It was a part of them: standing so tall, tapering gracefully and then fanning out in a movement of opulence.

"This year I'll be tall enough to go on the Parachute Drop and I'm gonna." Don had said in a commanding voice as the car followed along the Belt and it first came into view.

"We shall see, we shall see," his uncle replied, realizing for the first time the complications that may develop in the course of the day, the decisions that might need to be made.

The four children ran ahead and then back again multiple times, each time imploring the grown ups to hurry. But the adults were more than happy to maintain their leisurely pace. The children gazed with wonder at the sites that were coming into view, the landmarks capturing their attention along with the Parachute Drop and then the monstrous Cyclone roller coaster. They taunted each other to see who would be the first to accept the challenge that these rides offered. But the comments were benign as the anticipation of a great good time diffused through them, unifying their emotions, heightening their expectations.

"I bet you won't be big enough to go on The Cyclone this year," Don said to Tim and immediately they stood back to back to measure themselves. Don placed his own hand on the top of Tim's head and rested the side of his hand against his own head. He pulled away suddenly and no one said, but everyone suspected, that the action of pulling away caused his hand to tilt slightly. But no one called him on this and only Anne was tempted to do so.

"I'm at least 2 inches taller than you" Don announced after he had considered the distance between his hand and the top of his head. No one knew the truth, nor did they care now that they were running again, running to the next trial, observation of the wild, contemplation of some death defying act or freakish behavior of the men and women in the side shows that had not yet been sanitized out of these venues.

With other couples Jen and Mike would do things with, the men always walked together as did the women. But Frank and Jessie were almost inseparable. They left themselves open for some good-natured ribbing about this, but it never resulted in them changing this habit and preference. But after a couple of blocks the two men and two women had become paired as they walked along the street, in what felt a natural grouping. A small distance grew between them, allowing each conversation to be private.

Jen and Jessie liked each other but had little contact except at family gatherings. One of the main reasons Jen liked Jessie was because of how happy she made her brother Frank. So often the two of them seemed to float above the headaches and petty annoyances that the rest of them dealt with daily. They were the island of calm around the ever brooding storm that seemed to prevail. And Jessie admired Jen for keeping her family together. She doubted she, herself, would have had the fortitude to do the same. Mike was a good guy alright, but all the drinking and the nastiness that could come with it must have made life hell sometimes. She had seen Jen react bitterly to the way Mike carried on, and wondered how Jen was ever able to free herself from that bitterness.

When you got right down to it, the reason they were not closer was because of the children, the fact that Jessie had none and Jen's life was so taken up with caring for them and being the backbone of the family. But all that changed for them now, almost in an instant, and replacing that divide was the first intimations of a sisterly affection.

"So how's it going?" Jen asked in as matter a fact a tone as she was able to project.

"What can you say?" Jessie said and laughed in a quiet, nervous way. "There are moments when I can imagine us as a family, but then it all dissolves into some fight between the kids, or just total quiet with no one feeling comfortable with anyone else. Mostly I don't know what to say to them. Don't know what to expect from them or what they would like from me."

Jen looked in front of her, first at the 2 husbands talking and then the children up ahead running around and carrying on. She was supposed to be the one with the answers now, but she had difficulty discussing emotional topics of any kind. Why she could not say, but her whole body seemed to rise up against any strong expression of feelings, especially if they contained a quality of doubt about the choices she was making in her life. Some women seemed to know instinctively how to provide comfort to others, but even after all these years she was not able to say exactly what it was that her own children needed from her lots of times. Needs themselves were a mystery, and touching on them was like touching a train track's third rail. But neither did she allow herself time to reflect on questions of this sort much, as she was doing right now, as she felt she must do now. So she fought back against the rising tide within her that wanted nothing more than to remove herself from a situation where too much might be said, too much felt. The battle raging now, as always in these situations, was excruciating. Her heart raced, head pounded. But she fought these feelings and tried to stay attuned to Jessie, hoping she would be able to help her, and in so doing satisfy these needs, which were always a mine field for her.

"Every time I look in those kids eyes I can see how much they need their parents, and I have no idea how to help them, how to cross over that wall that divides each of them and me."

They walked on a couple of more steps and Jen found she was able to respond, "You've got to give it time. These kids are in shock. We're all in shock. You're doing fine with them and we are all grateful that you are giving this a shot." Saying these words felt good to Jen, but still she felt the danger in them without knowing why and she wondered why she had the desire to discredit them as soon as they were uttered, as if the fact that they were expressed primarily to give comfort devalued them.

They fell silent again and the images of the children's faces Jessie has been looking at these past weeks passed before her now. Even though Don would soon be coming onto his teen years, he was still a child whose heart remained concealed. Furious activity intermixed with frustrated lethargy; imprisoned in both modes, his eyes peered forth with a desperation that was not meant for someone of so few years. And Sara, usually the one to fly above and resist her brother's excesses, now morphed that quality to become vacant inside, instead of merely aloof, and her eyes were hollow portals reflecting this interior quality. But despite the sadness the horror of the parents' deaths had caused, Jessie could still see in both of them a child's beauty dimly shining through, and she wondered if the shadow of their parents death would ever not feel so close, so devastating.

The sidewalk led them directly into Coney Island. The atmosphere changed slowly at first, with vendors selling warm, soft pretzels, hot dogs and drinks, but then more quickly, taking on an enchanted carnival atmosphere that was uniquely its own. The children's eyes opened widely as they passed the sideshows and barkers. The Fright House emitted loud cacophonous noises of metal on metal punctuated by blood curdling human screams. Games of chance displayed potential prizes that were nearly as large as any of the children and every now and then a man could be seen walking through the crowds lugging along one of these prizes. And the games themselves looked so easy to the children that they could already imagine the stuffed animals sitting in their rooms.

But the plan was to bypass these entertainments for now and go directly to Steeplechase, the indoor amusement park with its enormously high ceilings that the children forgot even existed once they enter into its halls. The children were drawn to those simple, irresistible rides; those that, try as they might, they will not overcome because they involve laws of physics, the pull of gravity. This included the thickly walled cylinder that they walked within, or tried to walk within, as it continued its constant, slow turning motion. Occasionally they may be able to stay upright as they run from one side to the other by correctly compensating for the changing stable area beneath their feet, but that never supplied a satisfying experience. Instead they tripped or fell, on purpose if necessary. Once down, they would let the arc of the cylinder take them up as far as it might, resisting the tipping point, until they toppled into themselves falling in a heap and then starting the process over again.

They ran next to the slide that extended upwards a dizzying distance and had several humps placed along the course that your body flew over on the way down.

"Grab a sack," each child told the other. The burlap sacks were made from thick, coarse, jute and may have been used at one time to hold many 10 pound bags of potatoes but would now be sat on to give a faster glide on the way down the slide. Each child rifled through the piles of sacks strewn at the bottom of the slide; most searched for the "best" one, although uncertain of what constituted "best" in this case. But this uncertainty did not deter them from touting the virtues of their own sack compared to the others. Size, shape, density, and thickness of the weaved pattern were discussed, as were more esoteric topics such as the sack's ability to lay flat, their gradations of the color brown; each child propping up their own choice, while secretly suppressing doubts within themselves.

Soon they were on the staircase that straddled the slide and led up to the starting point. The line was long but it moved steadily. They critiqued the techniques applied by the kids they observed on the way down as if they were slalom skiers and the humps were moguls, things these kids knew nothing about at this time in their lives. Perfect posture included sitting upright, feet first, your body from the waist down in contact with the sack. Most important was to keep your arms folded on your chest in front of you at all times... This was critical! Doing otherwise was to open yourself up to the possibility of getting the dreaded brush burn on your arm.

Don pointed to one girl who took a tumble over a hump and lost control of the a priori slider's position. "Oh, I bet she got an ugly burn when she hit the wood." They all imagined the purplish streak that was sure to have marked that girl's arm. They followed her trajectory the remaining 30 feet of the ride. All peered at her arms to see if the marks had already appeared but the distance between them kept them from answering this question, allowing it to remain a mystery. But the greater mystery was the mark itself. How much did it hurt? What color would it become? They wondered separately if any of them were curious enough to get one, even if that meant grazing one's arm along the wood while descending, on purpose?

The parents and others in their groups stood huddled together down below. Some worried for their little ones but most took this opportunity to drift spontaneously and naturally into the otherworldliness of the situation. They experienced a moment's peace filled with idle talk, and something more than their own weight rooted them to where they stood; they understood subconsciously how different their lives were from these children with their slow, steady step by step ascent and clamoring excitement on the way up, which would be followed by the exhilarating ride down. But the parents, most of them anyway, had no desire to be part of the dizzying energy they were beholding, content instead to marvel at what they had helped to create. And the parents, these older ones, needed each other at this moment to gird themselves in the face of this immense mystery.

They went on the slide a few times, becoming more daring with each ride: searching out the humps, lurching forward for greater speed, intentionally wiping out and, in so doing, submitting to the possibility of a burn mark, which none of them were able to raise on an exposed part of their body. So in the end, the slide had been tamed except for the sensation of the brush burn that the slide withheld on this occasion.

As they walked away from the slide the children's good spirits were evident and were freely displayed. This was probably the first time Don and Sara allowed the pale cast by their parents' deaths to not dominate their mood, as it had since the reality of it began to sink in. They argued about who had the best rides, the worst wipeouts, the highest jumps, the best finishes, each focusing on their own experiences at the time and in the retelling, just as you would expect and hope for.

"So what would you like to do next?" Mike asked the kids.

After a short discussion the decision was reached to head for the bumper cars, which was one of everyone's favorites. They left Steeplechase and emerged back into the bright light of the outdoors.

The noises and smells of the strip they walked out onto were intoxicating and contained a promise of good times and excitement. Sweet smells of cotton candy and caramelized popcorn and nuts, mixed with the aromas of grilled meats and fried onions and peppers. Barkers called out to the unsuspecting and those whose defenses were weakening by the carnival atmosphere.

"I want something to eat." one of the children said with mild insistence, and soon this turned into a chorus that would be heeded. The girls opted for cotton candy while the boys went for the caramelized popcorn. They stood there quietly eating as Frank and Mike stood in line to buy drinks for the children.

A man was sitting on the ground off to the side under a small tree that was providing him cover from the sun. He had a smile on his face and called out to most anyone passing by offering them greetings, trying to tell a joke or get a conversation going. Don's attention was drawn towards him, and the comments he was sharing at this moment with someone walking by about the weather being too hot which Don felt was not the case. The man sensed Don's gaze and their eyes met. Don looked directly at his warm and friendly smile.

"Why don't you come over here young man, so we can have ourselves a little chat."

Don was only semi-aware of his actions and thoughts up until that moment. Once addressed by the man, he quickly cataloged that which had been effortlessly drifting between him and his surroundings. Don saw no reason not to accept the offer made to him and began walking towards the man, a distance of only about 10 steps. He took in the man's image, which was odd in some way but he was not able to determine how. He sat bolt upright but his hair was not well combed, and he had a couple of days worth of growth on his face. He was wearing a plaid shirt that rested outside of his pants and fell to the ground. But none of this explained the oddness that Don felt while gazing at him. Then, as he started walking towards him, the man's defining characteristic rose up within him all at once . The man had no legs, none at all. He was sitting, or more accurately standing, on a 2 X 6 pine board.

The man recognized and understood the thought process going on in Don's head. He continued to look at Don, without a trace of shame, still smiling and beckoning, still looking for a little conversation to help pass the day.

Don stopped immediately, as though he had just encountered an invisible brick wall. His mind became unfocused, unable to process this new information. He wanted, needed, his mother right then. There was nothing else that could help him sort all this out, make sense of his revulsion which was now augmented by his horrible sense of aloneness. And there was nothing there behind him either, no woman's breast and belly to be held against and comforted by. And so he ran and ran and ran. But what he ran away from was inside him, inescapable.

Then he stopped as though the brick wall had reasserted itself and he looked around. The direct experience of a simple truth arrested his movement, something he felt explode out of the back of his head and then spread down, touching every part of him: *There was no one, and no thing, that could change the fact that the man had no legs or that he had no parents.* They came and talked to him in the days following the deaths about how he was feeling but he declined these offers to speak. If he could express his feelings at all it was a dull numbness, and how do you express something like that, something that did not exist. He ended these inquiries quickly and the adults did not seem to mind cutting short these conversations, as if they agreed words were inadequate and more of a cause for embarrassment than anything else. In fact since the day of the funeral there was no mention of his parents in any way other than how their deaths were affecting him, and this was the last thing about them he wanted to discuss. But he was no closer to what he wished to say and doubted, himself, whether any words about them were worth uttering.

He looked at the booths and attractions running parallel on both sides of him as far as he could see, and saw them differently than before or at anytime in the past. The luster of the paint on the displays was faded, diminished; the beckoning calls from the games of chance failed to draw him in. The only thing that sparked his interest was The Cyclone roller coaster. It was not riding the ride that he considered, but instead he imagined climbing the wooden scaffolding that it was built upon, wooden support by wooden support. The idea of doing this made him smile as he saw himself ascending its heights. Then he looked around and saw people lining up for rides on one side to get in and exiting the other, and imagined this occurring over and over again. He would be different. He would want and do more than those around him. And he would achieve these things through his own power, now the only source of strength available to him.

He turned and began walking in the direction he came. They were chasing after him and by the time they met he was completely under control and focused. They were able to piece together what had happened back with the legless man and so did not question him, but instead asked if he was alright and he replied that, yes, he was alright. They wanted to probe further but sensed his aloofness and how removed he was, and didn't know how or whether to try to pierce through this strangeness.

Yes, he was alright and as long as he stayed like this he would be alright and he decided at that moment that he would stay like this the rest of his life.

They continued onto the Bumper Cars and made it to the front of the line and then when the chain was removed from the gate they rushed along with everyone else into the area where the Bumper Cars now lay idle. Don and Tim had already determined which cars they believed were the fastest and raced towards them. Sara took a car with her uncle and Anne with her father; Jen and Jessie grabbed cars close to their husbands. This left the boys separated from the rest of the family and each of them some distance from the other. Jen and Jessie considered this only as an after-thought when it was too late to choose different cars.

The buzzer rang and the sparks began to fly and crackle from the bendable metal wands that connected the cars' motors to the electricity emanating from the metal mesh suspended above the track. The action started slowly and politely, but soon the banging started. Don had never been allowed to ride on his own before and felt fueled by the idea of driving a vehicle by himself. During the first few turns he was cautiously driving the course, learning the art of the steering wheel and coordinating it with the gas pedal. He even took time to look beyond the track, wondering who in the crowd waiting to get on the ride was watching him, admiring how well such a young boy could handle himself. There was a boy who he was sure was at least a year older than he leaning against the railing, waiting his turn. He was surely watching him, admiring his control as he navigated the turns, accelerating at just the right times. Don was sure the other boy was thinking that he could not do it nearly so well himself.

Don's reverie ended abruptly when he was lightly rammed by his uncle Frank and Sara, who he had not see coming up alongside him. They continued on but his car was forced to turn around and all of a sudden instead of righting his vehicle, he was moving in the opposite direction of everyone else. He tried to right himself again but lacked the skill to reverse his direction as the cars continued to whiz by him. Within a short space of time he was the cause of a major pile up, with cars unable to maneuver around the expanding bottleneck.

Don looked around at the other drivers who seemed upset and cast annoyed expressions at him, as if to say why was such a young boy who could not control a car riding by himself. Everyone involved turned their steering wheel this way and that, trying to free themselves but few were successful. They were losing precious moments of the ride and Don felt their scorn coming from all points of the compass. A worker finally walked across the floor and roughly pried the cars apart until they were free to start moving again.

Don was now worked up and frustrated. He wanted, needed to free himself from the shame that cloaked him. Rounding a corner he saw a car stopped at the periphery of the track. Without forethought, Don came out of the turn and redirected his car to point directly at the midsection of this stopped car. The whipping motion of his car caused it to gain its maximum force and a moment later he slammed into the car broadside.

The driver of this car was a young black man who had been talking to a young lady in another car. He had taken himself out of play, or so he thought, and had no forewarning of the crash that rattled his car and shook his body. He looked over at the car that stayed pinned against his and locked eyes with Don. Don would never forget this expression. The man was very black, sweaty and angry. He had never felt as scared as he felt at that moment.

"What the hell you think you doin, white boy?" the man bellowed loud enough to be heard above the din around them.

Mike was close by and immediately jumped out of his car. He made eye contact with Jen who understood that she should get over to Sara, as Mike was about to leave her. He ran over to where Don was and just stood there, not saying anything. Motion in the other cars began to cease as the attention drew to the unfolding drama.

The young man now was standing too, and he and Mike now locked up, eye to eye. Mike knew, someone always backs down in these situations, even if that backing down is caused by a bullet or a baton cracked against the back of a head. Same results, the threat is removed. But until then, all aggressive emotions fire in unison, seeking out a flaw and any possible advantage, seeking dominance.

Mike broke the impasse by pulling out his wallet from his back pocket, flipping it open and flashing his police badge at the black man and said, "You know what this means." His eyes and voice remained level. He was carrying his revolver in his right front pocket but could tell already that there would be no need for it. And the black man did know, did know the way justice on the streets of this city was handled. Hurt a cop in any way and you'd be lucky to only get roughed up. Mike had been on raids of this kind. After an attack on a cop, word would get around and off duty cops from surrounding precincts would show up at a prearranged time in the neighborhood of the perpetrator and mete out one form of justice. And these incidents never made it onto anyone's blotter or news report; the police assigned to this neighborhood, not surprisingly, remaining absent during the assaults.

"Man, don't give me that bull." he responded but backed off, exiting the arena, relieving the tension, at least for now.

Don was the only one directly involved in this human interaction unaware of the different levels of meaning at work. All he knew was that his uncle had come to his rescue and for that reason was his hero. It was as if he had never really seen his uncle before and was looking at him now for the first time. Don never really had much direct contact with his Uncle Mike. If he was aware of him at all it was probably because he was yelling or laughing too loudly. But now he stood there, large and powerful, gazing out with full composure and concentration.

Maybe, Don thought, I don't need to do this alone. Maybe there is a source of power out there waiting for me, wanting to help me.

Back at his new home, Don reflected on the events of the day. After they left the Bumper Car ride there was still tension within the group, but not as much as he had expected. In fact, within some short period of time the tension was replaced with exhilarated high energy. Even though they had just snacked, they walked over to Nathan's and feasted on hot dogs, french fries, and cole slaw. The adults, particularly Uncle Mike, consumed large quantities of beer. The children drank large cups of iced tea. They laced it with sugar and the strong, biting taste of the tea washed down the food, enhancing the harsh, vinegary cole slaw and the ketchup drenched french fries, all of which they ate in abundance. They stood around a couple of round, formica-topped tables, situated inside Nathan's and outside on the boards. Grease stained paper products were littered around the tables and soon were all that was left from the consumed food. The mood was celebratory, a sense of victory pervaded, and Uncle Mike joked and carried on almost non stop. As Don thought about it afterward in bed, a better time was hard to imagine.

Chapter 7

When Rose and Ben were alive they would often get together with Jen and Mike for a game of Pinochle. It was a cheap night out they used to say, and laughed when saying it. It was some of their best times together, and now those times were over forever. One day, about 4 months after the tragedy, Jen was talking to her brother Frank about these times and all of a sudden they were making plans, themselves, to play. They would have to teach Jessie but that should not be a problem because she had been a Bridge player at one time and everyone always said how similar the two games were. Bridge always carried with it some quality of sophistication and snobbishness while Pinochle was a working man's game. Few people played both and only supposition about each crossed the barrier that separated them. In this light the notion that the games were similar could be seen as ironic, as everything else about them was different. They planned to get together the following Friday at Frank's home. Jen said she would bring the pizzas and Frank volunteered to supply plenty of cold beer and sodas for the kids.

Although it seemed like a good idea at the time, the closer they got to the date the more apprehensive Jen became. These had been special times and now she felt as though she were trespassing upon them. But if she had expressed these thoughts to Mike, she knew he would laugh at her and say something like, "What are you worrying about?" and swipe his hand through the air in front of his face like he was swatting a fly or casting off some evil intent. So she held this in and tried to discredit these ideas of hers.

They arrived bearing pizza that was still partially warm. They all sat around the dining room table that would double as a card table for the adults in a short while, casually discussing events that had occurred since they'd last been together. The main topic that was not discussed was Don's increasingly strange behavior. Frank, as he now looked down the table at Don munching on his pizza crust, carrying on and behaving every bit like the 11 year old that he was, thought about the time earlier in the week when he took Don along with him to pick up his car from the local mechanic.

He had been going to Nick's Auto Repair for many years and was friendly with the owner and mechanics working there. They weren't giving anything away but only did what was needed and did a good job, and because Frank had no interest in doing the work himself he accepted the cost of these services without too much of a sense of being taken advantage of. The shop was on a road that made no pretensions about itself. Junk yards, lumber yards, and auto repair shops made their place of business here, making it possible for the nicer neighborhoods it abutted to maintain their way of life, or jettison that which no longer fit into it. Frank did not mind coming down here, and even took some pleasure in it. Sometimes he waited for more than an hour, filling the time by reading the paper and casually speaking with the workers or the others waiting for the repairs on their cars to be completed.

This time they did not need to wait long and when Frank was handed the bill to review, he placed it down on the counter and pulled out his reading glasses. At this moment he sensed Don's presence beside him. It was not how he expected him to be, and he was still trying to decipher what had transpired in the short interval of time that followed. Don was standing there as if he considered himself the center of this transaction. He injected himself more by his body posture than by anything he said. Then there was the expression on his face which had nothing child-like about it, no indecision, no acceptance of an adult shape to the world that he should know better than to try to lay claim to. The little man-child was so bold as to reposition the bill in a way so that it was easier for him to read it and began studying it line by line. Frank and the mechanic looked at each other, only for an instant. Usually, a child acting precociously like this would cause a smile or perhaps minor irritation. But this was something entirely different, eery and unnatural. Frank pondered this again now. He had told no one about what had happened and would have found it impossible to put into words the effect it had had on him.

The meal was wrapping up and the table was cleared. The children went to the living room to sit around the TV but then Don returned to the table where the adults were setting things up for their game of cards. Drinks from dinner remained but everything else was removed and the sounds of the cards being shuffled and idle talk from the adults filled the air. His aunts and uncles were relaxing now, and they reminded him of how his parents acted at times like these. There had never been much contact between the kids and parents once dinner was finished. But this time he felt drawn back into the dining room and the game that was about to begin, the game that his parents had so recently participated in.

"I want to learn to play," he said with force and determination.

This was met with surprise, the result of not comprehending what drove his desire.

"Sure, honey, you come sit with your Aunt Jessie and we can learn how to play Pinochle together."

Mike and Jen passed an expression between them as this offer was being made because they had doubts Don would be able to grasp how the game was played. Just having one of the children seated at the table ruffled Mike's feathers a little. What's to stop them all from wanting to play he thought. And then what would we do? He believed this was a time that was decidedly not intended for interaction with the children. Maybe an occasional question for asking permission to do this or that, but that was about the extent to which he expected, or wanted, to pay attention to them.

The cards were dealt face up for the first couple of hands and the rules of how to play them and the corresponding bidding was explained.

The 2 couples sat across from each other and would be partners. Don picked the cards up for he and his aunt. He was told to sort the cards by suit and value order, alternating the black and red colored suits. When that was completed, he was to place the cards back on the table and then the practice hand would be played.

Even this seemingly simple task proved difficult for Don. At first he was confident he would be able to assemble them perfectly, and that they constituted a killer hand because of all the high cards he was looking at, but then his mind experienced a slight disconnect when he witnessed a pair of queens in his hand and both of them were diamonds. He stopped adjusting the rest of the cards and pointed at the 2 queens, with an expression that reflected his confusion.

His aunt was puzzled by this, and instead of seeking a cause for it, glossed over it, not realizing he had never seen a Pinochle deck before. Instead she said, "It's a start but I think we'll need some help if we are going to meld them. Why don't we get the cards on the table and then we'll see if they're worth anything."

These words were equally incomprehensible to Don so he went back to arranging the cards. The others had long before finished the task when Don finally place theirs on the table.

"The idea is to win points and there are 2 ways to get them. One is to place down meld at the beginning of the game and the other is to win tricks." Mike began.

Jen picked up the narrative, "Before you start playing your hand you need to bid it. The winner of the bid gets to call trump. Here is what gives you meld and how much they are worth."

Jen removed from her purse a piece of paper she had prepared earlier that contained a list of card combinations and their point values in the categories in which they belonged. Jessie placed the paper between herself and Don, and looked the list over quickly. She then motioned she was ready to proceed, and receive more details about how the game was played.

They continued to delve into the intricacies of the game including bidding which included subtle, indirect messages to your partner; and with each word spoken Don felt himself sinking further into an incomprehensible morass. How could this game that he had so often seen his parents play with an idle sense of concentration be so foreign and so complicated?

"Remember, the 10 is more powerful than any card except the Ace but it does not give you any points when you are counting trump at the end of the game."

"Any bid more than 10 is considered a "jump bid" and usually means that there is at least one suit for which you have no cards that belong in the run."

"During bidding you can 'pass' or 'pass with help'."

Aunt Jessie listened intently and Don tried to imply that he was doing the same. But all there was, was the look and the facade offered by the look, and he knew it. His only hope was that Aunt Jessie would ask questions that would help him gain some understanding of the game; because he had no basis of understanding from which to ask his questions. But as the hand moved from phase to phase it became clear to Don that Aunt Jessie somehow had grasped these instructions that for him were unintelligible. Each card played would result in some trifling detail being conveyed, filling in Aunt Jessie's understanding and at the same time stranding him further from any hope of catching up. These bits of information were for him all small cuts that he was forced to endure silently.

"So are we ready to get started!" Mike said, and looked across at the players. His gazed passed over Don's and Don obliged him by diverting his eyes from this inquiry.

Don's survival, as he understood it, was in entering into the world of adult certitude. It was the only thing that could free him from the nagging restlessness that was always there, always a part of him. *If I could just be that other way, that I can see and sense, but am unable to know.* How far he was from this goal he sensed when he saw how a game of cards left him feeling like he was cursed, thoroughly incapable, a sham.

As the cards were coming around, Don reached for them as he had done when the cards were laid face down. But after they had been sorted and placed on the table with their values face up, in the learning rounds, his involvement had been essentially non existent. Jessie had taken to selecting the next card to play and may or may not have looked to Don for concurrence, which he was always quick to grant when it was asked for.

Mike had directed the cards for this first real hand towards Jessie intentionally but watched as Don reached across his aunt to snatch them up. When the cards were assembled, Don stared blankly at them and Jessie peered over his shoulder. They played the first 2 hands in this manner, Don allowing Jessie to direct the play of their hand and learning a little about the strategy involved.

In truth, there was not a lot of play in the hands for them. They had little meld and lacked good playing hands. So they passed when it was their turn to bid and allowed the other team to direct play during the taking of tricks. Even this was not so disagreeable except that they were down by a score of 600 to 140 after two rounds of play.

Their luck appeared to change when Jessie noticed a king of each suit and pointed to them for Don to see. This gave them 80 points towards the minimum bid of 250. Their playing hand was not particularly strong but they were the first to bid and Jessie whispered into Don's ear that they should start the bid at 250 and he did so with gusto in his voice.

Everyone else passed so they won the bid and called for clubs to be trump. Frank passed 4 cards from his hand to Don, as the rules required. Don found it difficult to control them and the cards in his hand so Jessie picked them up and presented them so they both could see them. They offered little help to the hand and Jessie started to wonder if they would not be able to make what she had originally thought was a safe bid. She laid them into the hand and selected 4 others that she passed back to Frank. At that point, everyone laid down their meld.

Mike laid down aces, which drew a round of ahhhs from the adults. Apart from the 4 kings, only the 2 9s of clubs were laid down by Jen. The points were jotted down by Jen, who was the score keeper; the cards returned to the hands, and play began.

As the tricks were being played, Don sensed a disturbing trend develop. Whenever it was their turn to lead, his aunt directed him to place a card but then his uncle Mike invariably played a better cards and won the trick. All four of Mike's aces were played early and were winners. The flow of play shifted from Jessie and Don leading the cards, to the other team of Mike and Jen controlling play. Back and forth they worked the rounds, Mike being short suited in hearts but with more trump than the other team combined, and Jen with a near run of hearts. Frank looked on with a resigned expression and signaled that he was powerless to head off the assault being mounted by the other team. They would not make their bid and it did not take that long to realize it. Jessie carefully studied their cards but ultimately there was little they could do, so she directed Don to throw out loser after loser.

When the hand was played out, the carnage over, Frank asked Mike, "Why didn't you choose trump if you were sitting there with those aces?"

The cards were being collected and then would be shuffled and it was not unusual during the time between hands to discuss the strategy employed in the just completed hand. "When Jessie took the bid I decided not to bid against her. I had the four Aces and was short in hearts. I was hoping Jen would be able to make my clubs winners and it worked out that way."

Don, who didn't understand everything that had just been said, did understand that a trap had been laid for them and that they had fallen into it. "That's not fair. You didn't explain that rule to us," he blurted out, defiance and anger coursing through each word.

"I suppose you're right." Mike said, "I guess you just have to learn some of the rules the hard way."

Within an instant Don's rage was full blown, and he chose to direct it at Jessie, "You were the one telling me to play those cards, how much to bid. Now you see how wrong you were. And we lost because of you."

Everyone at the table was stunned. Mike and Jen were used to kids overreacting but this fury, coming from nowhere, left them shaken.

"Now just a minute, young man," Mike erupted, ratcheting up

the aggression so that his tone was even more intense than Don's. "You will not talk to your aunt that way." His eyes pierced right through Don, as he tried to master him, which he felt with the full force of his being was his right to do in this situation. The right to assert his authority at this time was something he believed in without question; not anyone or any force of nature would succeed in making him back down from what he saw as his responsibility.

Jessie looked on, bewildered at how quickly and unexpectedly shared hopes could be ripped down, left in tatters. What would Rose have done, what should she, herself, do? She wanted to calm the boy as she had seen Rose do, but was too uncertain of how to proceed to do anything. Even the simple gesture of placing her hand upon Don's which sat there beside hers on the table seemed too risky and the strength in her body to raise her hand to do so did not exist.

"Why don't we just move on, play the next hand?" Frank offered, but he also knew that it was probably not possible to just go back and start over; that there was no reset button to be hit after what had just happened. And so he drifted, removing himself to some safer, quieter place.

Nothing was ever easy for Don. In school he would look at other children working furiously along row after row of math problems. They would finish in half the time and got more problems right so he could reach no other conclusion than they were more than twice as good as he was... And there was nothing in his power to change that. He found it impossible to organize the small shelf enclosed beneath his desk that was intended for books and supplies. In his old school, his 5th grade teacher had seized upon this fact. Periodically, in the middle of class, she would tell him to empty the contents of of the shelf onto the top of the desk. After the books were removed, he would unearth layers of crumbled papers, tissues, and assorted paper and plastic wrappings. The teacher made fun in an evil, mocking manner. The children laughed not with him but at him. He said he would keep his space organized from that time forward, not letting the confused mess envelope him again, but even as he spoke these words he knew he would fail in these attempts. When he looked inside himself, he saw something as detestable and chaotic as these fragments of things, especially the used tissues left to dry and become encrusted together.

Layer by layer he conspired to hide his cursed nature from anything and anyone around him. His tools were lying, cheating, and fighting when necessary. He could also be charming and duplicitous. But what he wanted most was the freedom to escape himself, free to be one of those smart kids for whom school work came easily and quickly because that's where praise and acceptance were to be found. And when that freedom from himself would not come, the desire turned inward setting off seismic tremors of dangerous, blinding fury.

Don now turned and directed himself to his Uncle Mike. "You should play to win, not to make us lose."

Mike, at first was unsure how to respond to this attack, unsure if he even should. But then he said, "I didn't do anything that's against the rules. That's how the game is played." His speech had a hint of defensiveness to it, that even he was aware of and that infuriated him.

"I think it was sneaky. Anyway, why couldn't you have taken it easy on us and let us win at least one hand."

"Because we are playing for real now. And you are not the one making the rules. In fact, you weren't even invited to play in the first place."

"So," Don said, sensing an advantage, or the potential for one if he pursued the right line of reasoning which was just coming into focus, "that's why you played it that way. To make me feel bad so that I would leave you alone."

"If I wanted you to leave, I'd have told you to leave," Mike said. But Don's words had hit their mark. Mike wondered how his actions could get so twisted around. Unconsciously he wondered if there were not at least a hint of truth to what Don was saying. He had already admitted to himself that he would rather not have had children at the table playing. But tempers were now overtaking any clear thinking, something familiar if unnamed for both himself and the boy. Mike would never really think about why having children involved in the game was so disagreeable, how their presence took the fun out of it for him.

"Well, I don't want to leave. I want to learn how to play Pinochle. But why don't you give us a chance?"

"You're lucky to be sitting at the table at all. If it were up to me, you would not even be touching the cards."

"So I am right. You're just trying to get rid of me."

"I wasn't, but now I am. You need to go play with the other kids." Mike looked not so fierce as he had in Coney Island, but very nearly. Don jumped from his seat and ran, feeling triumphant in some way, as though he had just succeeded in exposing some strain of evil. But this discovery in no way cooled the fires inside him.

The row house had three levels, with the top level being rented to another couple. The other kids had run off to the lower of the two levels Frank and Jessie lived in, which contained the bedrooms. The two floors were as different as could be. The one the adults now occupied contained a dining room, living room and kitchen, and this area had a sense of spaciousness with its high ceilings and long dimensions. Exposed wood beams were stained a rich shade of mahogany and the entire area had a subdued quality. On the other hand, the lower level where the bedrooms and bathroom were, had almost a basement-like feel to it. In the colder months, the heating unit in an enclosed area rasped and groaned when it started and rattled the pipes when it was dispensing its charge. The bedroom Sara and Don were staying in had no window to the outside and, as a result, always felt cold and damp. This is where the three children had settled in. Anne and Sara were dressing some of Sara's dolls on her bed while Tim sat on the floor looking at his collection of baseball cards. Down the hall from the bedroom, a doorway opened out to the small back yard and, beyond that, the garage faced out to the alley that connected to the main thoroughfares at both ends of the block.

Don pulled a shoe box out of the closet with his set of cards. He took a seat next to Tim and the two boys began looking at their own and each other's cards. Don's shoe box had dividers that designated the American and National leagues, and the teams within those leagues. Another section of the box contained duplicates and these were the ones he would use for trading and flipping. Tim had just gotten a three ring binder that had plastic holders to display 9 cards on a side. He was in the process of going through his collection and separating out the best cards, which included any Yankee and any of the other stars past and present. This was the first time Don had seen the binder and was jealous of how well it displayed Tim's collection and, even more, how perfectly it protected the cards from harm and disfigurement.

The cards would be studied. Batting styles, action shots, and steady gazes into the camera were all pondered and internalized. The back side of the card contained players' stats, the first and probably only spread sheet most American youth of this era would study with religious fervor. Also on the back would be the briefest bio of the player; some trivial, whimsical fact about the man or a retelling of an exquisite moment he had engineered on the baseball diamond.

The study of the cards gave way to the most fundamental mix of competition, skill and gambling the boys would engage in perhaps forever and certainly for many years to come. The first competition involved "flipping" the cards. Both boys grabbed a stack of their own cards. With a round house motion of one's arm, you would hold a card on its width-wise edges with the tips of your fingers and let it go at just the right moment. This caused the cards to rotate rapidly and descend to the ground in an arc. Landing either face up or down, it was the job of the second boy to match this heads up or down position with his card. If he was successful he won his opponent's card, if not he lost his own. The margin of error was slim. A skilled player on a roll could make 8 or 9 out of 10 come up the way he had intended, but it required a steady, controlled, loose motion, not unlike a baseball swing itself.

Eventually, they tired of this, and chose to continue the contest outside with a different game. From a distance of about 10 feet from the back wall of the garage, they would flick the cards towards the wall and whichever landed closer was the winner. If they were fortunate enough to get a leaner, they not only won but got an additional 5 cards from their opponent. Leaners were not all luck, but included a fair measure of that, too. The controlled leaner was accomplished by skipping the card shortly before the wall which would cause it to rise up after making contact with the ground and possibly coming to rest in a leaning position between wall and sidewalk. The downside of going for leaners was that if you missed, it may skip off the wall and land further from the wall than what a safer, laser-like throw would result in. These were chances you calculated and were wholly dependent on how good you felt, how good the cards and your hand were communicating. They enlisted Sara and Anne to help them, whose tasks it was to collect the cards after each pair of cards were thrown. Normally, the girls would not be interested in helping, but they were growing bored with their own activities and consented to fulfilling this role.

After some time of competing in this manner, they commenced with the final variation of card tossing. This required throwing cards in the direction of the wall, as they had been doing. The difference was that you were not trying to get closer to the wall than your opponent. Instead, the goal was to have your card land on top of a card that had already been throw. This was the only version where more than two could play, and that was preferred because the number of cards that might be played before someone succeeded in topping another could be high, and the resulting loses could be large with only two players. This was also much more a game of chance than the others and this appealed to some players more than others.

Sara and Anne stayed on to watch although the games went longer and really did not require their assistance.

The first 8 cards were sent out in a hurried, random, spiraling array. The velocity generated from the properly executed flick of the wrist was astonishing. Good players could hone in on targets to a surprising degree, but not enough for the early stages of this game. So this was the time to have fun with the cards, release them in different ways so they would flutter through the air before descending to the ground.

"C'mon Tim, you can do it." Anne cheered, replacing her former role with that of cheerleader for her brother. Sara watched quietly, lacking any real interest in the outcome of this competition.

After the first sets of cards were thrown, Tim and Don focused their attention and got down to business.

The number of agonizingly near winners, for both Don and Tim, were incredibly large and Anne reacted dramatically to each one of these.

Soon a great panoply of shimmering baseball cards lay strewn about the ground, at least 40 in all; a collage of baseball glory and history. Now when cards were thrown both players secretly wished to not top another, to keep this extraordinary run of *bad* luck from ending, which had become something else, something of a greater magnitude and a source of extreme pleasure, that left them buckling over in spasm after spasm of laughter. Not wanting to win but recognizing that someone must win, something would occur to end this sense of wonder and disbelief. To try to force the game to not end somehow was artificial and that, too, would cause what was providing so much enjoyment, to end.

Tim threw a card and it landed directly on top of another. The game was over and he no longer felt the goodness that he had felt the moment before. Anne, on the other hand, cheered loudly, pumping her fists in the air and began collecting the cards spread around, as if they were wafers of gold.

Don felt crushed, wobbly inside. A plan hatched in his mind and he immediately pursued it.

"Wait a minute." he told the others, "I have an idea for another game."

He entered the garage which he had been in just a few days before when he and his uncle had returned from getting the car repaired. He took down from one wall a long piece of thick rope that hung from a hook on a peg board that contained tools of various kinds. He took it outside along with a ladder that could be opened up to be free standing.

"Here's how you play this game." he told the others as his

hands worked the rope. He had been intrigued by the hangman's knot, the beauty of the twisting strands that formed a passage way for the main strand of the rope to move through. He had seen the knot in a Boy Scout book and practiced tying it on lighter string until he was able to construct it without much difficulty.

The 3 other children were transfixed by the sure, rapid movements of his hands, not the movements one would associate with someone of their age, and mesmerized by his words. Everything began to move as rapidly as the tying of the rope, and felt just as unreal as the surgeon-like precision that Don was displaying.

"I'm going to throw one side over that tree branch a few times to get it secured," he said, pointing to the lowest branch of the only tree in the yard, an old maple that dominated the yard and stood 40 feet tall although was deformed in shape because of its close proximity to the building.

When he was done with the knot and was satisfied with its look and functionality, he continued his instructions. While he was talking, he got on the ladder and tossed the knotted end around a large branch of the tree 3 times so that the knot was elevated about 10 feet above the ground.

Then, as he was completing these actions he said, "We'll take turns but Anne will go first." And he beckoned to her to come to him.

Although she felt she should resist this directive, run from it, she was powerless to do either. Sara and Tim likewise were transfixed, dumbly willing to comply without question, as if this was somehow preordained and was a continuation of something that had happened long ago.

Don led Anne up the steps of the ladder and had her place her arms above her head. He attached the rope to her wrists and tightened the rope securely. Whatever trust Anne had was now gone when she felt the rope biting into her wrists, constraining them. But there was no turning back. She looked out at the wall of continuous brick, the other side of which were the homes of the people in the row houses. And something about what she saw suggested why this could happen here and not in her own backyard, or any backyard in her neighborhood, or even in Don's home where he had lived with his family. But here there seemed no bottom to what could happen, the spirit of the wall itself seeming endless and uncaring.

She had no control and Don pushed her from the ladder. When she hit the bottom of the pendulum swing, she sensed the desperation of the situation. The tendons of her scapular tore painfully and when she tried to assert her strength to stop the pain, she realized she had no reservoir of power from which to draw. She swayed painfully without control, consumed by feelings of panic.

The card game inside was interrupted by Anne's wailing. Mike was the first out of his seat with the others following close behind. The sight of Anne swaying in the wind was something horrible for all of them to see. And the other children, just standing there, made it even more disturbing. Mike got to the ladder and after getting Anne situated on it, removed the rope from her wrists. Her wrists were red and swollen but she was unaware of the pain her body was experiencing. Crowding out these feelings were ones of great shame and distrust. She ran past her brother and cousins and wondered how this could happen, how could they hate her so much to do this to her?

Jessie and Jen ran after Anne to attend to her while Mike and Frank stayed behind. The men looked at the three children who seemed as perplexed as they were and began the process of unraveling what had just taken place.

Chapter 8

Frank dialed the numbers to Jen's house. He watched his hand, which was trembling, search out each number on the rotary and twisted the dial harder with each turning motion. This action relieved some small amount of tension, not so much because of the physical act itself but because it represented another step towards the goal he was moving towards, which his body pursued more like a sprint than a long distance race.

In his mind, the experiment was over. The fact that it had ended in utter failure was secondary to the fact that he could now free himself from this virus of change. After Anne's hands had been untied, Mike and he marched the three kids back into the house. After a brief interrogation, that left no doubt in their minds about what had taken place, Mike took Donald over his knee and gave him several swift smacks on his butt. Frank looked at Don's form, which appeared too large to be treated in this way; his legs bent down towards the ground but his torso and upper body held stiff and parallel to the floor. Don took it quietly, letting out only the occasional grunt and when it was over ran into the bedroom he was staying in. Mike yelled after him that he was to stay there until he was given permission to leave, but Don yelled back at them that that was fine with him and he didn't want to see anybody anyway. Jen and her family helped clean up and then gathered their things together and left. They did not said goodbye to Don, who stayed in his room alone.

Now, two hours later, Frank was dialing the phone, and Jen had just picked up the other end. After greetings were exchanged,

Frank said to Jen, "Soon after you left, you'll never guess what happened."

Jen did not respond which left Frank to continue his story, "I heard a thumping noise coming from the living room and walked into it to see what was going on. Don was trying to move the TV console, the whole large cabinet and all. He got it halfway into the room by pushing it with his shoulder. When I asked him what he was doing, he said that it wasn't fair that he had to stay in his room and if he had to, he was going to move the TV in there with him." Frank went onto explain the struggle he had with Don and how he had to physically restrain him.

The house was like a powder keg. In Frank's mind there were no exits from the distress save one, and that was to jettison those children from his home. When he looked back, beyond these several months with Don and Sara all he saw was the peace, order, and serenity of his life alone with Jessie, the simple oasis that their home provided against the backdrop of the chaotic world surrounding it. The emptiness that could be there also, and the boredom and most of all the finality and lack of young life was something in these last couple of hours he had reconciled himself to, embraced in some way with a feeling of calm and purpose. Although he was describing to Jen the distressing details of what had just transpired in his house, his mind and soul were lifting because he sensed with clarity the destiny that would shape the remainder of his and Jessie's lives. If he were being honest with himself, his goal now was to determine the best way to disassociate himself from these kids. But he knew that he needed to take some care in doing this and part of that process was to lay out the causes for ending this relationship, which he was doing right now. He practiced on Jen what he would tell again afterward, changing the narrative slightly based on the audience, one of whom was his own conscience, which would need to be dulled if he were to unite again with his former confident relationship to everything around him.

"I had to force him back into his room, with Don all the while struggling against me. He continued knocking around inside it, banging things and throwing things around. All the while he is raving, pleading his case as if before a judge, trying to draw me into a discussion about his rights to behave the way he has. I ended up securing the door from the outside and walking away."

What he did not convey was his discussion with Jessie that took place after Don settled down. They began talking about their options and all of a sudden Frank felt the emotion welling up in him. The tears then began streaming down his cheeks. He was not given to outward displays of emotion and could not remember the last time he had cried, really cried. He knew that he was rattled by what happened but could not understand the tears, and was in fact embarrassed by them. He would never fully realize the source of this expression of emotion, which was the sadness he felt over their inability to make a go of it with Don and Sara, the failure on his part to bend the perspectives of these children to his way of seeing the world and behaving accordingly within it.

He had been visited by memories of his youth almost from the time Don and Sara had come to live with them. His memories of the past, the years of his growing up, were still crystal clear. The bulk of that time was spent in a small town on the outskirts of Pittsburgh, until the Depression hit. His father lost his job in one of the steel mills and then a job opened in New York City. A few months after his starting work, the family followed him east to the big city. And so, over the years that little town in Pittsburgh took on an almost mythical quality. He and his buddies, many of whom were related by blood in one way or another, had roamed freely over abandoned lots and undeveloped spaces. They grew strong and learned how to settle differences on their own. A ball and stick would keep them occupied for hours. Abandoned wood and other supplies would be scavenged for projects like tree houses and go-carts. The world was limitless, but also tightly confined and controlling, and there was no contradiction in any of this. To say that this was the world he fought to preserve in WW II was an understatement. It was the only world he knew or would ever recognize as desirable, convinced that deviation from it led eventually to chaos, the freeing of evil like that which sent him to Europe for all those years in the prime of his life.

He laughed as they all had at the family's first experiences in New York City. The family moved into an apartment right in the heart of midtown Manhattan. It was small but the six of them managed. What country bumpkins they were at that time, roaming the streets of New York just as they had in their little home town, searching for an abandoned lot in which to play, a game of stick ball to get chosen into. But even New York at that time had a gentler side, with little of the coarseness that was now so common. Strangers answered questions politely and offered help without asking. These were not the best of times but neither were they the worst. They were making a transition borne of necessity. Their needs were minimal and the world they were entering was not entirely hostile; the long tendrils of home back in Pittsburgh were something they knew were there and they would carry with them their entire lives.

The hardest thing that he faced now was his certainty that the life force connecting him with that youthful sense of adventure, that he began reliving when Don and Sara began living with them, would end with him. Those memories and experiences would not be passed on. He had come to accept this once before but allowed himself to consider whether there could be some continuity, whether life could be breathed back into them. But now he knew they would begin to dissipate; he saw clearly once again how it all ended with him.

Jen and Frank concluded their conversation by saying they would need to get back together the following day and consider what should be done next. It was late and the day's events had left everyone spent, emotionally and physically. Frank passed the children's room and heard nothing, so assumed they were resting; finally there would be no more crises to attend to. Jessie was already in their bedroom. She was attending to the rituals she performed at the end of each day and was sitting at her make-up table removing her jewelry.

Frank brushed alongside her, letting his hand graze along her shoulders and the small of her back, on the way to his side of the bed. Wordlessly he replaced his day clothing with his night clothes, mindless of his actions. Instead of doing the routine things that he did prior to going to bed, he simply slipped under the covers and closed his eyes and waited for Jessie to join him. Their ritual of kissing and holding each other briefly was done, but Frank felt only the mechanical aspects of these motions and was numb to the pleasure they usually gave him.

Sleep came quickly to him, deep, wonderful sleep. And he began to dream almost as soon as sleep descended upon him. He found himself in a large room, or something that reminded him of a room. All but one side extended seemingly without end, dimensionless. The wall in front of him was circular and curved out of sight. Doors existed on this wall, but there were no windows to suggest what lay beyond it. Conditions in the room he was in, if you could call it a room, were horrible. There was a stench suggesting rotten garbage and excrement. A cold wind whipped along the corridor and passed through him. He heard voices off in the distance, but they were in foreign languages and of no comfort to him, and the dark gray lighting made it impossible to see the people speaking these words. Other noises could be heard as well, but they were equally indistinguishable and sounded like the banging of heavy machinery off in the distance.

Within moments he opened one of the doors that led into the interior setting. This room was shaped like the room he was just in. The first thing he perceived was another circular wall opposing him, the same as the one he just passed through. The difference was that his senses were not assaulted to the same degree as they had just been, but still the sensation received from this space was far from pleasurable. The other major difference was that he could see people moving before him, most of whom he was familiar with, but with whom he would prefer not to engage. Frank sensed he was able to control the degree to which he was actively involved in his surroundings. If he chose to, he could remain invisible, as he was now, or break into the actions played out before him. He lingered in this corridor a bit longer but grew disenchanted with what he witnessed. It was not long before he made his way across the room and selected one of the doors on the opposing wall. The lighting again grew brighter and now the surroundings were noticeably more sparse. There were scenes of his common life, and members of his family and friends passed by. But now his focus shifted from the activity in the current room to what lay beyond the doors on the opposing wall. He ran to the door and opened it, and did the same several more times, experiencing only briefly the more and more pleasurable scenes that greeted him, never stopping to interact with any of the participants or admiring the increasingly rarefied surroundings. Then he entered a room that was much like his own bedroom. He saw himself and Jessie resting, then emerging from a restful night's sleep. The first sensation breaking through the haze of sleep was a summer breeze separating the sheer curtains in front of the windows before it swept over their two bodies.

The image registered with him and at first he lingered on it, contemplating the texture of this most intimate aspect of his life. But the room was not his room and at the far end of it was yet another door that he could not keep himself from running towards, opening, and passing through. There was nothing there but pure light, which lacked sound and sensation. Space itself was a mystery not to be unraveled. He found he could kick up his heels and was now floating, in a soundless, peaceful ocean.

He woke up at this moment. At first he felt calmed by the final episode of the dream, which he remembered in vivid detail. But then he became aware of his sweat drenched pillow and a cold, empty feeling that pervaded his consciousness as the dream seeped away. The night was now dark and deep and he felt at its mercy. He huddled into himself, searching out the warmth that his body could produce and the comfort of the bed linen. Soon he went in search of a deeper, obliterating sleep, one that severed all contact with the conscious world.

The following day was a workday but the three siblings and their spouses agreed to meet and discuss Sara's and Don's future. The whole day the sun stayed behind a thick, all encompassing wall of clouds and the six adults used the anesthetizing affects of the elements to harden themselves to what was coming, the unsettling options available to them. They chose to meet at Frank's house. This was not their first choice, but was selected because they felt Don could not be trusted with a baby sitter. Sara and Don were told to stay in their room on the lower level when the adults began the discussion mapping their future.

They took their seats in the living room. These row houses had a sense of permanence, of grandness even, that the stick built homes in the same price range did not possess. With their high ceilings and dark wood paneling you felt a sense of dignity that could either inspire or overwhelm. They had spent many evenings here, but none like the one in which they were about to take part.

They sat around chatting about incidental matters to begin with, and each was given a drink to take the edge off. But the real topic to be discussed was never far removed. They all searched awkwardly for some way to enter into this topic but they had no model for how to speak about something so unpleasant, how to preserve who they were while addressing a topic that had nothing but damning options.

Finally Jen attempted to begin the discussion that had brought them together by directing the following statement to Jessie and Frank, "So, I guess things haven't been going as well around here as we had hoped they might."

Frank allowed a small chuckle to escape from him and replied, "That's an understatement."

An uncomfortably long pause followed but then Frank forced himself to go on, "It's just not working. We gave it a try. But it's just not working out."

"We know you tried. And we appreciate that." Jen replied to her older brother, and at the same time, Jessie placed her hand on Frank's. Although some aspects of what would happen were not yet known, the greatest part of Jessie and Frank's future was made apparent to the others in that instant.

They had all looked quietly, inwardly into the future throughout the day, as they had anticipated these words. Mike and Jen had allowed Anne to stay home from school. Although they did not want to baby her, they knew she had strained some muscles in her back and could see how listless she was as a result of what had happened the day before. The idea of taking Sara and Don into their home was unthinkable. Mike and Jen had piled on the reasons to justify this decision but it did not do anything for the pangs of guilt this was causing them, particularly Jen.

Dan sat in his chair, but appeared agitated. He sensed his chance to announce himself, define himself to his older siblings and their spouses. What words of wisdom could he offer to make things right. He was the jester in the family, the clown, but sometimes he sensed that he spoke with such clarity that the force of his own words inspired him and, he was sure, those around him. But, try as he might, the source for that inspiration eluded him now.

"There must be something we can do," Dan blurted out and pounded his hand against the coffee table in front of him. The others turned towards him, as if seeing him for the first time, but none could find a way to deflect the embarrassment they all felt for him. Normally Rose was the one to calm Dan down, reign him in, raise his spirits in difficult times. But now they just stared at him as he cast his pensive gaze at the wall opposing him.

"We could take them in temporarily," Jen said. "But our house is too small and I just can't see that working long term." These comments were initially met with the same tacit agreement with which Frank's comments had been greeted.

But Dan would have none of that and responded, "We could get you some bunk beds and the boys and girls could double up. Sure, you could do it."

Dan felt he had struck upon gold, and maneuvered to have his idea adopted by the others, have it be seen as a reflection of his inventive mind. Instead, this was yet another instance of how the lack of nuance in Dan's thinking had the potential to get him in trouble. Undaunted, his comment caused the discussion to spin in an uncontrolled and unwanted direction: a detailed discussion of whether or not Jen and Mike's house could accommodate Sara and Don.

Sara and Don remained banished in their bedroom on the lower level. Sara sat in one corner of the room playing by herself. She had her dolls in front of her and a small set of clothes that were assembled in a miniature play closet laid opened before her. She could stay lost in this imaginary world for hours, robing and disrobing her entourage, imaging great balls and romance with each change of costume.

Don laid on his bed for a long time after dinner. He tried to look at his baseball cards but they could not hold his interest. Other than his cards, he had no hobbies that he enjoyed on his own and was not one to pick up a book and start reading to pass the time. He got up and found the tie that he had worn to his mother's funeral. His uncle Frank had not taken it back and he had in fact tried to teach Don how to tie the half Windsor knot with it. These had been only brief lessons and Don had never been able to perform correctly the necessary sequence of steps. He fumbled with it now, letting his hands pass over it and appreciate the feel of the material once again. He began to loop one side around the other and instead of mechanically trying to recall the steps his uncle had shown him, looked at the tie to determine how to maneuver it to acquire the desired shape. He tried pulling it roughly as he remembered his uncle doing but he usually tugged it in the wrong direction and did not accomplish what he sought after. Surprisingly, his failures did not bother him and he was able to undo what he had done and try again, which he did over and over.

His father always wore ties to work but he would never have thought to ask him to teach him how to make one. Usually he was away at his job as a traveling salesman. He told Don he sold insurance, which was some vague concept for him. When asked what that was, his dad joked that he was there to bail people out if they messed up or when something bad happened to them. Don had never given this much thought but now devoted some concentration to this idea, wondering at its applicability, and how one went about purchasing some of this insurance.

Mostly he thought of his dad as someone who did not have a lot to say even when he was around. When he died, Don kept waiting for some memories of him to enter his thoughts, but that was almost never the case. All he saw was his tall, lean body dressed in his business suit, his full head of prematurely gray hair combed straight back, not a hair out of place. He was restrained at home, not easily coaxed out of some protective covering, happiest it seemed when together in gatherings with Don's mother's family.

Don pulled from the closet the suit he had worn at his parents funeral and it brought back some of those memories of his dad. Sometimes when he returned from these trips to other cities, he would bring with him some little gifts that might include a souvenir of the local sports team or some landmark of that distant place. These would be met with incoherent expressions of joy. No matter what it was, it instantly became a prized possession and would be placed alongside the others on his dresser. Usually he would find some way to pack it away and bring it to school with him and be the envy of his buddies. He recalled other similar memories of his dad who, for no apparent reason, would run out to the local pizza shop and bring home a pie just before bedtime that they would devour whole, or the same that would happen after trips to White Castle that would result in him bringing home bags of those tiny hamburgers, with the fragments of cooked onion that tasted like nothing he'd ever eaten at any other time, each of which could be devoured in one or two bites. And so, these widely interspersed events made up for the lack of consistency in some way. And the memories he thought did not exist were now filtering back to him. His limbs and whole body ceased their motion, his hands lay open with the tie with which he had been wrestling wrapped around them. He sat on the side of the bed and let the rush of emotion come over him and the tears stream down his cheeks.

Dan had a captive audience and continued to press his various points, that could have, should have, been conveyed more succinctly. His comments floated on the most surface level of consciousness with the arguments for how great it would be for the cousins to grow up in the same house and the idea that somehow, "they would make do". Jen and Mike listened quietly but clearly, to everyone but Dan, they were beginning to chafe at these suggestions, the self satisfied tone with which they were being offered.

Between her own kids and Mike, Jen had her hands full. The

normal drinking and carousing were as much as she could handle. But then there were the not infrequent periods of Mike's binge drinking. These were times, days on end, when he would drink anything in sight. It was amazing his body could absorb that much alcohol and could function at all. During these times he was capable of becoming someone she detested: a mean, nasty drunk. His eyes set back in his head, peering out like a caged, dangerous animal. He never hit her, she had to give him that. But sometimes she secretly wished he had, so that the decision about whether or not to leave him would be made easier.

Mike also reflected on the utter impossibility of what Dan was piping on and on about.

"Sure, we could all pitch in and finish your basement. Make it a real nice place to play. Rose and Ben left a little bit of money. We can use that for materials."

Home improvements. It was all Mike could do to not reach over and grab Dan by the throat and throttle him. Every day for him was a challenge whose outcome was never assured. You do the things you were told, that everyone did. From school, to war, to getting a job and raising a family. But none of it made sense, none of it satisfied. At least with the earlier stages of life he could see change in the future, excitement, the notion that the gnawing inside him would go away when this or that happened. But now what? Now nothing. He was in his midlife. The majority of seismic changes were behind him and he had not attained to any greater peace of mind. He could sense that there was more to life than what he experienced, but he had long since given up hope that he would find a way to live any other way than the way he was used to. They talked him into going to some AA meetings but all they seemed to talk about was giving yourself over to some higher power: church, God, whatever, which was as much bullshit as anything anyone else was selling.

The truth Mike realized was that he was no more fit to be a father and run a family than his own dad was, which was not at all, nor his grandfather before him, and right on back to those potato farmers scratching out their existence in the hills of Ireland. Surely he was better off than them and provided better than they could have dreamed. But could they have felt any more empty than the emptiness that he faced daily, that left him with the feeling that he was ready to explode at any moment. And now Dan was preaching a religion of home improvements to make things right. At least, he told himself, he was not fool enough to believe that more square footage in their home would relieve the ache inside him, the ache he felt most times as he woke and that made his first conscious thought be whether or not his first stop after leaving the bed should be the liquor cabinet.

"How about you, Dan? Are you and Kelly ready for a ready-made family. We could help fix your place up, too. Just like you are offering to do to ours," Mike could not resist pushing this idea back on Dan for him to chew on.

"I wish we could. But we're just starting out and we wouldn't know what to do, taking on this kind of responsibility," Dan spoke with utter sincerity and a complete lack of self reproach for taking this selfish position. His hollow words were made more intolerable by his inability to see others in a similar light.

A silence permeated the setting for an extended period. Each of the six participants sat, withdrawing into their own lives, their own immediate needs and private thoughts. The walls absorbed the silence and this place would be changed by this short space in time. Time itself stood still and the experience that was occurring took root in each one of them, spreading out and taking space and no amount of drinking or subterfuge could hide or diminish how their lives, their essences, were being changed by their silence. They were abandoning the children, that much was for sure. How, was yet to be decided, and this they had some command over. But how the walls of this room and the foundations of their lives would be altered was something over which they had much less control. The nature of these things is that a significant decision made to staunch the bleeding rarely heals the wound. Such decisions are more resilient than the host and will return emboldened, convinced of its ability to dominate and mock contrived, weak arguments placed against it. Humanity perishes with such ill conceived expressions of itself. But not with great fanfare, not immediately, or even noticeably. Soon the pain becomes too great to try to perform a rescue or rewire these hastily made decisions. Time itself moves forward, plodding along at the behest of the monsters that have taken root. And even *time* becomes an ally of these darker forces, playing and replaying these tapes at their command, ensuring no escape. These tapes will not only highlight abandonment but the cruel irony of this act: had Rose been alive and the roles somehow reversed, this course of action would be unthinkable. But instead it was her children being let go and along with them the family's collective better angels, those things that give life worth and meaning in the face of incalculable longing.

"I was thinking about Liz and Carlo, Ben's sister and her husband. I spoke with them at the funeral about the kids. They seemed willing to take them in if things did not work out here," Frank finally said, breaking the silence.

This was not an outcome that any of them wished to consider. They did not especially care for the members of Ben's clan. In their collective view they were crude, living mostly in Flatbush, or some other run down area in Brooklyn that was more imagined than experienced. Carlo worked as a car mechanic and never looked like he scrubbed himself clean, nor did it seem to bother him. But now, all these reservations were swept away.

"It's worth a try," Jen said, with only a faint bit of resignation lingering in her tone.

After a brief, perfunctory discussion, Frank pulled his telephone book from the dining room cabinet and dialed the number that connected him to Liz and Carlo.

Don felt better after he cried, as if the tears had cleansed him. He was not aware of the natural process and flow of grieving and so each experience of it, the denial, rage, and sometimes the inner spiritual quiet, were experienced as if he alone knew of such emotion. If he were more accustomed to thinking of what had happened to his parents with an animal-like fury, he was, as now, capable of being made to feel light as a feather that is being held aloft by a calm but steady breeze.

He continued to allow thoughts of his old house and home life to pass through him, and he was realizing in larger and larger doses they were gone, gone forever. As tears continued to form at a slower rate, he got up from the bed and looked again at the suit that had just been by his side. For reasons he did not understand, he began taking off his clothes and replacing them with the suit. He found a bright white shirt in the closet that his aunt had ironed and placed there. After putting on the shirt and pants he addressed the tie and tie-making process again. Taking a pause from his prior attempts paid off and he was able to assimilate what he had learned into a set of twists and turns that approximated a half-Windsor knot. He pulled it admiringly towards his collar that he then folded down smartly.

He finished the dressing up by rummaging in the closet until he found his good pair of black leather shoes and after lacing them up put on his suit jacket. Why dressing up like this made him feel better, he could not imagine. His mother had always made a fuss about how he looked when he dressed up for a special occasion and even though he would complain about having to do so, he secretly acknowledged the power of these clothes to lift him out of himself and place him down differently in the world.

Don gazed at himself in the mirror for some period of time while combing his hair and allowed himself to think about the future for the first time since the death of his parents. This row house was not home, and never would be. But he liked his aunt and uncle and they were being good to him and Sara. He did not linger on the difficulty he had caused them, was scarcely aware of these things. Even the horrible event that occurred the night before was walled off from deep consideration and had undergone a transmutation in his mind that was an unhealthy trait that would cause him problems throughout much of his life.

He left the room and began the walk up the flight of stairs to where the adults were. Through the doorway above, he could see spectral lighting. He realized now he needed to move out of these basement surroundings of dark and dampness. The light came gradually and transmitted warmth to his body. Even more importantly, the upper level provided fresh air for him to breathe, and he filled his lungs greedily.

The adults were still in the living room as Don entered. The call was just completed and the desired outcome accomplished. The offer from Liz and Carlo was still open. The process for moving the kids was briefly discussed and although many details were still to be arranged they had tentatively agreed to move them this weekend. Before Don came up they had begun their own process of accepting this new direction, and they were pursuing it with determined speed. "There was nothing else that could be done," "They"ll do fine there," "We gave it our best shot," and the like they told each other. They were ready to move on, or thought they were.

Don moved onto the threshold separating the dining room and living room. He then walked up to his uncle Frank and asked him if his tie looked okay. The tie was, of course, perfect, as was the boy who had tied it. Uncle Frank, though, gave it a few shaping tugs and pulls which Don submitted to without reservation; in fact, he had wished for just such a reaction.

There was absolutely nothing to say. But Don was saying, this is who I am, who I aspire to be, who I can be... wordlessly, by his mere presence. And the adults had there souls torn and shredded by this sight, which they wished they could not see, were blinded to at this moment, because hope at this point was too difficult to bear.

Part Two

Chapter 9

It all started one night when Mike was sitting at a bar, enjoying a couple of drinks with one of the motorcycle cops, Eddie Mathews, who he ran with from time to time. It was about nine months since he'd been transferred to motorcycle duty, a transfer he'd been applying to get for a couple of years. He was as surprised as anyone that he'd been chosen for this job. There were a lot of applicants and he hadn't kissed anyone's ass to get chosen. In fact most of those in the position to offer this job he either had no contact with or, to put it mildly, were not admirers of his.

So when he was called into the captain's office he was expecting to be reprimanded for one thing or another but instead was told to sit down.

"Bet you think I'm here to ream your ass out about something you did, don't ya, Eaton."

"Can't imagine why you'd have the need to do that, captain," Mike responded, deciding to play along.

"I'm sure you can't," the captain said, happy himself to be participating in this game of cat and mouse because he had a clear sense of who was who, and he was the one with the upper hand.

Sure, Eaton was a fuck-up, there was no doubt about that. But the captain had read through his war record and was not surprised to read about his several acts of heroism. If you looked past the scheming that put him in positions where he was always trying to put one over on you, there was a certain quality in him that was at the very core of every good cop. One minute they could be talking the stupidest shit and the next separating fully grown men, tossing them aside with one hand around their collars like they were paper tigers, or taking directions over the phone to deliver a baby, or running after kids half their age, and normally twice as fast, until they were caught and apprehended. Eaton was one of those cops who did not take care of himself and was in bad physical shape but possessed more than his share of fierceness and power if he needed it and could dominate a situation if he had to. You did not teach this trait. Like old gun slingers in the west, you either had it or you didn't. And everyone knew it when they saw it. And Eaton had it, or could have it.

"Not sure why this is coming down this way. You certainly didn't do anything to deserve it," the captain continued, happy to string Mike along a little longer.

Mike suspected what the captain was saying about him was true, but was also becoming warily curious about where the conversation was going. He watched from the opposite side of the captain's desk as the captain opened his side drawer, pulled something from it and began to turn it over in his hands out of sight from Mike's gaze. Mike said nothing, deciding instead to let the captain play out his hand in his own good time.

"You fuck this up Eaton and there's no telling where you might land," and with that, the captain lightly tossed in the air the object he'd been holding.

Mike caught, snatched out of the air, the key ring with the two keys attached, and let them dangle a short distance from his eyes. He knew right away they belonged to one of the Chiefs sitting back behind the station house. He'd taken one out for a ride from time to time and loved to ride them, loved their feel. The Chiefs were being phased out by the new Harleys but being assigned a Chief was fine with him. He liked them better, didn't give a shit what anyone said about them. It was heavier than a Harley which meant, as far as he was concerned, you could work it harder, drive it harder. He couldn't wait to see which bike had been assigned to him, but was perplexed by this and other emotions he was experiencing, not knowing how or whether he should show gratitude, if in fact that was what he was feeling right then.

But the captain could see the smile streaming across Mike's face, even as he tried to make sense of everything.

"Its just because you're a good Irishman, Eaton... Now get out of here and go see what's going to give saddle sores all over your butt for the foreseeable future and make your legs bow like a cowboy's. One last thing, I think this might be just what you need. But if it does not work out, I'm not sure what will be good for you. So make this work! And if you do, it will work for you."

Mike left the office but not before saying, "Thanks, captain. I appreciate you sticking your neck out for me on this."

The captain did not respond but the two men looked into the other's eyes, measuring the truthfulness of the gaze, which was considerable, and what lay beyond it.

Mike walked down to the shop where the mechanics serviced the vehicles used by the precinct.

"Which one of these hot rods is number 8," he said to Emil, who was a regular at McGrath's, and someone he got along with reasonably well. The mechanics were a breed apart. They were incessantly angry about one or another car or bike, battling with frozen bolts, up to their elbows in grease. They started at a lower pay grade than patrolmen but carried themselves with authority, and, in fact, could be sarcastic, self-righteous bastards if they could get away with it. But you never wanted to screw around with them if you didn't have to because if you did you might find out that your squad car all of a sudden did not have heat in the winter and wouldn't be worked on until May, and all of your requests for service ended up on the bottom of the list. But you didn't want to be a kiss-ass either, because they'd pounce on you if you were. In fact, no one knew exactly how to deal with these guys and mostly you avoided doing so, which was fine with them, too. This included the brass as well, who put up with more shit from these guys than than they did from anyone else. They were, or had evolved into, a semi-detached entity as so often happens in large bureaucracies where small cliques of people gain power because they possess specialized skills and talents.

"So Michael Eaton has finally landed himself a Chief. I'll be goddamned. Now you don't have to come around here sneaking rides anymore." This must have been a good day for Emil and that meant there was at least a chance of learning something about this bike before Mike hopped on it, took ownership of it.

Emil was rubbing his hands on a rag, not so they would come clean but in order that they could touch a substance without defiling it. "These sons of bitches are temperamental," Emil told Mike and at the same time motioned for the keys, a request that presented Mike no response other than to comply with it.

Emil hopped on Number 8 and kick started it and drove it the short distance out into the yard, with Mike dutifully trotting behind in pursuit. Emil throttled Number 8 up and listened to the mellifluous sounds of the engine blasting forth in a fury. He could have been a violinist tuning up his Stradivarius or a sommelier testing the balance of the various textures of a fine wine.

"You see," Emil said, returning from his reverie. "When these Chiefs are not tuned just right you can't do this," and at this moment he opened the throttle full again which let out a lion-like roar that shook the windows in this small court yard they were in. "Those upper registers give you your power, your acceleration. But things get off just a little and it's just not the same. Instead what you get is the engine breaking up at high RPMs. What you hear then is is a sputtering noise, like what your kid's cap guns sound like. You hear something like that, you come back to me. I'll get it purring again."

And with that Emil shut down the engine, tossed the keys to Mike, which he snatched out of the air for the second time in less than half an hour, and Emil retreated back into his "operating room" to put the bones back into another of his wayward charges.

From that day forward Mike almost never had to numb his brain to get his body to walk through the front door of the precinct to start his tour of duty. And when he finished a shift, he felt that he had earned the fatigue that his body was experiencing. In between these beginning and end points, was a diverse world of experience. He could avoid for the most part the fucked up domestic disputes that became your primary pastime when you were in a patrol car, that made you suspicious of everyone, basically made you hate people, when you got right down to it.

But all that ended to a large degree when he switched over to being a member of the motorcycle police. Now he roamed the streets of New York, the vast stretches of Queens that contained both the local roadways, such as Queens Boulevard and Northern Boulevard, and the major arteries like the Grand Central Parkway and the Long Island Expressway that connected people, by bridge to Manhattan and the Bronx on one side, and Long Island on the other.

He always thought he had the imagination of a rock or some other inanimate object. His sister had the brains in his family, and look where it got her. Last time he heard from her she was borrowing money, having ruined her marriage, and trying to bring up a couple of kids on her own. He never envied her her brains that always made her seem so high and mighty and different from everyone around them while they were growing up. A few times he read something she had written, like the few letters he had gotten from her when he was overseas, and realized how differently her mind worked from his and everyone he chose to have around him. There he was, deep in the belly of the beast somewhere in France or Italy and he gets one of her letters filled with words he didn't know the meaning of. And the content of those letters made him want to throw up, too. After the first couple of paragraphs he realized that she was trying to impress him with her showy friends, and her "imaginative" writing style. He never got to the end of those few letters she sent him, except to check the way she ended them. "Namaste" was followed by her name. "Namaste", what the fuck was that? After checking for this salutation he crumpled them up and threw them in the trash and went back to whatever it was he had been doing. His sister taught him that "imagination", too, was a crock of shit, no more useful or relevant to his life than the other religions the know-it-alls of the world held up to him.

So what was it that was going on with him now? There was a reason they called these roads *arteries:* vehicles flowing, passing, avoiding congestion and blockage. And Mike was its agent, as much as any, responsible for promoting this flow, the flow becoming an end in itself, a worthy end. Like a flock of birds, he tried to keep the traffic moving with a single sense of purpose. All he needed to do was enter that flow every day and he was happy, genuinely, simply, happy. What the fuck was a motorcycle police doing being happy, he thought and laughed to himself, thinking and laughing to himself instead of hearing the tapes retelling of his failures and lack of worthiness that normally would play when he was left to himself. But now he was left to himself often, for hours at a time and it was not those stories that undermined him, that dominated his thoughts. He avoided asking himself about this transformation too deeply, recognizing that there was something important in play, something fragile and good that might not survive close scrutiny. So he combed the streets and highways of Queens eradicating problems, freeing blockage. And when he got bored, when things were going smoothly on their own, he knew a couple of stretches of land hidden away in remote sections of Queens, that were hilly and surprisingly rustic, and there he gunned the Chief for all it was worth, firing off those higher registers, wondering what more of life one could hope for, wondering at this great good fortune he never expected would befall him.

He had never thought about it before, but when there was a major accident on the highway, it was usually a motorcycle cop who got there first because he could snake through and around the accumulated mass of congested metal more effectively than anyone else. He was cool under the pressure of these situations and never felt the need to overreact to what confronted him. And he was treated differently by people when he was on the bike than when he had been in a squad car. Maybe it was the degree of danger he had to face or the fact that they could relate to the experience of riding the bike. He wasn't sure and didn't care. What mattered was that he felt he had found himself and was pretty sure he could ride out the rest of his 20 years strapped to the back of this Chief without any problem.

Jen, too, noticed a difference. Previously the subject of his work was rarely discussed; not that it was a taboo, but Mike saw no reason to bring it up. Work was something he had done simply to put food on the table. But then she started to notice that Mike would be all excited, like a kid himself, and looked forward to sharing with her, Tim and Anne the various adventures that he had with his new best friend, The Chief, when they sat down to dinner. At first these stories were only of high speed chases and rescues from auto accidents that he arrived at before the ambulances. All of this was welcomed by each member of the family because Mike was a good story teller and used this skill to his advantage at these times. While the children enjoyed the thrill of these stories, Jen was mostly happy to find Mike taking an interest in his work in a way that she would not have thought possible. At times, this new trend could be annoying, as when Mike felt compelled to recount his experiences of the day, even if there was nothing very interesting about them. The children did not seem to mind though, and Jen managed to bite her tongue when these details issued forth, and forced a smile through sometimes clenched teeth.

"I'm thinking of taking some First Aid courses, maybe even see if they offer EMT training for cops." Mike announced, as they were digging into their dinner that featured a meat loaf of his creation. "You know, there are things I could do while waiting for the ambulance to show up. You remember the crash on The Expressway the other day. Traffic was backed up for miles. The one guy was in a lot of pain and I wasn't sure of the best way to get him situated. It worked out though because there was an off ramp the ambulance was able to come down from to reach us. But it could have taken a lot longer if they didn't find that route to us."

"That's a great idea, Mike. It couldn't hurt, that's for sure." replied Jen, genuinely happy to provide words of encouragement for his idea. It was new, uncharted territory. They both kept trying on this enthusiasm for his new job, occasionally causing them to stumble like children walking together hand in hand, the weight of the world lifted, at least temporarily, from their shoulders. Their repeated efforts and missteps caused them no heartache or fatigue, which they were used to feeling when meeting up with disappointment, because now their load felt lighter, the journey easier.

After a few minutes, during which time they returned to their meal, Mike removed a piece of paper from his back pocket that had been folded several times. As he was unfolding it he began to explain its contents.

"Seems they have a motorcycle police competition every year. It's open to all the cops in the city."

Jen looked at the paper. It was a copy of an original and contained two small photos in the middle of the page that were sandwiched around text describing the event. The pictures were grainy, almost to the point where one could not decipher the images that were hidden within them. But as she looked more deeply she could make out, in one of them, two policemen straddling their bikes in preparation for the competition, a course that contained cones describing figure 8s that must be navigated. The other picture showed a large group of men congregating in some manner, presumably at a picnic area. Jen paused briefly while peering at this vaguely assembled society of men, who seemed so comfortable with each other, knowing just what to expect from one another, having shared the same world-changing historical events that left them there here in the same place, knowing and wanting the same things.

"I think it's a great idea, your taking part in the competition," Jen said as she pulled back from her reflection. "You've always been good behind the wheel of anything you drive and they say there will be a shooting match as well, and back in the service you got all those awards for marksmanship."

Jen's chest swelled and she felt a rush of emotion. It was the rekindling of her love for this man who gave her more trouble than any woman deserved to have, but who could also be magnificent, a star capable of shining more brightly than any other in her universe.

They were cleaning up after dinner when Mike came up behind Jen who was washing the dishes, placed his hands on her hips and slowly began to rock their two bodies together. Jen allowed this movement to continue, doing nothing to curtail it. The children were out playing and the days events had not totally depleted her energy.

"What's all this about?" she said, and stopped cleaning the dish she had been working on. She reached for the hand towel and wiped her hands even as she continued to allow her body to move rhythmically with Mike's, unconsciously making sure to maintain their many touch points. She was more surprised by Mike's advance than anything else. It was a long time since anything like this had happened.

Sex was not something that Mike reflected on at length. As far as he was concerned it was overrated, caused problems, and contained an unfathomable mystery and potential danger. His problems would occur randomly, without warning. Sometimes he would pull back as they were getting started, sometimes it would occur during or after they had completed, when he felt sated and everything was supposed to be fine. But the experience he was left with, when it happened, was essentially the same: from nowhere seemingly, he was hit with a force like the current from the third rail. When it happened, there was no defense for him from the terrifying free fall it placed him in. What could it be? How could it happen to him at the time when he was experiencing what he thought should be one of man's most enjoyable experiences?

The wound that he felt at these times would not close quickly. He could walk around for days feeling as if his mind and body were split open. He said nothing to anyone at these times about what was going on. Instead he walked around like an actor on a stage, trying to approximate some notion of normalcy. His sense of personal power would be nonexistent, as was his courage. It was a struggle to get out of bed, let alone perform adequately as a policeman. Every evening when he was being controlled by this unnameable force, he prayed to no God in particular that when he woke up that the world would be normal again, that the things that should be familiar were again starting to be within his grasp and that he could interact with them in a normal manner. If they were, he would be like an epileptic recovering from a seizure, exhausted but happy to be able to sense the familiar texture of the world around him. If they weren't, he would descend rapidly, wondering how he would manage to maintain the charade he was performing for one more day.

The injustice he felt concerning this was immense. During the first years of his marriage, he kept waiting for it to pass. He tried to suppress these feelings, which at the time they were occurring were excruciating. If they occurred while he and Jen were making love, he would shut down and just try bring the intercourse to completion as quickly as possible. His only desire was to get through it and retreat into himself until he was able to recover some stability, some coherent sense of himself.

That drinking diminished the sex drive, everyone knew. So he drank, but this logic assumed a circular quality. In his few instances of honest reflection into this portion of his life he came to realize that he often drank to induce his impotence, so that he would not have to face this amorphous beast that he did not understand, and even if he did, had no one with whom he could speak to about it.

Jen now turned to him, smiled and said, "So, is this what you're thinking about while you're up there on The Chief?" She put her arms around his neck, pulled him towards her and drew him into a long, sensuous kiss. They began exploring each other's bodies with their hands as if for the first time, and, in fact, it had been some time since they had pursued each other with such intensity, such desire.

When she let her hand slide down below his waist, she felt his fully erect penis, which she began to stroke tenderly, cautiously. That's when Mike was gone, took flight from himself. He was almost instantly removed from the act as soon as he sensed her hand descending over his belly. His skin convulsed and was highly sensitized, experiencing the touch as though he were being tickled instead of caressed, along the arc where her hand grazed his body. It was upon him and he was helpless. Why, he wondered? Why did this come upon him, just at this moment when the forces in his life seemed to be aligning themselves in his favor?

Within moments he was flaccid, their embrace, lifeless. But he chose differently than at any time since this had begun and said, "I don't know why this happens to me. There is nothing I want more than to love you at these times. It is the most horrible feeling you can imagine."

He sat down on one of the kitchen chairs, elbows on the table, hands in his hair holding his head.

"I had no idea," Jen spoke, comforting her husband. She then walked over beside him and stroked his back. The sexual encounter that had just engulfed them was over, a memory, but they were left with something more, a type of communication they had never attained to before. On some level they were aware of the importance of this, and were able to accept the fact that it had happened and the honesty, the caring for each other, made for a substantial force that could be used to confront this demon that had chosen to resurface at this time.

Mike came to realize that more things had changed with his job than merely moving from one vehicle to another. Although he retained his membership in the precinct, he also joined another, somewhat unofficial, organization. Each precinct had a handful of motorcycle police and they worked together across the boundaries of individual precinct jurisdictions. They also socialized and this resulted in Mike becoming aware of a new subculture that functioned independently to a surprising degree.

He and Eddie Mathews, on the night when change would take place, sat in one of the bars Mike would stop at during the course of an evening. They got along well enough, certainly well enough to share some suds, but then again most of them got along in this way that could be thought of as an easy fraternity. This local watering hole, its walls and ceiling mostly unadorned, placed the bar itself front and center making no pretension about why people entered the door to this establishment. The wood top was held to a high standard, gleaming with a recent coat of varnish and the racks of liquor bottles facing the bar and the mirrors beyond them drew one's attention like an altar and returned disjointed reflections of the enclosed surroundings. They had been talking about the events of the day but then Eddie decided to turn the conversation in a different direction.

"You seem to have worked into the job pretty easy and all the guys like you, think you are doing right by the job," Eddie began.

Mike, surprised but not displeased with this comment, offered some perfunctory response conveying thanks which he thought would allow the the conversation to return from this detour back in the normal direction. But instead Eddie continued with what he intended to talk about.

"Me and the boys have a little deal going that we want to get you in on," Eddie began, his speech taking on a more focused quality. He was a big, wiry guy. He had shocking, frizzy red hair that might have suggested an almost comical aspect to his appearance. But there was nothing else comical about him. He was hard as nails and it was almost impossible to know what he was thinking or feeling. His eyes betrayed no emotion and were distinctive because of their emptiness, the lack of light they emitted.

"I'm listening." Mike responded and realized this would be a very different conversation than what he had expected.

"Here's how it works... You stop a speeder and you can tell he's a player. Drivin' a big caddie, doing the circuit from the City to the Hamptons, or something like that. After the normal explanation of what he's being stopped for, you find a way of explaining there's a way for him to avoid having to pay the fine, go to court, get his insurance rates jacked up; however you want to ease into it is up to you," Eddie began, throwing out the final comments without much interest and then threw back the last of his beer.

The bartender came by and asked if they were ready for another round and they said they were. After receiving their beers, they sat quietly for a minute in their own space, before Eddie resumed his explanation.

"If they show an interest, you explain they can purchase this pass from you." And at this, Eddie pulled from his coat pocket a small hard backed piece of paper, about the size of a business card. The wording on it was, "One pass for auto violation," and below that was the name Marty Herman. The border around the card had a type of double line graphical quality that lent the card a somewhat official appearance.

"You explain that this pass costs 40 bucks and is good for this infraction and maybe the next time they get stopped by a motorcycle cop. Tell them that if they want to use the card to ask the cop if they know a cop named Marty Herman."

Eddie continued, "Marty Herman doesn't exist. It's just a code name that we use to let the guy being stopped know whether or not the cop who pulled him over is in the game. If the cop does not acknowledge Marty Herman, tell him not to try to use the card."

Mike was always being asked if he knew this or that guy when someone was trying to weasel out of getting a ticket and thought he remembered hearing this name more than once.

They stopped again to take some pulls on their beers, and let the first bit of information settle in before Eddie resumed explaining how the operation worked.

"You get the cards from me. They cost $5.00 a piece, and they're the only ones you use for this scam. The money goes for protection in case the wrong people ever catch wind of this; the less you know about that the better. You come up with a number and put it on the back of the card, and you let the rest of us know what that number is. If someone offers you a card that looks legit, you accept it. When you get it, you return it to whosever number is on the card, either in person or through the mail, and they will send you back $15. You can either have it sent to your home or a Post Office Box if you want to play it safe. So you either make $20 when you issue the card or $15 on the return. Everyone makes out this way and it keeps the players, out there, in the game. I've even sold a couple of these at a time. The big rollers just leave them in their glove compartment. I don't know, must make them feel like they're immune from the law. Ends up being a nice chunk of change if you play it right. Any questions?"

Mike thought for a while about what he was listening to, trying to make sure he fully comprehended the circular nature of the financial transactions that were being conveyed to him.

"So this is just between the motorcycle police, no squad cars are involved?"

"That's right, that's the way we keep things under control."

"Is everyone on a bike involved?"

"You got it. We can't allow anyone to take a pass on this. It would put the whole operation in danger. If you don't want to play along, you have to go back to a squad car." Eddie said and took a long draw from his beer. He completed his statement with finality by saying with a menacing tone, "Any other option you wouldn't like."

What Eddie did not say was that everyone had their little scam going and this was theirs. You couldn't hardly make ends meet on a cop's salary. Guys often picked up second and third jobs to get by. Mike painted houses when he could find a job. These types of schemes were built into the system and everyone acknowledged them with a wink and a nod; and you were a sap if you didn't take while the taking was good. He did not need to be told that the key to making this work was to keep his normal quotas up. The importance of that had been made clear to him from day one. You had to bring in a certain number of speeding tickets a month to add to the till. Fail to make your quota, whether you are working something on the side or not, and you would be called up before the sergeant and have to explain yourself. "Make some shit up if you have to, but make your numbers," you would be told. And as long as you made your quotas, there was a wide range of activities that could fly under the radar.

But this knowledge and the foreknowledge that he would

participate in this parallel form of justice sent an imperceptible shiver down his spine that cast him into a different relationship to his work, his world, in an equally imperceptible way. The almost carefree nature and, at times, sheer enjoyment of his job would be at least diminished and maybe destroyed as soon as he began taking part in this scheme. And although he was not conscious of how much the job had lifted his spirit, it had. And he would have to wait and see what effect losing the sense of goodness he had derived from his work would have on the rest of his life.

Chapter 10

Three years had passed since the cousins lived in the same neighborhood. That the span from 11 to 14 years old was an eternity was something both Don and Tim knew with certainty, but neither would have been able to explain what changes took place during that period of time. Tim had helped Don pack up his stuff and even visited him in his new apartment in Flatbush a couple of times during those first months of separation. But promises of staying in touch were not kept as their lives became caught up in the demands of their every day activities.

Even though his parents verbalized their desire to keep the cousins in contact, Tim sensed that this effort was doomed from the start, and wondered if his parents were just playing along until the cousins themselves displayed less and less desire to plan events together. Those early trips to Don and Sara's new home were always tense and uncomfortable. His parents would talk about all the things they could be doing instead while in the car on the way to their visit. Another topic of conversation was their worry about what they would have to say to the aunt and uncle that were now Don and Sara's guardians. Tim and Anne's parents told them to address Don and Sara's guardians as Uncle Tony and Aunt Liz, which was something they were more than willing to do.

This was the earliest experience Tim had of uncovering someone's duplicitous behavior; *duplicitous* was a word given to him later in life and that set off a cavalcade of images within him at that time, giving form to a host of unrealized thoughts. At the same time his mother and father were mouthing encouragement to him to stay in contact with Don, they were putting up road blocks of a very indirect type. His and Don's relationship reminded him of a balloon that was losing air slowly and as it did he could see what was once full and round becoming misshapen, disfigured. But if he ever would have confronted his parents he would have been hard pressed to come up with a single example that supported his belief that they were trying to lessen the bonds between the cousins. Even though he recognized this inability, his suspicions lingered. Unfortunately, having possession of this idea did nothing to slow the separation he was feeling from Don, which increased each time they were together.

Uncle Tony and Aunt Liz were always real nice to Tim but his parents seemed to have developed a strong dislike for them. They were always criticizing them for the way they lived and acted, but they did not seem very different to Tim from those he was used to seeing in his parent's group of friends. The early trips for these visits were accompanied by recountings of their supposed failings and, although his parents tried to put on an act while they were visiting, Tim could sense his parents discomfort and could tell these visits would not continue for very long.

That's why it was so surprising when the request for a sleep over was granted. It was the summer between 8th and 9th grades for Tim and 9th and 10th for Don, and the idea came up when the two boys were talking on the phone, something they continued to do from time to time.

Tim's friends in his neighborhood went to Catholic school and he had talked his parents into letting him attend their school before the beginning of 8th grade, even though his father was perplexed by this request, and wondered if his son had found religion. The nuns could be mean, hitting and humiliating kids for no reason sometimes or if you did not do well on an exam, but it was the price you paid and the kids seemed to accept that. He took on the styles of speech, demeanor, and dress that was preferred by these students. Penny loafers or wing tips were the desired footwear, khaki pants or chinos and any type of plaid buttoned down shirt were the final touches applied to this wardrobe that intended to promote a casual, confident quality to anyone that chose to outfit themselves in this way. Rounding out the youthful male image was a crew cut or near crew cut hair style. The demeanor that went along with the physical appearance was one of incessant joking, the laughter needing to flow whether anything funny had been said or not. Truth to tell, Tim found keeping up with these requirements tiring but he pursued them accordingly, following the leaders who seemed to understand the parameters of correct style and behavior. He accepted on faith the correctness of their choices and fastened his limited world view to the dictates of those acknowledged leaders.

There was another reason why Tim wanted to go to this new school, which was to change the person he was becoming. The life of his family had been deteriorating for some time when he had hatched the idea of switching to Catholic school. His mother had always admired and commented on how nice the boys and girls looked dressed in their uniforms on their way to school. Tim and his family were Protestant so the option to join them was not an obvious one. But then things began to happen that Don could only comprehend vaguely. He could sense that his dad was in trouble at work but could never figure out exactly what he had done, or what was being done to him.

He still was a policeman but instead of being stationed in the local precinct in which they lived, he was moved to one far away. His dad no longer talked about his work like he had done when he was riding a motorcycle but occasionally a story would slip out and it always presented the world he worked in as one of misery, decay and danger, and the behavior he described left everyone listening feeling upset, sickened. He used to enjoy listening to his father's motorcycle tales, but these more recent stories were ones Tim would rather not have to listen to, and his mother yelled at his dad for saying many of the things he said. It was as if his father could not stop himself from speaking of these things and many times this led to his mother and father hurling hate-filled comments at each other across the dinner table.

Tim sometimes was unable to finish his meal because his stomach was tied into knots and he would ask to be excused from the table. One of these times his father had asked him, "What's wrong, can't you take it?"

Tim's mind cramped up at this question. He wasn't able to answer then and still could not. Or more correctly, none of the answers that he could summon forth came even close to expressing the feelings he was experiencing while these arguments were taking place.

But then the idea for Catholic School popped into his head and seemed maybe to be the answer he was looking for. He would make them proud of him, so proud that they would forget all the problems that seemed to have twisted them into different people. The laughter and closeness that had existed in his immediate family and the wider extended family and family friends, had become mostly a memory, one that he could not map a path back to. So he would become that path with his new clothing, considerate manners and joke-a-minute personality. But if this approach did not work he could not imagine what the solution was to this problem, a problem that had become a burning issue for him.

The nuns were constantly beating into them that only the best students would be good enough to go onto college and from there be able to move onto a successful career; and even some of these students would falter when they were confronted by the rigors of any of the better Catholic High Schools to which some of them would be heading. The rest, and this accounted for nearly everyone sitting there before them, would not amount to much. Tim was only a naturally average student but he heard this message clearly and related it to his home situation and was determined to make his parents proud of him through these achievements of college and a successful career that his education would provide.

Don had taken up with a distinctly different group of kids. His friends were part of a group who were linked through gradations of age to a gang of young adults that ran in that part of Flatbush. The rules of the street applied here, and acts of violence ranging from small skirmishes to full blown gang wars, usually over issues of turf, honor, or retribution for past grievances occurred infrequently, but acted as the glue that held this band of friends together.

As Don and Tim talked on the phone that evening it was clear they had little to say to each other and to partially relieve this discomfort, Tim suggested that he come to visit for a sleepover. Much to his surprise, his parents had agreed to this request and now he was on his way, wondering at how this visit had come about, worried about its outcome.

His parents came into Tony and Liz's house with him but did not even bother to sit down. They explained how Tim's sisters were also away at sleepovers and that they were taking advantage of the situation to go to a show in Manhattan and were running a little late. Tim had known about these plans but did not understand their consequences and before he knew it he was flying solo in this unfamiliar house inhabited by people he hardly knew or had known in the past but was not so sure he did anymore. He was a little put off by the fact that Don was not there waiting for him but tried not to dwell on this fact. He could tell from his parents expressions that they had felt the same way.

Aunt Liz placed the book she was reading down when they entered her house. She told Tim that Don had been delayed at a game of handball and would be home shortly, stating this information as a matter of fact instead of an offer of apology. Handball was a game played widely throughout New York City but not among Tim's friends. There was an area in his neighborhood park to play handball which required high cement walls, maybe 15 feet high, and two teams with one or two members on each team playing. It intrigued him but it was simply not engaged in by his group of friends so he never got any closer to it than watching the games, or matches, or whatever they was called, while he was walking past the courts on the way to some other destination. Although he went to this park on an almost daily basis, he had never entered the handball court area because a different group of kids hung out there.

Sara was also out as was Uncle Tony so it was just Tim and Aunt Liz all of a sudden, and a wide patch of unknown territory laid out between them that neither was sure how to enter into. Aunt Liz's only child, a 16 year old daughter named Lana, was upstairs in the bathroom taking a shower. Tim had not had any contact with her for a couple of years and was not even sure where he had last seen her.

Liz took in the image that Tim presented and was much impressed. He was more clean cut than any teenager she had seen for a long time outside of the TV shows, that featured families that were equally unfamiliar to her.

"We don't see kids dress up like this very often," Liz said, smiling to herself at the degree of understatement in her comment.

Tim felt encouraged by this comment, which made him feel a little more comfortable in these surroundings.

"This is how we all dress at home when we're going out. These are the same clothes I wore to the end-of-year eighth grade dance at school. My mom washed them since then, of course." At this mildly humorous joke he let out a howling laugh like the ones he had learned from his friends, his mentors. At the same time he clenched his hands into fists and knocked the middle joints of his two hands together several times. He was not sure why he did this but it was something else he had acquired from one of his friends who employed it in convivial situations for reasons, if Tim were asked to explain, would be unable to produce; but it always played well with his set and had become a standard part of his repertoire.

Liz watched all this, and was partially dismayed and partially endeared to this young boy who she hoped would not bruise himself, and also hoped would survive the evening.

Tim heard a great shuddering of pipes from the 2nd floor of the house, which was followed soon after by the sound of doors slamming open and shut in quick succession, interspersed with feet hurrying across the floor in what was a decidedly no nonsense manner, almost as if each step set off little explosions of fury.

"That's just Lana," Liz offered with what could only be interpreted as a sigh of infinite resignation when she saw Tim's eyes tracing the distinct path of motion from above.

"She's always late, or at least acting that way. Been that way for a couple of years now, I'd say. Best not to get in her way when she's like that, which as I said is just about all the time these days."

Don walked through the door at about this time. He was carrying a couple of Pensee Pinkies, small rubber balls that contained compressed air that Tim recognized immediately. They were of a softer substance than the Spaldings that he preferred, which had a coarser feel and was better for stick ball, the game he used them for. He could tell Don had been sweating but otherwise did not appear to have just come from playing ball. Tim did not know how to describe it but Don looked well appointed like he had combed his hair, pulled his shirt in within his pants after finishing play, something he would never consider doing. Don was dressed in basic black, and both his tee shirt, stretch tightly across his torso, and tightly fitting jeans would not emit even a speck of light. He noticed, too, that Don had put on weight, and was probably 15 pounds heavier than he was but that he carried it well and this set off some other memories that he could not define. If he had been able to, he would have realized that Don reminded him of his Aunt Rose in the way they acted, except that there was an additional, more intense, quality in Don than what you would have seen in Aunt Rose.

Don looked at Tim and was at first only able to focus on the plaid shirt that Tim wore with its criss-crossing oranges, browns, and reds. What alien force had mis-wired the brain of his cousin who was once his close bud and confidante. He had skimmed one of his aunt's nature books once and studied the picture of a cockatiel, and now could only see that picture as he looked in amazement at his cousin before him.

Looking across a bridge of time and experience that neither had willingly chose to erect, they sought awkwardly to find touch points to their old selves, too young, still, to manage the ache this effort set off inside them.

Aunt Liz had put together a plate for Don and had kept it warm by covering it and placing it on top of a pot on the stove that had water simmering in it. She set the plate of food on the kitchen table and Don went to work on it. Tim had eaten dinner before coming over but accepted an offer of cookies and milk that Aunt Liz made to him.

"After dinner we can go and hang out with my friends. They're a ratty group of guys but I think you'll like them." Don joked.

"That sounds good. Where do you guys hang out?"

"We'll probably start at the park and then go from there."

"That where you play handball?"

"Yep, where I spend most of my time. You ever play?"

"No, always wanted to try but my friends just never went in for it for some reason." The reason, which they both suspected they knew, was that it was a cultural phenomena. Kids who played handball didn't play other sports. And kids who played other sports did not play handball. They looked at the little pink balls and separately considered the cultural divide that they embodied.

At about this time when Don was describing the fine points and strategy involved in handball, Lana breezed into the kitchen. Her's was a stiff breeze and she sailed by herself along it. Tim tried to say hello to her but she merely responded with some snorting type of response. He could not determine if she was putting together her own dinner or if the sandwich she was eating was just a snack. Everyone seemed to be keeping to their own schedule and this too was unusual for Tim to see, leading him to think the whole way of life in the house was different than anything he was used to.

He could not help staring at Lana. Her shoulder length red hair was parted in the middle and flipped up at the bottom. Her eye brows and lashes were heavily painted with black mascara and she was also covered in basic black clothing. Her body was slender and he could not help noticing her breasts which were small but articulated and emerging. Her perfectly chiseled facial features did nothing to soften the image that she presented to the world, as right now with the banging of drawers and crashing of plates. What do you say to such a girl, Tim tried to puzzle through, not realizing that this was the first of many times he would ask such a question, the answer to which would remain relevant yet elusive.

Don watched his cousin and could intuit what was going on inside his body and mind; it wasn't hard to do. And he felt close to him at this moment, closer than he had felt since his life had changed with the deaths of his parents.

Don said he'd like to take a shower after he finished his meal and he and Tim went up to his bedroom. Don and his sister had been sharing the room until not long ago but then Sara moved over to Lana's bedroom, giving Lana something else to complain about. Tim laid on Don's bed while he showered, and took this time to study Don's room. Hardly a spot of wall was discernible between the assemblage of posters filling them. They were all of cars and nearly all were Chevys and among these there seemed to be a preference for '57 convertibles. He admired these posters displaying cars that could be sleek and yet larger than life at the same time, the lines of chrome running from front to back conveying a sense of timelessness. The paint on these cars was perfect, vibrant, reflecting the world and so giving back to it. It made him smile to look at them and lifted his spirits.

He had never considered cars this way before, had never taken an interest in them or was friends with anyone who did. So even as he was now lulled by their beauty he was aware of something else, something like a code of behavior that he had adopted and may now be violating, and this reflection acted like an insect bite needing to be scratched.

After Don got dressed in a duplicate set of black jeans and tee shirt as what he was wearing previously, he spent considerable time combing and shaping his hair. He had already run a largish gob of Brylcreem through it in the bathroom and now back in his room he was engaged in the grooming process. He had a hair brush that he attached to his hand, much like what a horse groomer would use but smaller, and he ran it over his longish hair many times before performing the maneuvers that would result in a massive pompadour extending down to the middle of his forehead. The hair on the sides of his head then was again the focus of a brushing movement from front to back, and as Tim caught the reflection of light on these strands of highly greased hair, he was reminded of the glossy fins of the cars he had just been admiring.

The whole process of preparing his hair only took Don about 5 minutes but struck Tim as the most lavish act he had ever observed. It was both compelling and disturbing to see his cousin, his peer, spend so much time on his appearance. It was, in fact, a revelation, something up until this point he would never consider doing to himself and seemed wrong to him in some way.

"These cars are really cool, aren't they?" Don said, noticing the catalog of new 1963 Chevys that lay in front of Tim on the bed. He flipped through the pages, pointing out different design features, engine sizes defined by horse power and engine displacement, and the result of zero to sixty time trials the way Tim might do with a magazine containing baseball players and their statistics.

"I'm going to work on them when I grow up," Don announced with a level of conviction that left no doubt. "I'm going to the Vo Tech High School to study car mechanics. Started last year. I wish I could work on the cars all day. But I still have to take some of the normal classes."

Settling for being a car mechanic, even before being forced down to this level by the rigors of high school... the nuns would not approve. And yet Tim sensed Don's excitement about it, his looking forward to learning about these beasts and how to tame them with a hunger he could not lay claim to as he looked at his own coursework or towards his future.

Don had been considering whether to offer Tim a change of clothing but decided against it. He would be okay as long as they were together, and he would shield him from any abuse that may be sent his way. They made their way to the door, stopping long enough to provide a brief itinerary for their whereabouts to Aunt Liz that was short on details, and then sailed out into the night.

The distance between the area of Queens Tim lived in and this part of Brooklyn could be traveled by car in 30 minutes but could also be measured as worlds apart. Tim knew only row after row of single family homes sitting on small, mostly 37.5 feet wide, lots; but they were undeniably separate. Porches did not exist in the front yards, and if people wanted to take to the outdoors, they spent their time in the back of their homes, separated from those living around them or walking by on the sidewalks.

They walked down the steps of the row house that Don lived in and Tim saw a different version of life than what he knew. Now that the dinner hour had passed, life had spilled out onto the streets on this sultry summer night. The older neighbors clustered on or near the steps of theirs or their neighbor's homes. Throw pillows were placed on the steps to sit on or aluminum folding chairs were brought from inside the houses for the same purpose. The buildings, themselves, contained a beauty and sense of timeless presence derived mostly from the brick construction and stonework that occasionally included an ornate pattern or sculptured image.

The younger children played close by, taking advantage of the triple wide cement blocks that separated the row houses and the street. Their safety from traffic on the street was essentially assured by the rows of parked cars lining the curb. The children ran after each other and rode their bikes. With chalk in hand, they constructed games of hop scotch or satisfied their artistic urges with colorful designs or images of people that they drew on the sidewalks.

Don said hello to a few of the people as he walked by but did not seem compelled to do so. There were simply too many people to carry on this exchange with everyone, and no one took offense if they were not greeted. But there was a recognition, a sense of safe passage that Tim felt as he walked with Don along these streets that Tim realized were propelling him into an unknown world.

As they strode down Flatbush Avenue, Don seemed to hit upon an unexpected idea.

"Follow me," he said and ran across the street, dodging between cars, both stationary and moving, along the way.

They ran in this way a couple of blocks and then stopped outside a Chevrolet car dealership. Tired slightly by this run, they stopped in front of the showroom window. Tim studied these cars in a way he had never done before. The difference between Chevys, Fords, and Chryslers was something he had never had the interest to commit to memory. Names like Impala, Galaxie, and Thunderbird did little to excite his imagination.

Standing now before these stylish, new, shiny, metallic creations awakened something foreign inside him that demanded attention. The showroom was magnificent with its towering ceilings and light emanating from every direction. The stark contrast from everything around this building added to the effect that it conveyed. Rows of storefronts, containing retail stores like butchers shops, barber shop, candy stores and dry cleaners made up the rest of what Tim could see, and right alongside them was this place that had the power to transport him to somewhere unreal and wondrous.

After looking from the outside of the plate glass window enclosure, Don went to the door to let himself in and Tim could do nothing but follow him, although his preference would have been to stay at this safe distance outdoors. The temperature in the room was cool and the carpeting muffled sound, allowing those inside to walk around in contemplative comfort. Just seeing cars parked on carpeting was startling for Tim. The central floor space of the display room was taken up with a deep red Corvette. This is what they walked towards first and the image of it made Tim think that it belonged on another planet from the one he lived on.

"This is the only one they've got here, and its mostly for show." Don explained. "You'd be lucky if you could get your hands on one of these, even if you could pay for it."

They moved on to the other cars in the showroom and at this time Don's expression began to dim. The large, boxish Impala and Belair seemed to be the cause of his sullenness.

The showroom was empty and one of the salesman, probably more out of boredom than anything else, walked over to Don and Tim. Tim expected to be told to leave, which was what Don thought would happen as well. But instead the salesman, in a friendly, likable way began speaking to them.

"So which one of these beauties are you boys ready to buy."

"Not this one, or this," Don snapped back. Pointing to the Belair and Impala, both painted in some nondescript aquamarine blue/green. "What are these trunks going to be used for anyway? You could fit a swimming pool in them if you wanted to."

Tim could not believe these words, their boldness, and realized there was still something crazy about his cousin. He felt like he had entered a church and now his cousin was blaspheming its holy sacraments. He would have liked to run out the door before the salesman had a chance to respond, but knew he could not and stayed glued to the floor where he stood.

The salesman gave a quick laugh and measured Don now with a different look that may have been more respectful, and he found himself taking on more of the tone and attitude of a salesman, which is what he was essentially, than he had expected to.

"Sure, I understand what your complaint is. So maybe you could see yourself in one of these." And he motioned the boys over to a cream colored Chevy Nova convertible.

"Yeah, I can see myself in one of these babies. Sure I can," Don said admiringly.

At this they all rested in respectful repose and admiration for this newly installed member of the Chevy family that Don and the salesman knew would carry on the proud family line.

A real customer had entered the showroom and the salesman said to Don and Tim, "Well, let me know when you are ready to sign on the dotted line and I will draw up the paper work. And remember," returning to an avuncular tone, "you're here to look not to touch. And you should be moving along pretty soon now that you've decided which of these beauties you're interested in." And with that, he walked over to the couple that was doing about the same things that Don and Tim had before them.

The park they went to was only a few blocks away and not unlike the one where Tim played ball. There were a lot more people there than he was used to and as he surveyed the area he surmised that those of different ages stayed pretty much to themselves. Don explained that there were three loosely formed groupings. He was part of the youngest that included kids through the 10th grade who were called juniors. The next group were the lieutenants or leuts for short and extended through the end of high school. The third group extended into the early 20's and took only the name of the park that symbolized their gang and that all three groups were connected by, Wyanda Park. The two younger groups provided services to the one above them, usually little things like running to the store for sodas or running after a ball that had found its way over a fence. In return, the older group provided protection and a sense of guidance to the younger members of the gang.

They passed by a group of older gang members, who were lazily hanging around the outside of the park, leaning on or standing around their parked cars. One or two of the hoods of these cars were popped open and some of the guys were slouching over them, peering deeply into them while discussing the best ways to boost power or unmuffle the sound of the exhaust. They were all dressed in essentially the same deep black clothing and the only thing that differentiated them were the insignias on their garments announcing their affiliation with the Wyanda Park gang. Don looked greedily into the engine compartments as they walked by the cars while Tim stole glances at these characters, most of whom were tough looking and muscular, their impassive expressions suggesting that little could disturb or upset them and that finding that something was not advised.

They met up with Paulie and Augie, two of Don's friends. Tim could see just how out of place he looked now and figured he was being analyzed much the same way that he had done shortly before with the Corvette, except without the sense of appreciation that he had felt.

When they arrived, Paulie called to Don, "Here comes the Chief." It was a nickname that surprised Tim at first but not as much as he thought it might, and opened a window to a side of Don that he was only now coming to see and appreciate. He also felt a twinge of emotion as he was reminded of his father's motorcycle that he had not heard about for what must be over a year.

It was about 8:00 PM, not too late but not to early to be hatching plans for the evening.

"You want any of this," Paulie said, pointing to a couple of brown paper bags. They made quite a pair, did Paulie and Augie, Tim thought. Paulie, half a head shorter than he and Don, and Augie half a head taller. Paulie, all nervous action and excitement; Augie, already well studied in the art of menacing cool that they had just observed in the older crowd.

"What do we have here," Don said walking over to the packages, the contents of which contained a bottle of Gypsy Rose in one and a bottle of Thunderbird in the other, both wines of a certain quality. And taking a swig from the opened bottle of Thunderbird, Don said, "Ah, nothing but the best for the *junior* crew." And after doing so hoisted it in front of Tim and asked him if he wanted any.

Some of Tim's friend had already been initiated into drinking but he had not, although he figured it would not be long before that changed. What felt odd to him was that it was there, right in front of him, all of a sudden. No build up, time to consider the right and wrong of it, the ramifications, the guilt now and later. It was bottoms up. There was no other choice.

The wine ignited his mouth, full circumference of his throat and belly and did not stop there. His arms, legs, toes, and fingers were all aflame. He thought he could sense every closely cropped hair follicle on his head and was sure that they stood even more upright as a result of the foreign agent that had just entered his body. When he recovered from this experience, he had a sense that it was not altogether unpleasant.

"It looks like you're on your way to a fancy party," Paulie said to Tim after taking a drink from the bottle. "Not sure we got anything to do where you'd hafta be so spit and polished." That said, he passed the bottle in the direction away from Tim.

Tim allowed the comments to be made without responding to them, realizing there was little else he could do. Paulie was the clown of the group so let him be one, he figured. Don responded instead, having expected something like this comment.

"Hey, he's from Queens. Leave him alone. That's how they dress in Queens, man."

Paulie shrugged his shoulders. He had made his point that he thought Don's cousin looked foolish, pathetic even. He was willing to overlook it now and move on with planning the evening, but wouldn't have been able to if he hadn't gotten this off his chest. Augie was there to provide the muscle if anything got out of hand, which might have meant slapping Paulie around or this new kid if he got mouthy. And if he couldn't figure out who was causing the problem, Don was there to lay down the final verdict. At least these were the shape of Tim's thoughts as he watched the interaction of the group in their first half hour together. More than anything else, he was impressed that his cousin had risen to the role of leader of even this small band of friends.

"So what's it going to be, gents," Paulie said as he polished off the Thunderbird and threw it onto the roof of the school building that abutted the playground. The dilemma at hand was whether to plow into the second and last bottle of wine now or after they got into one type or another of some mischief.

"I say we show Tim some of the sites around Brooklyn, our fair borough. We could take the train to Brighton Beach, walk around there for a little bit and take it from there," Don said, as if having already made up the mind for the group. "Bring the bottle along. I'll hide it with my shirt." and with that he took off his outer shirt that he had put on just in case this type of need developed.

The air was moist and hot. Usually air like this would slow you down half a step but now the sense of newness and the effects of the alcohol lifted Tim and carried him along these city streets effortlessly, making a sort of fuel out of even this balmy evening.

Once they made it out of the park, they chose a direction that led to the train station. The tracks were elevated above the ground and quiet now, and it wasn't long before they were standing within view of the tracks.

"Follow us," Don said to Tim, after checking that the coast was clear, "and you ride for free."

Paulie was first to bound along the well worn path. They squeezed between a steel girder and metal fencing that they were able to dislodge just enough to fit their bodies between. From there it would be a short climb diagonally up a man-made elevation of rock and dirt, and then a 3 foot jump to the steps that you would reach had you used a token. The only problem was between the two landings was nothing but a free fall of some 20 feet directly onto pavement that might kill you, certainly one that would break some bones if you came up short of the landing.

"Don't scrape your khakis." Paulie yelled behind him as they were making their run up the hill. Tim ran along, trying to keep up, but lagged behind. The footing was poor and it would have been easy to have your feet go out from under you; still he made his way between shadows that cast darkness over stretches of the hill.

The noise had been building as they ran to the spot where they must make their leap. At mid distance it was easy to associate the noise with that of an approaching train on the tracks that were directly overhead. But once it approached closer, and then closer still, there were no earthly comparisons that could be drawn. It was pure cacophony and then more so, if you were listening. But only Tim was listening because the others lived it into the realm of normal experience, the way people who live near Fire Stations no longer hear the bells and sirens when a fire is announced. But it terrified Tim -- the thrashing of metal to metal accelerating, noise beyond noise, beyond comprehension.

The others had already made it across but Tim stopped just short of where he should have jumped, barely stopping and then swaying back and forth. Tim and Don's eyes locked. It was the first time in the three years since Don's parent's death that anything close to real awareness of the other registered in either of them. The changes that were brought about in their lives were like the train, unstoppable and more powerful than either one of them, and each choice, conscious and unconscious, propelled them into a life whose path they could no more control than the route of this train approaching them now.

Their look, held no more than a few seconds, expressed questions they were too young to understand, that asked whether their lives would ever again intertwine or whether their distance, now a few feet but mostly unfathomable and that could be observed in their clothing and future plans, could ever be bridged because of a deeper significance, of meaning, of love between them.

"C'mon, you can do it!" Don implored Tim and smiled his mischievous smile which left no doubt that what he said was true and would happen. And after taking a few steps back, Tim ran forward and then leaped and reached the others with plenty of room to spare. They continued up the steps, racing to beat the train that was applying its breaks. Paulie, first up the steps, held one hand in the door, forcing it to reopen and the others scooted in behind him as he held the door open, laughing as they did so.

They reached the Brighton Beach subway stop and got off the

train. Walking the streets of this foreign neighborhood, without a parent in close proximity, gave Tim a sense of freedom he had never experienced before, and he found this both appealing and disquieting. The liquor, which they continued to consume once they reached the boardwalk, continued to work its magic. They nestled in under the boards and heard the wood creaking above them as people walked by. There they drank, talked of cars mostly, and laughed, mostly at Paulie's antics. When they tired of this, they walked onto a commercial strip and entered a diner that had the shape of an extended train car.

The lights in the diner were blinding compared with the evening outside. Light reflected off of every mirror, formica, and silver surface in the room, which was about all the room consisted of. The front of the building was covered with plate glass windows and they sat themselves in a booth in front of one. Paulie rushed to one of the inside seats and immediately began pawing through the case containing the tunes on the juke box. Each booth contained one of these mini juke boxes that would accept your quarters and play music through speakers intended just for your table, a seemingly incredible extravagance but something virtually all diners had, and something that, in fact, expressed the essence of a diner's charm and personality.

Tim was feeling the effects of the alcohol. The stream of movement and sound left him feeling out of control and giddy at times. At others, he was totally removed from the other three who seemed to mesh so well together and with their surroundings, leaving him to feel like one of the moon beams he had been watching while on the boards and took refuge in that memory and the tranquility it offered him.

The waitress had already taken their orders and seemed none too pleased that they were just here for sodas and not to eat. The fact that she was even serving them without an adult present was surprising to Tim, but she seemed unconcerned.

When she returned with the drinks she laid them on the table and then placed one in front of each of them. Conversation ceased instantly. She was drop dead beautiful in an obvious and direct way. Her pink, polyester waitress uniform could not have been stretched any tighter. Her body did not seem to be touching the dress but rather the dress was like a second layer of skin which had a perfect contour the first and second time. It was like a body suit that a diver would wear and, in fact, it gave her skin surface the quality of a marine animal, and each boy imagined touching its soft but firm, rubbery, moist surface. Her hair was platinum blond and was raised in a beehive and lacquered into place. Black eye make up completed this dazzling display of "B" horror movie beauty that was as unattainable as the images coming through that celluloid medium.

When she left, Paulie was the first to comment, "Wouldn't mind getting my finger wet with that one."

"She's probably got some guy working on the docks looking over her, ready to cut off your finger and anything else you tried to touch her with," Don joked.

"He'd have to catch me first," Paulie responded and darted his body in various directions, avoiding imagined assailants in pursuit of him.

The tremendous pull towards sex was everywhere, all the time. Tim felt it here and back home with his friends; the girls at school whose bodies were beginning to develop and the boys who were left to ogle them and make up stories of supposed conquests. Tim had recently learned to play chess and was exposed to the Queen's Gambit opening. In this opening, one of the white pawns is intentionally placed in harm's way. "Go ahead, take it, go ahead!"

was the offer being extended to the opponent moving the black pieces. This player could either accept the gambit by taking the pawn or deny it and develop his/her strategy in other directions. Sex offered Tim the same perplexing options. It was being offered, if not yet in any real sense, then in every other possible way. Accepting the gambit or not could result in helping either side, but the one thing for sure was that it would change the game irrevocably. So with this, with the offer of sex, the gambit it imposed on his life, the space it assumed in it. But if he were to compare his life to a game of chess what he most wondered about was who or what was moving the white pieces and how could he possibly know the effects of the moves he made on his own *game* and all of the games that were going on around him.

"I'd screw her in a minute and run like hell when Mr. Longshoreman came looking," Tim found himself saying, and the other three looked up from their drinks in genuine shock. It was the first time in their view he came down from his perch and said something they could believe he meant and relate to.

"Listen to the prep meister, mister Ivy League. Wouldn't believe such a dirty thought would come from your mouth." Paulie said.

"Take her right down, would ya? Beat her with your tool till it was raw and bloody?" Don decided to join in.

"She wouldn't stand a chance," Tim responded, staying with it, feeling comfortable with these kids for the first time, and laughing loudly, loudly enough to turn the heads of those around them. And he didn't care that it was him they was looking at.

They walked out of the diner and onto the street. They were several blocks from where they would pick up the train and began their walk in that direction. The street turned back to a residential area of well appointed brownstones and small apartment buildings that projected an upscale quality.

"Remember what we did before the dance at the high school? Let's do it again," Paulie suggested with conspiratorial glee.

Without a nay vote being offered, Paulie explained how the three of them would make like they were jumping him, making a lot of noise along the way, and when the neighbors came out to see what was going on, they'd all get up and run away.

Paulie walked ahead of the rest of them, rounded a corner and leaned against a tree waiting for his would be assailants.

Don, Augie, and Tim rounded the corner and immediately gave chase to Paulie who feigned to run away from them. Soon they had him surrounded.

"So where's my money?" Don yelled at Paulie, after he was spun around by Augie until he was face to face, nose to nose, with Don.

"I'll get it for you, really."

"You've said that before and never paid up. Why should we believe you this time?"

Although Tim knew this was all an act, it felt real on some level and totally foreign. His father's stories from the war and his more recent experiences with the gangs in his new precinct were threatening, but also contained something undeniably alluring. And he sensed now, even in this mock confrontation, the heightened emotions that must rage in battle and their intoxicating effect, the clarity of focus brought into play as each moment ticks forward to some unknown climax.

"I will this time, I promise," Paulie responded. They had been talking loudly before but now Paulie's voice was screaming and pleading at the same time.

"This time it won't be so easy, though." And with that Don pushed Paulie into Augie who shoved him to Tim who roughly shoved him back to Don. Don threw a punch at Paulie, that grazed off his chin and sent Paulie sprawling on the ground, acting as though it had struck him fully. All three took turns making like they were kicking and punching him, as he lay on his back like a bug being crushed, reacting, overreacting probably, to every blow. They were collectively screaming through all of this, Paulie the most, as he yelled for help while trying to protect himself from the mock attack.

In the midst of the beating Tim looked up and saw standing at a nearby doorway, an elderly woman. The street light was directly in front of her home and she came out onto the front step as though onto a small stage. She held her night coat closed, wrapping her right hand around so that the loosely fitting garment was held tight. It was made of a faded cotton print and her spindly legs protruded beneath the bottom of the coat. The expression etched on her face was one of fear and impotent rage.

His attention was then turned in another direction, across the street. A man yelled out, "What the hell are you kids doing?" and was coming at them fast.

The 3 assailants took off running, leaving Paulie on the ground. The man came up to Paulie, asked him if he was alright to which Paulie, too stunned to comprehend everything going on, mumbled enough of something to satisfy the man.

The attackers began to slow their pace but then turned and saw that the man was hot on their trail.

"What the hell does this guy think he's doing?" Don said and again they picked up their pace, running into unknown parts of the city and the night.

While Don and Augie ran with delight, each street they passed left Tim felling less and less connected to the mayhem of the evening. He hadn't any idea where they had been since the train had left the station in Flatbush so he wondered how it was possible that he could feel more exposed, more lost, with each step. Perhaps it was that he became aware that Don was also lost, and that he could not look to him for guidance and support; and then he realized he did not want to depend on Don anyway.

They were able to walk now because they lost the man. Tim sensed that he should be laughing it up with Don and Augie now that they had pulled it off, lost the big crazy guy and scared the crap out of the neighbors living on that block, just like they had planned, capping off a blissfully cool night. But Tim felt in the atmosphere an oppressive quality, pressing down like a vise.

"Did you see the look on Paulie's face when the man came running towards us?" Don said, the sweat now dripping freely from his face. "He didn't know whether to get up and run with us or stay put. His look was like 'oh shit, what do I do now?' Made me want to pee my pants. But we didn't have time for that with that crazy old guy closing on us like freight train."

Don laughed with Augie and slapped hands with him, but Tim could only issue a faint half-smile, realizing something changing within him.

They came upon a train station and boarded the train back to where they had started the evening. Tim was glad to be on the train because the noise made it easy for him to distance himself from the two who had been his companions until a short while before. He looked beyond the two of them, towards the nameless, disconnected people on the train, staring in no direction, whose minds were filled with thoughts he would never know, never care about.

He wondered what it was he did care about. The image breaking forth from this reverie was that of the old woman, standing on her steps, expressing the effect of the supposed beating on her, which he was responsible for, and knew that it was fear he had caused her, plain and simple, and knew right then that this image would be the one that defined the evening for him, the one that would be brought forth unsummoned. And he was shamed, not exalted like Don and his friends, the one with him, and the other tunneling himself back like a worm to their home base that Tim wanted no more to be a part of.

And what else, what else did he pull back -- his family. Why did they not go to each other's homes with the friends and family as they once had? Why did they speak longingly, already, of times only a few years ago as if they were from another life and time? Always someone had been over back then, it seemed. His parents' friends and their families or his uncles and aunts and, of course, Don and Sara. The card games that occasionally the children were allowed to play, the silly games, the made up games, like when "No Peek" became "No Squeak" and you had to throw a dime into the pot when you said something and more often than not people would end up in howling laughter because someone else had to have their say about the luck of the cards or some stupid play and would throw as many dimes into the pot as was necessary until they had said their peace. The laughter, constant and loud, everything always loud. The music, barbecues and impromptu get-togethers were always there, always could be counted on. In this setting he was prepared to grow up, wanted to grow into, accepting all the family had to offer, the guidance, the sheltering sense of belonging, even the prejudices and the pettiness would have found an acceptable level of tolerance. None of these things he understood completely, but they were there and he felt them now fully, longed for them in their absence.

It was his family which he felt for and fiercely wanted to protect and recover from wherever it had been lost. And he looked at Don, laughing now with his buddy, Don, who had no family, not anymore, not really. That was over and Tim could do nothing about it and he felt himself turn away from Don, much like the elders had done. But Tim was not aware that this had occurred and he felt stricken that he was reaching this conclusion, but clear in his own mind that undeniable, unrepentant logic was forcing him now to sacrifice his relationship with his cousin in a way that he could only dimly comprehend, and that this turning away needed to be done by him alone.

Chapter 11

Tim woke slowly after his first night back from his stay with Don. It was Sunday and his mind drifted into and out of gauzy sleep. He passed between these states several time, until his eyes no longer remained shut and slumberous sleep no longer carried him off.

He was unfamiliar with the effects of a hangover and the fact that it could carry into a second day made him consider whether this could be a permanent condition. But despite the lingering effect of the alcohol, or perhaps in part because of it, his body's fatigue was accompanied by an overall sense of subdued happiness. He looked about his room, that was not as decorated as Don's was. Although he would have liked to imprint the walls with things that interested him and related to him, he had not done so and making a statement of this kind never seemed like an option to him. The few items laid out on his dresser held little significance to him – a snow globe of the Statue of Liberty and awards associated with ascending the ranks of a cub scout that he had received years before, things he had long since forgotten about and no longer appreciated. The single item on the wall was a Yankee pennant which was dwarfed by the wash of blank space surrounding it. But these shortcomings were not what focused his attention. The strongest sensation he experienced was the feeling of the newly cleaned sheets on his bed, their texture still ruffled by the cleaning, not yet flattened by use, by human sweat. He rolled on their surface, luxuriating in the sensation like a dog rolling on warm summer grass.

But the material things around him held little weight in his emerging consciousness. What he experienced instead as he emerged from the coils of sleep was the feeling of safety that returning home afforded him.

He wasn't sure what had happened. But he knew that the joy and laughter that had permeated his house, even with all the bickering, was now mostly absent. He rolled on his side and then raised himself from the bed. He walked into the room where his sister Anne was sharing a room with the new addition to his family, a little girl of two. She lay still in her crib and he beheld her. It was as if she, in the morning's new beginning held the answers to the problems that weighed heavily on him, on all of them in this household. He broke the cardinal rule regarding this little hellion, this ball of fire that tried to draw all the world into her vortex, and raised her from the mattress even as she slept, something he had never done before. Her sleep remained undisturbed as she rested into Tim's shoulder and chest, melding into them. He rocked her slowly, cradled her in his hands and arms. Her weight was real and considerable and he would soon need to place her back in the crib. But for now he was equal to the task and experienced the pleasure at having this warm body resting, pressing onto his.

Tim looked out the window onto their small back yard and then out onto the other adjoining yards. His gaze rested on a power line that ran alongside the row of houses to his left. A row of birds, maybe 30 in all, sat on either side of the post that held the wire aloft. The birds fluttered this way and that, pecking each other when they felt encroached upon, and actually stepping along the wire to close the ranks of spaces that they perceived to be too great. They seemed like senseless animals engaged in senseless movement until that movement stopped and Tim could see they had achieved perfect, or near perfect alignment, as with their individual bodies, too, angled perfectly so the rising sun could touch and warm the greatest surface of them. Were they only aware of the spacing of themselves and those directly on either side of them or could they be aware of the symmetry, the beauty they created together, and that Tim was able to perceive from this distance. Tim pondered this for some time and, as he looked at them, was reminded of a row of robed monks. His answer came when a group of them eventually flew off. They had left the line in a ragged order and those leaving immediately formed another group, flying off together, leaving the remaining birds to search again for balance, consistency. This seemingly random movement was all the proof Tim needed, showing him the understanding of the group that each bird possessed. And he recalled now seeing sheets of birds flying and swooping in the air as if they were one, and perceived these movements in a different way than he ever had before.

He placed the baby back in the crib and she remained sleeping as she had throughout. He regretted that she would never remember this experience of him holding her. But then he thought of the birds and laughed, questioning what exactly we do remember, what exactly comprises who we are and what we are aware of. He stroked her back and caressed her thin, tallow colored hair that fell in soft curls to the side of her head. His hands grazed the exposed parts of her arms and the sensation was like nothing else, maybe like an unripe plum, vulnerable and smooth but firm despite the smoothness, and cooler than one might expect. In fact, an unnameable surprise and wonder was all he was aware of as he gazed at his younger sister.

He returned to his room and lay on his bed, staring up at nothing in particular. The question that he considered as he looked out across his room was how do you keep the sense of happiness that he was feeling while holding his sister, that he was still feeling to some degree, but would surely leave him as the day wore on? The visit with his cousin came to mind and, in response, his eyes flickered rapidly several times and his body tensed, trying to cast off the images of the evening romp that would inevitably lead to the look on the old woman's face, as it surely did.

He got up from his bed and reached a decision even before he knew that he was considering a question. His mother had been taking him and his older sister Anne to a local Methodist church but this ended during his mother's recent pregnancy. His mother had been sick after the baby was born and they simply never started going again. He was not aware of missing church, which consisted of Sunday School with Bible lessons read to the kids of his age, followed by a few questions from the teacher and then some snacks. He and his sister would attend these classes each Sunday morning during the school year and never think of the church again at any other time.

It was Sunday morning and his friends had invited him to Sunday Mass, but he had never taken them up on this offer. All at once now he knew that was what he wanted to do, what he knew he had to do. He had never been to mass at a Catholic church but remembered the first time he accompanied his friends one evening during the summer the year before into the court yard that was surrounded by the church, the convent where the nuns lived, and an elementary school. This was the same school that he had attended the past year but had no idea at the time that he would be switching to this school. This complex of buildings was only a few blocks from his home, but he had not even been aware that this courtyard existed before they entered it that evening. The walls of all the buildings except for the church were austere and economical with minimal wood work around the windows to offset the office-like cement walls. The courtyard also contained a minimalist quality but had elements that changed the atmosphere of the entire area. Interspersed around the perimeter were sets of comfortable looking wooden benches and beside them, potted plants and small, well pruned bushes and other landscaping. As the boys stepped into this area, their voices echoed within the chamber created by this enclosed space and this caused their voices to grow quieter. Then, as if by some prearranged agreement, one of the boys yelled to the wall containing the residences,

"Sister Margaret Mary, Sister Margaret Mary."

They stood and waited for what seemed a very long time. He had heard of her before. She was the favorite teacher of the boys one year older than Tim and was responsible for teaching them what was, for most of them, their least favorite subject, math. She was no longer young and many of the boys had older brothers and sisters who had already been taught by her. She was even starting to see a second generation of students from the same family coming through the doorway of her classroom. She seemed to love not so much the math as the children she taught and had an unending energy for her students, and patience and love for the boys and girls of this difficult age group. It was these qualities of hers, which could not be faked or learned, that compelled her students to do as they were told, study as she required, drill the lessons as she instructed them.

She emerged from the archway that brought her from the building that none of these boys would ever enter. She was clothed in full habit that covered her body except for face and hands. The cloth was all black except for the white portion of the head piece that raised the cloth up off her head.

She stood before them, as she did every summer with other

small groups. It was mostly boys who would come, which had surprised her at first. She was done now with most of this group but they needed to come back, say their goodbyes again, look for what little assurances she was able to provide them. But it was not her way to be sentimental. That would never work with them and what they needed now was a little nudge pushing them onward to the to the adventures waiting for them, their destinies that were beginning to unfold. She enjoyed these visits but she had never been sure how to navigate them, how to perform her role. This thought, this indecision, was something she never felt in the classroom but did so in almost every other area of her life. Outside the classroom, the calculations of how to address people and fit into the roles ascribed to her, wore her out. It was one of the things she liked most about being a nun, narrowing the expectations placed upon her by others so that she could live her life simply and in service.

"Must be a slow night for you boys," she started off. "But it is very nice for you to come by and see me."

"Don't worry, Sister. Jonesy didn't come by to explain why he doesn't have his homework." Ronald Jones was a big boy, maybe a little slower than the rest in agility and mental acuity. This made him an easy target, but he took the kidding mostly in stride. The other boys tested his good nature constantly, attempting to evoke an eruption. And when they accomplished this, they scurried off in all directions away from the seismic tremors he was capable of producing. He talked about wanting to be a priest, but that would become a distant memory by the time he finished his first year of high school. Joking about missed homework with any of the nuns would be strictly off limits during the school year, but Eric, who made the joke, announced their newly graduated status with this comment, and had planned it beforehand just for this reason.

"How about you Eric? You bring another apple for the teacher?" Another boy jumped in, to take the spotlight off Ron and provide another target for further kidding.

They peppered Sister Margaret Mary with questions and provided updates on the progress of their summer which had really just begun. The successes and failures of their sports teams, baseball in the first part of the summer and then basketball as the summer progressed, were relayed. The topic of family vacations was also mentioned and then they talked about the upcoming school year. She knew all the boys here except for one, and knew that of the five she had taught, four were going to attend Bishop Reilly High School. This was a middling academic school and would suit them. The one boy who would be moving off in another direction was Eric, who would be going to Malloy High School, a more demanding academic institution. Although he did well in the eighth grade, she did not see any real talent and superior intellect in him and hoped he would not be disappointed when he saw what the wider world would confront him with.

"You boys have not introduced me to your friend," Sister Margaret Mary said, and motioned to Tim.

Tim had been standing off to the side, observing the interaction between the nun and his friends. Nothing could be further from the stories of terror his friends had filled him with concerning the treatment the nuns meted out to them. He searched his mind and could never remember having a conversation with any of his teachers outside of school and would not have known what to say to them if he had. But there she was dressed in these robes that conveyed to him a sense of strangeness but also dignity, a sense that she would always be there for them and that she would always project the clarity and humor that she was expressing to him right now.

"This is Tim. He goes to public school but all his friends go to Catholic School." Everyone laughed at this, whether it was intended as a joke or not. His friend Mark Pinder made this announcement. Mark was different, more subdued than the others. His younger brother had Down's syndrome and it was as if you could see some strain of this disability in all the members of Mark's family, but it was only fully expressed in the youngest boy. But Mark, despite his oddness, projected a level of comfort with who he was that all the other boys recognized unconsciously and bestowed upon him a level of respect and leadership in the group one would not have expected, and was, for that reason, confusing to newcomers to their circle of friends.

Tim did not expect the attention to be turned in his direction and could feel his face flush when this introduction was made. He took a short step forward and issue a respectful hello.

"Well, thank you for coming to visit me with this rowdy bunch of hooligans. You look like a boy with a good head on his shoulders. Don't let the likes of these boys turn it in the wrong direction." She said with a sweeping arm movement but also with a wry smile.

"Okay, I'll do my best." Tim replied. The other boys ended their remarks to her with the respectful *Sister,* and he would have liked to have done the same but felt it was not his place to do so and left that emptiness hang in the air.

"I'll bet you never had a teacher drill you like Sister Margaret Mary does," one of the boys issued from the crowd. "I bet you she put 5 miles on every period, walking up and down the aisles and across the front of the room, pounding her theorems and math rules into our heads."

"I had to do something to wake you boys up and get your brains working," she chided back. "But you boys will do fine.

You're all ready for what they will expect from you in high school."

Certainly this was not what Tim's math class was like, nor any of his other classes. Life in his junior high school was a circus and he felt a pang of regret as he heard about this world that his friends had been a part of but that he believed he would never know. This feeling came from nowhere because his friends were always bad mouthing school, but now he saw a different side.

The evening air was perfect, hot but not oppressive, as was the setting in this small court yard, and for these reasons no one felt a need to hasten the end to this time spent together.

When there was no longer anything any of them could think of to say, they said their good byes. Sister Margaret Mary's final words were an admonition to be sure to come to Mass every Sunday during the summer. This was not necessary for most of them as they knew to not do so was a mortal sin. Tim had never attended Mass with his friends, who viewed it like any other ill tasting medicine. But he felt as if her words were intended for him as well. And now, a year later, he felt as though this offer was being presented to him again, by this woman who embodied so many wonderful qualities. He sensed it as an option that opened up to him a whole new set of possibilities and spoke to him directly, deeply. It was this interaction that had started him thinking about attending Catholic School and an invitation that he now realized encompassed much more and one that he decided he would accept.

He met Mark Pinder on the steps of the church. He was the

best choice for this initiation. In some ways, important ways, he was everyone's best friend. He seemed naturally to be able to balance when to be serious and when to have fun. And because of his unique style, whatever the effect of that recessive gene was on him, you often did not know what he was up to until it was too late. But his seriousness also translated to taking religion and this church seriously, more so than the other boys. Every Saturday afternoon he would disappear for a couple of hours and deliver The Catholic Chime, the newspaper from the local diocese. He only made a couple of dollars and everyone wondered why he bothered, but nobody was really surprised that he did so.

Tim had kept Mark company a couple of times when he was delivering the papers. The route took several times longer than it needed to because Mark would be drawn into conversation with many of the old ladies who subscribed to the paper. Most seemed desperate for this contact and Mark was willing to submit to the conversations, repeatedly answering all the questions about his family and school. As he walked away from each of these houses he could be heard issuing forth a low level rumbling noise like what the character Lerch, from the Adams Family TV show, had made famous. But by the time he reached the next house he had dispelled the Lerch-like cloud of dissatisfaction that the previous house and conversation had forced upon him.

Mark walked him through the ritualized steps, pointed to him when it was time to kneel, snickering at times at the repetition of these movements. He whispered to him the significance of the various sacraments; the incense was to transport you away from earthly troubles, the priests spoke in Latin because it was the purest of languages, the language of *The Church*, the italicized nature of these two words resounded even in his whispered speech.

The priest was a young man, not having yet reached his 35th

birthday. But he carried himself with a sense of grace that bestowed upon him a presence, a sense of purpose and enlightenment beyond his years that was impossible not to be influenced by. This was Father Daniel, brought to this parish to energize its membership which had not been growing as the diocese felt it should. It was thought that if he could turn this church around, he might have a bright future.

Father Daniel Ward's focus in the church was the young families. He was convinced that the way to draw them in was to speak to them in the language they used, at least some of the times. Occasionally the service would include a folk song or two, with guitar accompaniment. He had a hard fight for this, mostly with the older members of the congregation. But he had made allies within the core group of powerful families and they supported his efforts which gave him the strength to pursue them, even if it meant losing some of the more established members along the way.

But his real strength was in his oratory, which he believed connected him with the Holy Spirit and allowed him to act as a conduit to those beneath him, his flock. This transference of the Holy Spirit was a matter of the utmost seriousness to him, the thing that sustained him, and them through him he believed, and this was the bond that held them together. Such a heavy responsibility he felt, which went even deeper when he considered his ability to wipe clean the stain of sins borne from bad behavior and impure thoughts that they all experienced every day, perhaps every minute of the their waking lives. But he knew he was chosen for this life and accepted with all his heart the responsibility and authority this life placed upon him, and thrilled to the challenge it offered.

"I will speak to you of the divine as I know it," the sermon began. "But before I do so, remember that we are mere flesh and bone and that means we cannot know the kingdom where God's love reigns, where the light of his wisdom pierces and annihilates those who would stand against him. No, not until we venture beyond this life will we know with even a glimmer of clarity of the gloriousness of what awaits us if we accept Christ as our Lord and Savior in this lifetime. So why bother to live with a sense of purpose and striving if the glories of God remain hidden from us? Why struggle if we can never emerge from darkness, living with the full knowledge that our earthly shell will always buffer us from true knowledge, true beauty? And, at times this earthly shell will indeed deflect us from appreciating those few glimpses into God's wondrousness that he might choose to make manifest to us. Make no mistake, your bodies are often not your friends and point you away from the light of our Lord and are not to be trusted."

The preacher's voice contained a lushness, the words issuing from him in such a way that the body seemed a property of the words instead of the opposite, seemingly normal relationship. When he stopped he was aware of the intense quiet that filled the sanctuary, a pause taken so that he could dab at the sweat that streaked his face and forehead. He felt a sense of rapture as he looked down at those who had come to be nourished by him and by their God who he tried to conjure, to awaken so that He may shine through him. His gowns were heavy with embroidery and flecks of gold plated metals, glass beads and mirrors, that were woven into the vestments, contrasting the pure white linen garments covering his body, exposing only his head and feet at the extremities and hands waving, punctuating the air.

That was it, Tim thought. How well the priest described his own feeling of unworthiness. Why he felt this he was unsure, but that is what he felt with force, as though a great hand had slapped him in the chest, taking his breath from him.

The priest blinked and his body shuddered perceptively. Tim recognized these motions to be like his own eyes closing to ward off dark images trying to assert themselves. He believed that Father Daniel was doing this to redirect his mind and spirit in another direction and Tim waited anxiously to see in what direction the priest would lead.

"I will tell you what is left for you, the faithful. But before doing so, you must realize and accept that all of us, every last one of us, is tainted by the temptation made manifest by Eve's partaking of the apple in the Garden of Eden. But all of you have been given the choice to follow our Lord who sacrificed Himself so we could be led away from the sordidness to which our bodies would have us be slaves. The way we acknowledge and exalt our Lord is by doing good deeds. Look at the missionaries we support in Africa. They are teaching the farmers better farming and irrigation methods not primarily to help the farmers themselves but to exalt God and the glory He has bestowed upon us. Not all of us will be called to do missionary work, but we must all follow the lord's example and teachings. You young people must obey the authority of your parents and you parents must provide the example to your children that will help guide them in the ways of our Lord and our religion. The sanctity of the family is second only to the loyalty to God himself."

The priest continued with his sermon but Tim, engaged in his own thoughts, strayed from the thread of the priest's words. His father and mother seemed to always be unhappy, angry, or fighting if they were together at all. Usually they would eat as a family, but even before the meal was served there would be arguing and bickering, poisonous and gut wrenching. He would follow the priest's admonition. He, Tim, would be the shining light that reconciled his parents and restored the order that he so desperately desired. But he would need to strengthen himself for this task and learn patience, waiting for his parents to see through him the joy of their family long forgotten.

Chapter 12

Michael Eaton was laying back on his bike in a little secured woodsy area along the Grand Central Parkway. It was 10:00 PM on a Thursday night. It was the middle of fall and the mystery in the air filled his lungs, body, and mind. He'd grown up not far from here but most of the tenements his family had lived in, and they lived in several, running from one to another in the dead of night to avoid the bill collectors, had been torn down and replaced by fancy high rises. But the loss of the buildings he grew up in left him without any feelings of remorse, and to them, he said, good riddance. This was one of his favorite times and places and it was in places like this that he could recall his past and family life growing up without excessive churning, with an air of resignation neither positive nor negative, simply accepting what was. In the middle of this reverie, a new black caddie, flared wings and all, flew by him. It had to be traveling at least 80 mph.

Mike stomped hard on the starter petal and was off, flying down the road in pursuit. A pig in a poke he thought, like lassoing one of those little oinkers and then tying their legs together in a rodeo. He closed the distance and could tell the driver was aware of his presence first because he slowed his speed and then when their eyes met in the rear view mirror of the car.

Mike walked up alongside the car and made a quick determination of the occupants. The man behind the wheel was older, mid 50's probably, and was decked out in an expensive looking charcoal gray suit. His hair was a little tousled and his face was flushed, a sign he knew all too well that pointed to him having been drinking. Sitting beside him was some young tart, half his age if that. She looked expectant and wide eyed, apparently enjoying this spectacle and the tinge of fear, or was it danger that she imagined, that shot through it. The old man would probably get a hand job when this was over if he played his cards right, Mike thought.

"License and registration, please," Mike said while shining a flashlight at the occupants and the contents of the car. The color scheme of the interior was black and white. The front seats were two luxurious, deeply cushioned bucket seats, that were connected by a small area just large enough for an arm rest that could fold up or down. The leather covering still expressed the distinctive odor of new leather and was discernible to Mike even from outside the car. The interior portion of the seats were a clean bright white color while the outer portion was a correspondingly dark black. But what really caught Mike's eye was the steering wheel, which also consisted of an alternating black and white pattern that flickered even in the dim light cast from the light in the middle of the roof.

The man in the car reached into the glove compartment and pulled not his registration but instead one of the cards he had previously purchased.

"Maybe this will do instead," and the driver gave the card to Mike.

It was legit and Mike was satisfied and was prepared to offer his canned response and let the man go on his way.

"This will do fine," Mike said, pocketing the *free* pass, "just be careful the rest of the way on your trip tonight. Looks like you've had a few."

"Yes, officer, we've had one hell of a night and its not over yet." the response came, and the driver flashed a little *mano a mano* look back to Mike.

"I'm glad to hear that," Mike felt inclined to reply, but what he really felt was angry, disgusted to be talking to this high roller this way, having to listen to more come out of his mouth than he cared to.

"Yes sir. Me and Angie are on our way to the Hamptons for a long weekend, a little quiet getaway." Again the conspiratorial glance, accompanied by a wink.

The driver reached into glove compartment a second time and pulled out a fresh, new 20 dollar bill. "Why don't you take the little lady out for a bite on me, officer. Great little system you're running here. All my best to you and yours." Mike felt as if he were being dismissed. With the twenty still in his hand the driver pulled the car back into traffic and Mike slowly regained his place on the bike, but the mood that had been his was now lost, and this loss was incalculable.

Mike did not much care about the scam that he felt forced to take part in. The extra money was nice and it wasn't like he thought he didn't deserve it. Nor did he think the dishonesty bothered him that much. Still it gnawed and he wished he could rid himself of that feeling. He would have preferred to have pulled that asshole out of his car and send him off to jail on a drunk driving charge. He had no use for idle talk masquerading as a bond, camaraderie, with these upper class fools. They always turned it around so they were the ones in control, and that was his complaint with the scam, and with what had just happened now. But there was nothing to be done about it. Nothing either to do about the anger welling up inside him except of course to drink it down until it was dulled to an acceptable level, or let it explode in a fit of rage.

Mike headed back into work the next day. Everything ached and it would be amazing to anyone not initiated into the world of excessive drinking to see how much people could consume and still stand on their feet, function in even a nominal manner. But before he could get onto his bike and out of the precinct, he was summoned into the Captain's office.

He mounted the steps to the office, one by one, trying to shed the effects of the poison coursing through his system. His entire body oozed sweat and he felt like he had just jumped out of a pool. Mike stopped at the bathroom and threw some cold water on his face. He was 40 years old, had 12 years in the force and was determined to make it to 20 for the pension. He looked at himself in the mirror and was a little stunned by what he saw. The youthfulness was gone and he wondered, where, how, it had been spent. Meaty jowls sagged on both sides of his face, his hair was sprinkled with gray, especially around the temples. But mostly he saw the lines etched into his face, set from innumerable repeated motions that set his expression, freezing it, into a scowl that he could only assume best suited him, best portrayed his true attitude towards life. Also on display was the reddened, inflamed quality of his skin and the tiny blood vessels that had been pushed to the surface on and around his nose. So he was developing a Rummy's nose; at least he was well studied for this look, he decided. But what scared him most were his eyes. He imagined they were like what you would see when looking at some small, feral animal, trapped in a maze too complex to make sense of, bend to its desires.

He entered the Captain's office and knew right away this was big trouble. Also in the office was a suit from internal affairs and a rep from the Police union. Captain Marks told him to sit down directly in front of him which resulted in him being flanked by the other two who sat on either side. Clearly he was the object of interest, and the only one without foreknowledge of what brought them together, which the Captain set forth explaining after introducing everyone in the room.

"You really screwed this up, Eaton. I gave you a shot to do what you wanted to do, thought you'd be good at it, too. But you couldn't let 'well enough alone', could you?" He stated, and started opening a folder that lay in front of him. "Do these mean anything to you?"

Captain Marks placed before Mike some copies of some of the fake tickets. Most had his identifying number on them, which was the month, day, and year he was born, 062820. He had been none too creative with a moniker, but he doubt it would have mattered much if he had been.

He looked up. The feral animal was now subdued, cornered by forces seen and unseen, and laid exposed, waiting to see what would come next.

He looked around the room and realized there was not an ally among them. None of them had ever walked a beat, been in the community in any direct way. The suits and the captain had their book knowledge. But how do you compare that with delivering a baby whose mother went into labor while in a traffic jam that only he on his motorcycle could get to. Or the time he jumped into the freezing water around The Throgs Neck Bridge to pull a woman attempting suicide back to shore. No, these guys knew nothing of these things. They pushed paper, probably were looking to get as many convictions out of this as possible; he was just another notch on their belts.

He looked over at the union rep, Jack McCann, the one who supposedly was looking out for him. Mike had watched this guy for years and kept his distance. One of those uptown Irish wannabes. Once in a while he had something good to say but you couldn't trust him, because the next day the calculations might point in a different direction and different words would spew out. He would go out drinking with the guys and made like he was one of them but was always surrounded by his coterie of Jack McCann wannabes. The whole thing made Mike sick but Jack had his role, some power that you needed to recognize. So you did not tell Jack McCann how you detested him, but sidestepped him like you would a dangerous snake, which is what he was. In response to the look Mike gave Jack, he thought he saw a nearly imperceptible nod, an ascent that answering the questions was all that was left for him to do.

"Yeah, I know what these are," he responded, a little defiantly, and placed them back on the Captain's desk, not wanting to look at them any longer.

"How stupid could you be? Did you really think you could get away with this?" the Captain snapped at him.

Mike felt like he was being spoken to like a child, but a child has no knowledge of the world and the first times spoken to this way believes he/she is the worst speck of excrement in the world and accepts this truth and builds a world view around it and then becomes hardened to these words when they are delivered subsequently and believes there is some triumph in this hardness.

"That wasn't really the point."

"What do you mean by that?"

"'Getting away with', 'being stupid about doing this'. It's not the point. The scam was in place. You did it or got another job."

"Don't give me that shit, Eaton," the captain began

sermonizing. "Don't feed me this cheap baloney that you had to do it, that you had no choice but to go along with this. You could have said 'no'. You could have stepped forward and exposed it."

And he supposed they thought he could dance on the head of a pin or jump over the moon, if only he tried, he wanted to say. What did they know or care really? They had their uptown scams going and could now feast on the little guys out on the streets. Choice, what choice, now or ever? When do you change the course of your life perceptibly, wake up in the morning and find you are something different, different in shape or thought? No, you are who and what you are. And the forces propelling you will either tear you apart or buoy you up. But choice, no, choice was another one of those fancy uptown ideas they manufacture to allow themselves to look down on you.

Instead of putting to words any of these thoughts, all he said was, "If you say so Captain."

"Well, if you weren't helping to run this thing and felt like you were forced into it, who were the ones running the operation?"

Mike was waiting for this question. It was the only question that really mattered and he weighed it heavily. If he got bounced from the job he wasn't sure how he would support his family, or if he could. And the assholes pressuring him into the scam weren't worth going down for. But none of that mattered.

"You're right captain. I was only a minor player," and then after a pause, "But if you want someone to name names, you're going to have to find that person somewhere else."

"How did you guys expect to get away with this? Running your racket all over the fucking city. Were you guys out of your minds?"

Mike tried to keep his mouth shut. Speaking truth would only work against him and he already felt like he was impaled on the captain's bayonet. But he could not hold himself back.

"I've been thinking the same thing, wondering how something like this could operate, go undetected and not be squashed as soon as it started. It does make you wonder." After making sure the captain understood the meaning of his words, he turned his attention from the captain and he took in the figure of the Internal Affairs rep for the first time, dead pan and impassive throughout, the perfect hatchet man. Mike wanted to give him one glance, narrow him in his gaze one time, like there was no one else in the room so that he could convey to him how completely, how utterly he hated him, and wished he could rip his heart out at this very moment.

It was impossible to distinguish their reactions to this exchange – probably disappointment that they had come up empty, and some anger. But he wondered if there was some degree of relief, too, because you never knew where a lead would take you. You just never knew who or what you might pull out once you start digging into one of these schemes. Regardless, Mike knew he did the right thing and hoped that he would never live to regret saying just what he said and nothing more.

The Captain sat back and considered his options in an unhurried manner. He had few illusions about what went on out on the streets, and he was willing to look the other way at many of the minor trespasses that came before him. But this was different, much bigger, and could not be swept under the rug. Heads would roll and most of those decisions would be made by his superiors. With minor exceptions he would simply be following the orders passed down, which was fine with him. This was not a situation to get any closer to than what was required.

"You understand that that decision won't help you any. Things might go easier for you if you gave up the ones running the operation," the captain said to Mike.

"I understand."

"'Code of silence' and all that, I suppose," the Captain replied when it was clear Mike would not be saying anything more.

"That's it. It doesn't always make sense to me, either," Mike responded. "But it's all I've got left."

"Then you leave us no other choice," the captain said and then paused until he received a visual confirmation from the Internal Affairs rep, who still had not uttered a word. And when that cue was received, he continued "but to suspend you without pay effective immediately. You can leave your shield and gun with me now."

Mike surrendered these things to the captain, placing them on his desk, and the captain let them lay there.

"We're done here now," Captain Marks said, bringing the meeting to a close. "We'll be in touch but until then you should stay close by. Be available to be called in for further questioning. I suspect you will want to have some words with Mr. McCann before you head out."

"Yes, sir," Mike replied, but he had no desire to talk with Jack.

He could not get out of the precinct fast enough. But before he could collect his stuff and get out of there, Jack was was there beside him, matching him stride for stride.

"Before you bolt out of here, I need to talk to you. What do you say we slip into here," Jack said, and opened a door leading into an interrogation room.

"You handled yourself okay in there. Although I could have

done without some of the bravado." Jack said, laughing to himself, like he had just watched a good show on the television. "But you did good, you did right by not calling out any of your fellow officers."

"Oh yeah, I did so good I probably got my ass fired from this fucking job... And for what?"

Jack seemed disturbed by the sound of these words. The certainty and cockiness he'd heard in the Captain's office, were replaced here with a defeated quality.

"Listen, Eaton, I know this thing is bigger than you. But you can't give into it. Just keep playing it tough. Everything will work out for the better."

Mike snapped out of his introspection and looked up as if for the first time, and began eyeing Jack differently.

"What do you mean by that, Jack... that you know it's bigger than me."

"Well, I know they've pulled other cops in on this, just like you. And I suspect they aren't done yet either." Jack said after a pause and with an air of caution.

And remembering the cut that was taken off the top, it was all becoming clear to Mike, or at least he thought it was. But nothing was ever really clear, and the further you dove into something like this, the more confused and disfigured things became.

"I certainly appreciate all the attention you are paying to my case, Jack." Jack was immune to subtlety, so the true nature of Mike's words never occurred to him.

"That's right," Jack responded. "All I want to do is right this ship and get it back into port. Get us all past this crisis."

The man could talk, no doubt about it. Mike had heard him before, shouting with the best of them; he even made sense some of the times. But it was the shout of his own voice that he loved the most, the power in the union hall it gave him on occasion. It was an end in itself and Mike was convinced that if Jack ever got his hand on the whip he'd use it to bloody those who crossed him more effectively than any boss he'd ever had since joining the force.

Mike's elbows touched upon the table while his upper body leaned across it. But with a presence too charged to be resting any weight on them, he cut through the niceties that had been voiced to this point.

"What do you mean, Jack? You've never cared a rat's ass for me and now my welfare is all that seems to matter to you?"

"That's not fair," Jack said, with feigned hurt feelings. "I'm always looking out for all the men in the union."

That was it, more than Mike could take. "You lying piece of shit. What's in it for you? That's what I want to know. For all I know you've already gotten yours from what was skimmed off the top, and now you're just doing what you've been paid to do. And if it means letting me go down, I know you wouldn't think twice about letting that happen."

"Mike, you got to remember which side your bread is buttered on," Jack said, trying to gain the upper hand in the conversation, get it moving again in the intended direction.

"I'll show you which side my bread is buttered on!" And with that Mike leaped over the table, threw Jack against the wall and began throttling him. Jack tried to defend himself, but was ineffectual. His screams were the thing that saved him as others charged into the room, breaking them up. Blood gushed from Jack's nose. He was yelling at Mike in his high Irish tenor, things about him being a stupid animal, not knowing what was good for him.

After the fight was broken up Mike fell silent and reasserted control of himself. He walked away, down the hall and collected his stuff from his locker. He was not sure what his future would bring but was quite sure he would never walk through the doors of this building, not, at least, as an active duty policeman.

Word got back to the captain about the fight while he was sitting alone in his office. He smiled to himself and then let out a long, deep roaring belly laugh. Eaton was a fool for doing it, there was no doubt about that. But Mike was a good judge of character and the captain reflected on how he would love to take a shot at that loud mouth himself. If you were looking for a litmus test in the precinct it could be how you felt about Jack McCann. There were those hated him straight up, and he was not surprised to include Mike Eaton in this group, and he felt a strong affinity with anyone counted among them. Then, on the other side were the group of whiners who were more than happy to let Jack do their bidding, willing to bury their manhood under his protective wing. Then there was the middle group that recognized in Jack, and so many others, the necessary evil they represented. This last group was the one the captain found himself in, knew he had to be a member of. But damn, he would have liked to have been the one to administer the blows to Jack, would have paid a handsome price to witness the exchange. Eaton was stupid, alright. But if he had a chance to save him from losing his job, or worse, he would stick his neck out a little to see what he could do for him.

Mike went home and sat around the house for several days waiting for the call that would lead to his knowing his fate; they could fire him or bring him up on charges or any of a number of other disciplinary actions as well. It wasn't worth worrying about but he wasn't able to avoid doing so. Here was something he enjoyed doing, could have sailed through the remainder of his 20 years doing as long as his body held up. The experience of enjoying his work was new, foreign. He had not fully gotten used to it and now they were taking his job away from him. His suspicions about the improved quality of his life proved to be warranted.

Mike told Jen as much as he knew about what was going on. He would have preferred to say nothing but he had to explain why he was home so much and probably why a paycheck would not be coming, as they had been every 2 weeks for the past 12 years. He expected to have a row about it, have to listen to the tales of stability that characterized his brothers-in-law. These he would rebuff, offering some stories of his own that highlighted their shortcomings. This would escalate into shouting and eventually they would make up and then there would be relative calm for some period.

But things were different with Jen and he wasn't sure how to characterize it. She was pregnant again with their 3rd child, not something they were planning for, or wanted particularly. It wasn't like things made her angry in the way she was capable of becoming, but instead she seemed to have become absent minded, unable to focus or pay attention for very long. Even important matters like him getting suspended did not register like he thought they should.

It was almost two years since Rose and Ben died in the accident and life still had not returned to normal, and normal was becoming more of an ideal than anything tangible. Nobody talked about it but the innocence that they worked hard to recover after the war was shattered with their deaths. And nothing replaced it but a void that they collectively failed to acknowledge and tried to ignore.

Jen listened to Mike's story of the suspension and absorbed it like so much other bad news that came her way. Her ability to deal with life was predicated on her ability to keep it at arm's length. If she could do this she believed she could manage her affairs. But her ability to maintain this sense of control so that she could deal with Mike's drinking, run the household and manage the kids, was evaporating. Others saw this change but she steadfastly refused to acknowledge it and, instead, attempted to keep pushing through the requirements of the day. But what the others saw was the lack of fluidity in her movements, the way she would become distracted and lose focus.

What she admitted to was how much she missed Rose, the utter emptiness she felt because of her absence. What she would not bring to the conscious level was the distance they experienced for many years before her death and the reasons for that distance. Rose's free-thinking ideas were abhorrent to the family, threatened its very existence. Jen had wondered how Rose could not see the family's response, why she would not stop sharing her ideas or at least not be so public about it.

So Jen set up a boundary between Rose and herself whenever Rose started expressing any of her notions. Jen's ways of interacting with her sister began to narrow, and replacing a rich variety of experiences was the single determinant of whether or not to try to stifle Rose. Her thought process was that if she became non responsive to Rose's actions, she would have the power to stop her carrying on in her disruptive ways.

And it went deeper, beyond Jen's conscious awareness. Jen knew she had been angry with Rose for taking the family in directions that were taboo, and because of this anger her nonresponsiveness was a form of punishment. And the reward of Jen embracing Rose back into the security of the family was granted when Rose resumed a more respectable topic of conversation and way of acting. But complications arose from these tactics. The problem was she could not enable and disable this barrier with the ease she assumed this task would require. For how long can you turn your emotions on and off at will? Was she always able to determine the tipping point for the transition? Was it always an all or nothing proposition, or were there gradations of rewards and punishments?

But now she was gone, gone forever. And Jen was crushed by this loss, adrift and unable to find stability, push through as she had always pushed through. She failed to recognize the true reasons for the distance between her and Rose or learn from them, because that level of introspection did not exist in her and would be steadfastly resisted. But the core of her strength, based on the notion of resisting and overcoming obstacles placed before her, had met its match in Rose's life and death, and she would not be able to easily vanquish this adversary. Any alternative to this model of behavior was too treacherous, too outside of anything she had ever known, experienced, comprehended. So she waged her limited war with what was left of her power, much of which was lost, lost forever probably. Those around Jen recognized a change in her. Just shy of 40 years old, she aged perceptibly and physical ailments became more common.

So she took the words of the suspension from the police force without much fight and fiestiness, because this is who she was becoming and the direction her life was headed. The demons lurked below, content for the most part to live parasitically, sucking the marrow from the host, spreading a low grade sorrow over her life.

Chapter 13

Mike woke slowly, groggily. His mind cast about, becoming aware of a realm other than the one it had just inhabited, emerging warily from the depths into clear consciousness. At first the only thing was light, there, gone and then back again; the steady pace of the arcing brightness was measured across his field of vision, even as his eyes remained closed.

When he opened his eyes he realized immediately what had happened. The small cot that he lay on looked out from a little alcove onto a hallway. Someone, or something, must have knocked the light hanging from the ceiling out there. He wasn't sure what woke him, maybe the movement of light or the noise of the initial contact.

"Sons of bitches have no respect," he mumbled to himself and rolled over onto his other side, which put him within a foot of a cinder block wall that was pock marked with mold that was flourishing in this dark, damp environment. He tried to make his mind blank so he could return to the deep slumber from which he had just been summoned.

Several days passed without contact with anyone related to the case after the incident with Jack in the Station House. He thought about how it was possible that his world was coming apart. He was a master of schemes and took part in them unapologetically.

But even at their worst they only had the potential to exact real harm on himself. This was big, larger than anything he could control and for that reason he hadn't liked it from the start. He had issued very few of his own "tickets", enough to show that he was a player, but only a fraction of what most of them did. But he did return the ones that came back to him through the mail and if that's how they tracked the operation he would appear to have been as caught up in it as much as anyone else.

He drank at home and out with the boys. But it did not lift his spirits, or change his focus or even blot it out. The world was closing in and the feeling of powerlessness, a feeling he had always known, was now like a rampaging fire, burning him from the inside out. How did other people do it, he wondered, sail through life as though on some perpetual happy pills. Take his asshole brother-in-law, Frank. The world could be going to hell in a hand basket and it wouldn't phase him. He would keep the same slow, steady view of the world he had since Mike had met him more than 20 years before. Now he could be seen with a cigar twirling in his mouth most times, a paunch grown around his middle, and graying, thinning hair. But when you looked into his eyes nothing had changed, nothing penetrated and he was committed to not allowing change to happen. It was easy to be envious of that, but just as easy to be enraged by it.

A man's house should be his castle, that's the stuff he had grown up on. But that was turning into another lie that he was beginning to see through. He loved Jen, that was for sure, but somehow that love gave him no peace. They say opposites attract and maybe the problem was that they were too much alike. Neither of them gave an inch and expected so much, in terms of living by a certain code of behavior, from others. This hardening to the world outside the home had resulted in a distance between them as well. And now things were changing again subtlety. This pregnancy had almost come to term and was really taking a toll on her. She would not get out of bed some days and that left the remaining three of them to fend for themselves. He handled this better than anyone expected, even took some satisfaction in performing a few simple chores to keep the family going until Jen was back on her feet.

The little he had decided about what it would take to be a good father started and ended with providing for the members of his immediate family. If you put a roof over their heads and food in their mouths, you were doing your job; if you didn't, you weren't. He was doing the providing, so why didn't he feel better about it, why didn't he feel the closeness to them that he expected would develop from being the provider?

After two weeks of sitting around and brooding, he was called into the captain's office. The meeting was swift and somewhat unexpected. He learned that he would not lose his job but would be transferred to another precinct. He had been reassigned to the precinct in Bedford-Stuyvesant, one of the worst, most dangerous parts of the city. He was going to be a foot patrolman again and would never be allowed to ride a motorcycle for the police. In fact, there was no place left for him to go. The motorcycle incident was on his record and it was essentially the kiss of death. It was ride it out in Bedford-Stuyvesant or find another line of work.

He faired better than most, and never understood why. Most everyone else was fired from the job and some were brought up on criminal charges. There was something of a media splash, with articles in the papers and the TV news covering it. He was told to not tell the press anything but the opportunity never presented itself. It was the first time he was ever involved in something that was reported in the press. It amazed him how wrong they got almost every detail of the operation, until it was barely recognizable even to him; what he saw was how the whole process was embellished, mangled, and the characters who were singled out for prosecution became villainized, thrown to the wolves. So he kept his nose clean, accepted his marching papers and tried to move on.

He knew poverty and violent neighborhoods, had grown up with both. But nothing prepared him for what he walked into in Bed-Stuy. Gang violence ruled this area, gun shots rang out regularly. The year was 1961 and the whole country was experiencing a sense of change of a magnitude that was unfathomable. For Bed-Stuy that meant an accelerated movement into chaos. There was no counter to this centrifugal force that showed in the disrepair of the buildings, the garbage on the streets, the lack of discipline exerted by an established social network.

In this precinct you had a partner and went everywhere with him. About the only time you were left alone was when you took a piss. He was teamed up with Nick Randazzo, a lanky Italian. Nick was a bundle of energy, could not sit still which was a problem when you pulled a shift in a squad car and drove around for most of your 8 hours.

The hardest thing Mike had to adjust to was the mistrust that was directed towards him from the other police officers. Everyone knew about the motorcycle police bust and now one of those that survived was among them. In addition to being one of the most dangerous precincts in the city, it was also one of the most corrupt. Like so many other things, the schemes being run in this part of the city were of a magnitude that Mike had never seen and now he was perceived as a potential threat to them. He was made aware of the danger this put him in almost immediately, and he did his best to figure out how the game was played and how not to stray outside of its boundaries, keeping his eyes open all the time.

Get moved to another precinct in another part of the city and all of sudden your work day increases by two hours. That's what Mike experienced with the added commute. He thought of the trip more as an elevator ride. Instead of being on a level roadway, the trip to work was straight down, and coming home was in the other direction. The people back in his section of Queens, along the border with Nassau, took what they had for granted: tree-lined streets that often formed canopies over narrow roadways, individual homes and yards that were just large enough to afford a degree of privacy. No, that was heaven compared to what he descended into every day, entering it with the hope that he would make the return trip at the end of his shift.

When he worked days the traffic was the worst, and he fought his way through the rush hour traffic on both sides of his journey. These days he would eat with the family, maybe help prepare the food when he got home and then shove off to meet up with the boys or stay home and watch TV. He had been at the new precinct for about a year and during that time he'd found himself becoming more and more disconnected from his family, less and less comfortable in his own home. The battle to compress and then decompress eventually wore him out, and this forced a shut down of feelings at the outer reaches of his emotional life. In this way, he tried to survive the hand he'd been dealt. Marking time until he got his 20 years in became his mantra. The pitfalls of this strategy were many, but considering that was a luxury he could not allow himself.

One night the family sat around watching TV. They were on their fourth half hour television series. It was a Tuesday night, which they considered an unusually strong night of TV watching.

They all knew what the offerings were on the various networks although the paper was open to the TV section as it was every night to make sure no "specials" marred the expected sequence of shows. The first three had been sitcoms, relating to families, experiences, and locales that looked like nothing they knew and that probably did not exist anywhere but in some TV producer's dream scape. But this did not take away from the enjoyment of the entertainment.

The fourth show was a buddy series, taking place during WW II that occasionally hit on slightly more thought provoking material. Jen laid on her back on the sofa as she watched. She had just gotten the baby to sleep and once she settled herself down, she was content to just sit in front of the TV set. She would drift in and out of conversations and the story line of the shows. She had little control over her lack of focus and other family members had begun to joke when she had that far away look in her eyes and someone might snap their fingers in front of her face, to bring her from wherever she was back to the current circumstances.

This particular show featured the regular cast of characters, that was comprised of a squad of five or six men, who needed to travel deep behind enemy lines to perform a dangerous rescue mission. The guest actor knew the whereabouts of the person needing to be rescued and was given the responsibility of carrying out the mission. The squad's sergeant was reluctant to surrender control of the squad or turn over the safety of his men to this outsider from Central Command, and much of the half hour was spent watching the two of them spar for control of the minds and spirits of the men and each other. The sergeant was habitually unkempt, with a several day's growth of beard and deep set eyes that said he did not like what he was doing but would do it anyway and no one better get in his way. He was gritty and working class and charismatic in a quiet, intense way. He carried a rifle that looked like a bazooka because of an unexplainable extension attached to it. The outsider spoke the Queen's English, stayed on topic which was the mission he was sent to carry out and, oh yes, was black, probably the only black person ever to make an appearance on this show.

Tim enjoyed watching war shows with his dad. Sometimes Mike would take the opportunity to point out the poor job the shows did in portraying the rules of engagement, or the wrong guns and armament that were being used. Occasionally a show would evoke a memory of combat or some other event occurring during his years in the army and Tim would drop whatever else he was doing and listen intently, trying to glean from these stories the world at that time and the man that his father had been.

But this time it was different. Mike deflected a couple of questions that Tim posed to him and Tim understood that his father did not want to be bothered. One look at him showed he was deeply engrossed in the action of the show. His chair was an incliner and usually he would send it into full glide, leaving him in a position that was essentially lying down. But half way through this show he positioned it upright and then it became clear he did so because he was too agitated to remain in his former position.

Towards the end of the show it was clear that the sergeant and the outsider were able to work through their differences and had gained a degree of respect for each other. As they prepared for the attack, crouching in the brush because they were within enemy range, the sergeant pulled out a tin of black shoe polish and smeared a streak beneath each eye. Without thinking, he turned to the outsider and offered the shoe polish to him. He did not immediately move his hand to accept the tin but their eyes met and each man's expression froze the other. The sergeant, who never smiled, broke into a sardonic grin. This evoked a good-natured response from the outsider, that he, also, had not expressed until that moment. No words were spoken and the sergeant placed the tin on a large rock that sat between them and had been serving as a table. Their smiles remained as the sergeant moved off to his troops to check on their preparations for combat.

"What are they putting this shit on TV for?" Mike bellowed and his fury froze every other thought and activity in the room. Anne held her doll whom she had been dressing, tight and close to her. Jen needed no snapping of fingers to get her attention, and Tim, who had been watching every moment of the show wondered exactly what caused this. What had he missed? But Tim did not have long to consider such things.

Turning his attention to Tim, Mike said, "Do you have any idea why he did not take the shoe polish?"

Tim felt the answer was obvious. He assumed it was because his skin was dark enough and he did not need it. But his father's intensity froze in him the ability to respond, formulate a thought that could be communicated.

"I knew it. Of course you can't. They shouldn't put stories like this on TV. Things that kids can't understand."

He was up, out of his chair, pacing, ready to explode. "I don't want to let this crap into my house. They're always cramming this shit down your throat. Why can't they leave things alone, let people live their lives, especially when they're in their own damn house."

Tim and Anne were unable to understand Mike's response. How could this story of friendship and developing trust evoke this response from their father. The discussion went no further and was never brought up again. But Mike quietly committed himself to finding ways to block unwanted opinions such as these from reaching him, especially while he was within the walls of his home.

Tim and Anne knew better than to say anything. But even if they were allowed to ask for an explanation, they could form no coherent thoughts around what had just transpired. Instead, what each was left with was a deep sense of apprehension. If Mike was trying to shield his family from something wrong, something bad, the result of his actions was the opposite: filling his children with a sense of the world being intrusive and deceitful, and that this was the nature of the world they were entering.

The next morning the air was bitter cold. Mike had battled his way to work along The Belt Parkway. An accident on the other side of the road had snarled traffic on both sides of the roadway. Rubberneckers, Mike concluded. The stupidity of people never ceased to infuriate him. When he did finally reach the accident scene, he assiduously avoided turning his head to survey it and accelerated instead of slowing down. When he almost crawled up the ass of the car in front of him, which had slowed down so the driver could assess the damage, he stomped on his brakes mere inches from the fender of the car and laid on his horn for a good 30 seconds until the driver resumed his speed and attention to the road ahead of him. The fact that justice had been served, that he corrected the behavior of the driver in front of him, did little to improve his disposition, his outlook on the world. In this frame of mind he continued his daily descent, shutting down any emotional sensors except for those directly involved in his survival.

He and Nick were assigned a squad car for the day. They followed a predefined route, making their way along the rows of shops that still operated and provided an ever so slight economic heart beat to the community. Mike, who was driving, looked out at the groupings of men hanging about the street corners. Various shades of brown and gray defined the monochrome landscape.

The morning was still young, the sun was just starting to break into view when the eastern horizon could be spied between the buildings that dominated the landscape. The air was biting, uninviting. But it was also light and crystal clear, as if descended from an unearthly source. And there were the men out there perpetually standing about, dressed in little more clothing than what you would see them wearing on a cool autumn night; maybe a woolen hat, maybe a thread worn jacket or two. But their warmth mostly emanated from the bottle, opened and covered in a brown paper bag, held tight within their hand's grasp.

They received a call and were told to respond to an incident on the corners of Jefferson and Nostrand. Within moments they turned the corner that was a block away from the situation they needed to investigate. As they approached the scene, Mike surveyed the block that he had not remembered being on before. It was decimated; piles of rock, garbage and building parts littered the entire area. He felt like he was back in the war; this could be Dresden he thought. How was it possible? Travel a few miles from here and you were on the Brooklyn Bridge and then over into Manhattan, and the Financial District with its unimaginable sums of money. And then back in the other direction, not many miles really, to where he lived in the relative prosperity of modest single family homes that people took care of. And here, in the middle of these two seemingly disconnected lifestyles was a hell that was rapidly descending into a deeper hell. You needed to blame someone so you blamed them, out there, living no better than animals, shooting each other up all the time. His life was hard too, hard beyond anyone's imagining. Each and every day he wrestled with the bottle and the demons that the uninitiated could never appreciate. Not the kind of a have a few drinks type of drinking, but the kind that commanded every thought, recognized no limit once it was engaged and sought an exhilaration that could only come from annihilating one's self. No, there was nothing left of him after this battle. Every shred of will and strength and determination were spent in this single, constant struggle. So he did not care, really, about what he saw outside the windows, mainly because there was nothing left of him to care with. And he was left with the conclusion that if this was how they lived then it must be their own fault because not everyone lived this way. And if they behaved like animals then they must be animals and be treated accordingly.

The sunlight behind him edged through to one of the few intact walls in his purview. The brick of that wall became brilliantly lit up; light of a blinding kind glinted off its windows. The sight of the investigation contained a garbage truck, the garbage collectors assigned to the truck, and a few of the local residents. As Mike and Nick approached the scene, the participants remained in darkness. The wall that received the sun was behind them but the reflected light glanced away from them, in a way that seemed to defy the laws of physics. There was no detail to the scene. Instead there were the undefined darkened forms creating a cameo of the nearly motionless setting. Now, as he got closer, it was not Dresden Mike thought of, but the featureless surface of the moon.

They got out of the car and were directed to a garbage bin and looked within. An infant had been deposited there. The burial grounds: waste and fetid garbage. He or she had on a diaper that was relatively clean, in contrast to detritus of its surroundings. Maybe it had been placed there with some care instead of what one would assume. Maybe it had died of natural causes instead of neglect. These were questions that would never be answered, and even the asking had an indulgent quality.

They looked around at the others. All were sullen. Eyes teared up in some. Quiet pervaded. Mike and Nick had joined the scene and felt a part of this featureless landscape and were undone by it, realized that this was the only burial this infant would receive. But not for long would Mike allow himself the feeling of remorse and sympathy. As quickly as possible he would reinstall the walls and barriers that would allow him not to feel, for to do otherwise he was certain would hasten his own demise. In fact, each situation like this that he encountered hardened him a little more, justified the racism that had grown to become a pillar of strength for him.

Mike, now in street clothes headed back towards work. This was unofficial business but business every bit as integral to the job as any on-the-clock activity. A couple of fellow policeman from his precinct had been harassed while braking up an incident on a corner two days before. It was nothing major they had responded to: a fight between 2 guys that drew a crowd. But when the police entered the scene the crowd would not disperse. The cops worked their night sticks and things got a little out of control. Punches were thrown in all directions, stones and bottles rained down from the rooftops. Before the melee was over, both cops had received minor injuries and had called for assistance.

Word had spread throughout the local precincts and it was only indirectly that Mike heard about the plans to reassert order. He would have taken part in this action regardless, but now hoped his taking part would get rid of any lingering doubts and suspicion about him. He had been stationed here for over a year and still felt like an outsider.

Twenty to twenty five white men descended onto a bar on the

outskirts of Flatbush. They drank, some heavily, waiting for the appointed time. They were all carrying their weapons, and were none too concerned about whether they were concealed or not. Their ages ranged between 25 and 45 years and each was capable of expressing war-like aggression. When the time came they walked outside. A hand drawn map was circulated. The point of attack was noted by an "X" in the middle, which was where the policemen were injured and where the group responsible for the attack hung out. The intersecting streets spanning outward were noted. Four circles were drawn 2 blocks in each direction from the point of attack. Four equally sized groups were formed, and each took ownership of one of the attack points.

There was little said but one man took the lead and with military precision issued the few instructions that were needed. He was an Italian with wavy, dark hair. His dark eyes narrowed with intensity that spoke to the fact that he was several steps ahead of the rest of them on the road to aggression, the road towards dispelling doubts and questions and fears and replacing them with fierceness and a sense of the rightness of their cause. Anything less or contrary would not be tolerated from those assembled here, who had come not by force but by choice. The leader was not tall but was powerfully built and wore a black leather coat and seemed comfortable with taking charge and the others accepted his authority.

Within the crowd there was a full range of emotions and dispositions. On one hand there were those who hated to be there and doing what they were about to do, but knew they would want this backup if the tables were turned and so did what they felt was their duty. At the other extreme were those that actually enjoyed everything about the rumble, had done it since childhood and could just as easily have ended up on the other side of the battle line.

The strange thing was, both perspectives and all the gradations that spanned these polarities were necessary to get this done. All, for this brief period, were accepted and held together in this one body. And, in much the same way, this is how and why the gangs themselves flourished.

"Check your watches gentlemen. I have 7:23 right now. It is only a 15, 20 minute drive to where we are going so we should be able to get into position and be ready to engage them at 8:00 PM. I would say take as few cars as possible and plan to come back here after this is done. Any questions?"

"What's there to ask about? Just another beat down, the type we have to administer from time to time to let them know who's boss," issued from one of the boys to the rest of the fraternity. Again, no one would argue this point, but the way it played in each man's mind varied widely.

Mike met up with his partner Nick who had been talking and hanging with two other cops from their precinct. They were also partners but could not be more different. George, the loud one, had an opinion on everything. He was likable enough but only a partner like he had in Tony could put up with the incessant chatter. With Tony you had to practically pry open his mouth to get a word out of him. With pompadour hair and muscular good looks he could have been a movie star but was content to be George's side kick, going through life doing the things that needed to be done.

Mike was glad to be teamed up with these three as they walked off together towards George's car. The calendar said it had edged into springtime but the weather was still frigid cold, with no sign of letup and when the heater in the car kicked in, the warmth saturated them, down to their bones. A bottle was passed among them and Mike drank lustily from it. He was drunk, but was a drunk on a mission.

George said to Mike, "I didn't expect to see you here with us. But I'm happy to have you along."

Mike had had little direct contact with either George or Tony, which was true of most everyone in the station house. Mike had a stigma associated with him and was still looking for a way to not be seen through that filter. Hearing a comment like this was welcoming for him. If he were being honest with himself, the experience of male camaraderie was the thing he enjoyed most in the world, and he now felt himself sink calmly into it. At this moment, while feeling better than at any time in recent memory, he would not have been able to lay claim to a single feeling for his wife, kids, or other family members. This manly warrior spirit now on the way to battle, and heightened by alcohol, fitted him more surely than any of those ideals placed before him every day that he tried to live up to. "Fuck them all," is what he thought just then.

"I appreciate that, I really do," Mike responded, almost child-like.

Nick sat beside Mike in the back seat. He was psyching himself in his own way, was consumed with his own preparations. When he was nervous he would scratch uncontrollably at his arms, legs, and various body parts and now he scratched all over as though he were going to jump out of his skin. He was crazy wild, as Mike was also becoming.

"So what do you do for fun?" George asked, wanting to keep the banter alive for this was his way to prepare for what was about to happen, to not think about it until it was upon him and then allow every pore and receptor in his body to fill with aggression and rage, amped up 0 to 60 in seconds.

"Other than drink, I guess you mean."

"Yeah, other than that. We all do a lot of that," and they all let out a hearty laugh.

"Well," Mike had to think about this. The only thing that came to mind was the motorcycle and that was the last thing he would mention. The fact that nothing else came to mind did not even bother him much. And after some mining through his memory, he continued his response, " I do like to bowl, although I haven't gotten out much recently."

"Did you hear that, Tony?" and before Tony had a chance to respond, which he would not have done anyway, George continued, "We have a team at the station that plays in the police league. Just so happens, we have an opening on the roster. Don't suppose you'd consider joining us?"

Mike took a long draw from the whiskey and fumbled in his mind for the best way to say, "Yes, truly, yes.".

"So, you ever been on one of these before, Mike?" George asked, continuing to warm to the conversation.

"No, can't say I ever have. But I can't say we ever really needed to in my old precinct." and then giving it some more thought, "but then again, we didn't have many colored there either."

"That's it. That's the problem exactly," George said, growing contemplative. "If it wasn't for these niggers, the job wouldn't be half bad. But you throw them into the mix and our lives turn into a living hell. Lookin' over your shoulder every two minutes to see what trap they're laying for you and even if you're careful they find ways to show you things you should never have to look at, right in front of your face."

The image of the infant in the garbage can rose up before Mike and something clicked inside him. Or rather, whatever remorse or sense of commonality he felt for the people in the community he was servicing dried up and was gone.

"I know what you're saying." Mike said, feeling that what was being expressed in the car was true and good. Whatever those uptown politicians were running their mouths about had nothing to do with what they were doing down here in the trenches to keep things from exploding into chaos. "Like the man said, 'what they need is a little beat down from time to time keep things running smoothly and let them know who the boss is."

The cars had traveled in a caravan until they reached the exit closest to the point of attack and then they fanned out in the four directions they would advance from. They were only a few minutes early and waited a block from the point of engagement.

Nick was crazy now in movement and thought. "Why don't we just drive up there and get things rolling, kick their asses? I hate this fucking shit waiting!"

"Cool it Nick," George said, "You'll have you chance soon enough. We all will." He was now in the process of amping up, letting free the fury he had kept walled up behind an avuncular attitude that he knew would keep things reasonably calm while it was necessary to do so. But that time had now passed. Only Tony remained most like he had been throughout the trip, but there was no doubt that he could be counted on once the action began.

They shot off from the curb and sped to the site while cars came rushing in from all sides at the same moment. Car doors flew open and they were moving, spreading out. They kept their hand that carried their night stick down, along the length of their leg, concealed as much as possible. Shouting and taunting commenced from all directions. There were around 10 - 12 males, mid teens to mid 20's, that they surrounded. Within seconds a few of them started to run, trying to find cracks in the wall of men facing them. A few of the cops gave chase to them while the rest continued to move closer, sealing the gaps. This made everyone restless, everyone but one big black man who seemed to refuse to be fazed or impressed by what was unfolding. Mike and this young man made eye contact and locked onto each other's gaze as if they were destined for each other. Even as pandemonium broke out, their gaze remained fixed. Mike came at him with his night stick raised and as he did, the man picked up a bottle that was on the ground and flicked the bottom of it against the wall. The bottom of the bottle broke off, leaving a jagged edge. The man held the bottle at the base of the neck, turning it into a weapon, extending it towards Mike.

They circled each other and then Mike cracked the man's arm with the club, sending the bottle flying. Even though the pain radiated up his arm, the black man's face still lacked any trace of submission which infuriated Mike. Mike took the club and cracked it alongside the man's head resulting in a horrible, thunderous, bone crushing sound. The man crumpled to the ground and Mike was upon him, kicking him, stomping him.

Most of the other fighting had moved to the periphery and was dissipating rapidly. Two cops Mike did not know came over to him. A look of horror developed when they saw the state of the man on the ground.

"Jesus Christ, what the fuck's going on here?" one said and pulled Mike off the man on the ground that he continued to pummel.

"Man, we don't want to kill anyone here. We're teaching a lesson, not starting a war. Settle down. Calm it down."

Mike returned to his senses and looked at the results of the beating he had administered to the man. He wondered how, why, this had happened. And he was left again in limbo, questioning everything, wondering in fact what, if anything really mattered, wondering if anything that made sense now would make sense even minutes later.

The captain in the precinct where Mike worked was sitting with two of the sergeants who reported directly to him. Captain John Myers sat on one side of his desk, while Sargents Dick Maloney and Frank Smith sat across from him in chairs set back a few feet from the desk. The Captain had before him a folder filled with papers. His fingers tapped nervously upon the papers he was about to address.

Myers opened the folder and the first sheet of paper contained a medical report. It told of a young black man who was struggling for his life in the County Hospital as the result of injuries sustained to the head during an altercation on the corner of Lafayette and Marcy two nights before at around 8 PM. He recited these and a few other details of the matter, and then began his inquiry of the two men before him.

"Neither of you two happen to know anything about this incident, do you?"

Maloney and Smith looked at each other with a sense of indecision and nervousness and Maloney, who had seniority over Smith replied while rifling through the call log, "There was no report recorded of any incident like that between 8 and 10 PM at the switchboard that night."

"Myers laughed in an ugly, mean way and let the moment dangle in the air. "Let me guess, there weren't ANY calls at all during that time frame, were there?"

"No sir, there were no calls."

"Not one."

"That is correct, sir."

"So this incident never happened, sergeant?

The two sergeants looked to each other uncertainly and then Maloney spoke up again, "There is no official report of it, sir."

Again, a thick, penetrating silence took hold while the captain considered the direction to take the conversation. He lowered the stridency of his tone with his next comments, as he had decided on what needed to be said.

"Look, you two know things are changing. The days when we can just go out there and break a few heads are over. This incident is getting a lot of play in the community, it might even reach the press. A gang of white men rough up a group of unsuspecting colored standing around on a street corner in the middle of Bed-Stuy and there are no records of it at the local police station. It would escape the head of steam that is building out there if they had just been roughed up, maybe a few stitches and black eyes, like what we've seen from time to time. But we handed all those bleeding heart liberals a poster child with that boy in the hospital.

"You know they are starting to let colored on the police force and we've been chosen as one of the first precincts to have some. It doesn't matter who likes it and who doesn't. It's going to happen. It is reality and it is my job, our job," he said while poking his index finger first at one and then the other, "to make it work. If we have shit like this going on when they get started, we'll have a race riot right here in our own precinct. I've got five years until retirement and I mean to make it through til then, regardless of what this hell hole throws at me."

Sergeants Smith and Maloney looked at each other, and sat quietly for a brief period before Maloney spoke up again.

"What do you want, captain?"

Without pausing, because he knew exactly what he wanted, he

replied, "I want to know the fool who almost killed that man."

And then saying the words that caused Maloney to cross a line he hoped he would not have to cross, he replied, "It was Eaton Captain, Michael Eaton."

Captain Myers knew the case well. He wasn't thrilled to bring him into the precinct when he read his record. He, along with everyone else, wondered how he had escaped the bust up of the motorcycle scam with only a reassignment. But he had no choice about bringing him in, so he kept his eye on him like everyone else since he came on board a little over a year ago.

The captain considered his options and then began to speak his thoughts as they were unraveling.

"I won't be able to shop him to anyone else because he's already damaged goods."

And after another pause, "And this never really happened," he said, with an unkind smile in his voice, conveying that he was once again closing ranks with the two men sitting across from him.

"So, I can't officially discipline him or have charges brought against him."

Again he let his mind wander, looking to see what options were available. His fingers tapped the cover of the folder again. But the quality of the cadence and touch were different. Instead of strumming rapidly, each finger tap seemed more confident than the last, as the captain's plan to reassert order took on more detail and form. Then with an air of finality he said, "I don't ever want that son of a bitch on the streets again. He's a bad cop. There's nothing else to say. Keep him washing the fucking latrines if you have to, but don't let him out on the streets again."

The sergeants shook their heads and understood what needed to be done. And then, with a concluding statement, that did not have to be said, the Captain stated, "This meeting never happened gentleman. The incident in question never happened, to the best of our knowledge. Eaton's reassignment just happens. And hopefully we ride this out without too much flack from everyone out there who has no reason to be involved in our business anyway."

But Mike's mind would not comply with his wishes and the anesthetizing sleep that he sought would not be achieved. Instead he dreamed crazy dreams of espionage in which he was being chased down by superior forces that were always several steps ahead of him. The crimes he was accused of were never explained or understood. Only the fact that he was prey to superior forces was clear in the dreams. In and out of these chase sequences he would emerge, forgetting their details but retaining the unease that these unnameable foes had instilled in him.

After awakening in a frenzied state a few times, he realized real sleep would not return and swung himself up onto the side of the cot which was housed in a room only slightly larger than a cleaning closet. He joked to his band of buddies that this was his office. Alongside the cot, a broom and dust pan rested against the wall of which, again he joked, were the new tools of his trade. He sat on the cot and looked out at the opposing wall, only a couple of feet from him, wondering how long he could stay like this before some circumstance would force him to become ambulatory.

Through the partially opened door he could see to the other side of the cellar, where the prison cells were. A few drunks sprawled on the benches and cots, nodding off, sobering up. Mike did not consider that they would be visited by the same reflections as what he was experiencing, but as he looked through the bars he had a sense of vertigo and wondered who was on the inside, who on the outside. And the dizzying affect of these thoughts were accelerated by his questioning in this semi-conscious haze. How does one get out? Where exactly is out? What does out look like?

But he was not long on this path of questioning, for soon he was reminding himself how good he had it. Since he was reassigned to station house duty a year ago, he could come to work and essentially disappear. The message was made clear to him that the less he was seen by his superiors, the better. And he was more than willing to comply with these wishes. He came to work, as often as not, to sleep off the drunk of the prior night or day. As long as he could keep his mind numb for the eight hours he was at work he was okay. If he could do that, he could avoid thinking about his close affinity to those on the other side of the cell bars. And he had settled in with a group of guys at the station. If some of the cops looked at him as a "bad cop", a "rogue cop", there were plenty who appreciated what he had done or at least didn't think much one way or another about it. Up until recently, it was standard operating procedure. A new regime was trying to instill change, but that would never get more than lip service from the majority of older cops who believed they knew what was necessary to retain order.

He did not reflect much on the beating he gave that man. Those he surrounded himself with expressed tacit agreement that what he did was okay. Probably the best thing that had come from that evening was learning about the bowling team and league. He joined shortly after hearing about it and felt it was the best thing that had happened to him in a long time. It was the closest thing to a regularly scheduled fun experience, other than drinking, he had gotten involved in since he was out on the streets playing ball with his friends as a kid. No, his life was okay, he assured himself, as long as he did not think about it too much. He got up and stretched his limbs and then picked up the broom and dust pan and began to make his rounds. He looked for dust motes and cigarette butts littered on the well worn walkways in what could be thought of now as his primary residence.

Chapter 14

She knew this last pregnancy was going to be tough on her. It was unplanned and she felt distressed and older when Dr. Holmes confirmed that she was expecting again. Because she was beginning to show signs of complications, she was told to stay in bed the last month of the pregnancy, which she tried to do as much as possible. That was right around when Mike was having all the trouble with his job that resulted in his getting transferred to a precinct way on the far side of Brooklyn. In a way it was good that he was around during those days to help out, but in some ways it wasn't.

The lying in bed was the most exhausting experience in her life, something from which she had still not regained her energy after two years. She was never one to be at rest, alone with her thoughts. But now she had no alternative and the images and thoughts rising up before her were as unpleasant and startling as they were unwanted. Without the ability to move and stay busy she found herself defenseless, passing into and out of a dream world that she barely knew existed and one that disregarded the barriers, the rules that for the vast majority of her life had seemed impregnable.

She had thought about Rose before this time and thought she had grieved her death, although would not have thought to use such a word to describe her feelings, a word that seemed self indulgent and showy. No, the thoughts she had about Rose at that time were about all the good times they had and what a good person she was and how everyone liked her. These thoughts had never kept her from caring for her own family or slow her down much. But then each day as she was lying on her back in the last month of her pregnancy, her mind forced her to consider more deeply the relationship she had had with her sister.

Frank was always Jennifer's favorite. Eight years older than she, he always seemed involved in activities of great fun and excitement, far beyond her interests and with what she was familiar. He was considerate and even when still only a teenager, projected the sense of importance he felt for family and looking after those within their immediate circle. These early memories went back to their days in Pittsburgh and the images of homes being built into the sides of mountains, which she came to realize on subsequent visits were only rolling hills that eddied throughout the communities. From these early memories she recalled that Frank would have some type of job, things like selling newspapers or delivering groceries. And this meant he always had a little money with which to buy penny candy, which he shared freely with Jen and his other brother and sister.

What she got from Frank was a tremendous sense of security. At the time, the little games they played like trying to guess which hand held the candy, or spelling words that Frank thought up to earn a piece, or guessing a color he was thinking of for the same reward, were fun and she always pressed him to play, something he was willing to do to a surprising degree. Little did she realize at the time that these were among the happiest moments of her life, the most carefree. And now, as she lay on her bed, she experienced these images and memories more strongly than she had for years.

But Rose was closer in age to Frank and not so in awe of him. And her disposition was always different, different from Frank's, and Jen was coming to realize now, different from hers as well.

Jen watched the two of them go at it when they were growing up, arguing over the stupidest things. And now Jen felt the lurching feeling she had known at that time, leaving her unable to catch her breath when all she wanted was for the fighting to stop, for Rose to go along with whatever Frank was saying, which Jen, herself, was more than happy to do.

Frank believed that it did not really matter if you were the smartest or the best at something and, in fact, the pursuit of such goals were potentially embarrassing and disruptive to the unity of the family. But Rose so often baited him, challenged him, jeopardized these and other fundamental beliefs.

These thoughts that occupied her during the first few days of her bed rest veered sharply, unexpectedly. Jen was unable to deny that Rose tried early and often to establish sisterly affection with her. And almost with the same frequency Jen used the opportunity to assert her own power even when the vehicle used to accomplish this was a cruel act directed at her sister.

One early memory of this type of interaction occurred when Jen was about 10 and Rose 14. The family was sitting around on the front porch of their home in Queens that they had relocated to after their brief time in Manhattan. Rose came running from up the street to join them. She had made a small amount of money delivering circulars that advertised the specials of the week for the local butcher. It was a hot summer evening, with nothing much going on. Their mom and dad sat on their outdoor chairs. Both had long since passed away and many of Jen's memories of them were like this: both spoke little as they enjoyed their perch on the world as evening edged closer. Her dad, tired from his day at the Port Authority where he worked as an electrician, would casually flip the pages of his newspaper, rarely reading an article from start to finish and her mom usually kept busy darning socks or working at some other handicraft. Frank was also sitting there on that evening, although her younger brother Dan was down the street playing with friends.

Rose's energy was at odds with the relaxed atmosphere that the others were sharing, but she was unaware of this as was usually the case. She held in one hand a bag of candy that she had purchased with her own money. She had brought it to share with her family members, something she had never done before.

With great excitement in her voice Rose said, "Jen, if you can guess the number I'm thinking of, you can pick two pieces of candy from the bag. The number is between 1 and 20."

Jen felt different threads of thought and feeling course through her. She could image the wonderful small bits of candy sitting within the bag which produced a strong desire to have some of it. Individually wrapped pieces of taffy, five to a set and compactly held together with another piece of plastic, were her favorite. But there would also be chocolate silver dollars, red licorice stamped in the shape of coins, and necklaces of hard candy contained within that bag of treasures. Her body ached with slave-like discipline to their allures. But then, as she considered the question being posed to her, she felt a pull in another direction, from another part of her brain.

Answer this question posed by Rose and she would lose something, something so fundamental that the loss of it or even the potential loss of it filled her with a dread that she she could not ever remember feeling before that moment. This special game, this give and take, this acceptance of roles of control and submission were what defined the bedrock of her relationship with Frank. She would play this game with Frank gratefully, endlessly, because it brought her a sense of joy and security that would end, she feared, the moment someone else took on the role of task giver.

"I don't really want any candy," Jen said, even as her head was banging from within, as it indeed wanted what was contained within the bag. "I don't think I'll play your game."

Rose was stunned, totally deflated. She had planned this for a long time, looking forward to the time when she could be the one asking the questions, dispensing the prizes. She took a few moments to regroup and then asked,

"How about guessing colors?"

"I don't think so."

What about spelling words? Want to see if you can spell 'chartreuse' ?

"I'm not in the mood."

With each question and response Jen experienced a new feeling. She sensed that her denials were giving her a sense of control over her older sister, something she had never laid claim to before. The experience was stunning. She was filled with a type of energy and power, the nature of which she had never comprehended until these days of contemplation on the bed at the end of her third pregnancy.

But at the time it took place, all she knew was that she had retained, and perhaps even enhanced, the special relationship with her brother and altered, fundamentally, her relationship with her sister in a way she found alluring, but darkly so.

"I don't think this dog will hunt," their father said. It was one of his favorite sayings and found a wide range of applications. But its primary goal was to cause whatever was happening to end, usually in quick time.

Rose snatched up the candy, which was never seen again. She rushed to the doorway leading into the house, swiftly opened the door and let it crash behind her. Jen felt an odd sense of victory where she knew there should be none. She thought she saw a slight smile spread across Frank's face, but couldn't be sure. She let the desire for the candy run its course, while at the same time sensing a strange power radiating through her body.

In many encounters like this, she experienced ephemeral emotions of power and control. Her victories against Rose were parlayed by an increased closeness to Frank. He never advocated for these skirmishes but also never used his authority, his place in the family, to curtail them and Jen sensed a conspiratorial ascent coming from Frank. Although he only rarely gave voice to his feelings about battles between Jen and Rose, Frank commended her on occasion for the positions she had taken. Offering a "Just what I would have said," or "Where does she come up with those harebrained ideas?" Jen could sense Frank's thoughts whenever Jen tried to "knock Rose down a peg or two". And she sensed, at these times, an ally in him.

When they had children, the differences between them only became more accentuated. The behavior of her own children compared to Rose's, specifically Don, became a source of pride for Jen. Every time Don crossed over the line, Jen would make a mental note and felt a small victory because she was convinced she had the greater degree of control over her children's actions. And this sense of control became all the more important because of how she perceived it elevated her above Rose in the eyes of the rest of the family.

She thought of all the events that occurred that formed this pattern in their relationship. And then her mind leaped to a truth she wished to never uncover. Rose had, from time to time, tried to draw closer to Jen, engage in conversation that could only occur between two women, two sisters. But Jen consistently rebuffed these approaches. She could not now escape the truth that her primary reason for rejecting these attempts at closeness was because she was concerned about the dominoes that might fall if she accepted these overtures. How would it affect her own standing in the family and her special relationship with Frank if she drew closer to the agent of instability? She did not want to be linked to Rose's way of thinking, having to defend it in the way that Rose was forced to do. She was not well equipped to be the target of questions and derision. Instead she took pleasure in being aligned with the stronger, dominant view and was willing to sacrifice almost anything to maintain the status quo, even the sanctity of her sister's right to see the world through the prism refracted light that emanated from within her.

Run, gallop, run some more, stay busy, avoid any but properly vetted thoughts, feeling, ideas. Slam down anything that evades their simple, singular, form of correct thinking. Smash closed the doors on anything in opposition. These are the things she had lived by, formed the basis of what girded her up.... And then Rose died. She died and was gone and would not return...ever.

Jen lay there in bed, made immobile by her body engorged with the new life that was all but fully formed, able to embark on its own, starting empty, ready to be filled with experience, with life. But she herself was now empty, less than empty. Those defenses and walls that had sustained her had been scaled, become porous, washed away as if by a tidal wave of emotion that found no defense, spreading, overwhelming her total waking and sleeping self. She thought she had felt grief when Rose first died, but that was an easy grief compared to what she experienced now, which threatened to unhinge her mind. This was a grief that came face to face with how she had failed her sister, how she chose against her, against what Rose, in herself, felt most strongly about saying, being, doing. How she, Jen, worked strenuously but surreptitiously to suppress her, to silence her. To what end, she now wondered, did she pursue this way? What was so great that needed to be preserved? What danger did Rose, in any of her guises, pose to them? What cowardice did they show by denying her this right to express herself?

"Things don't just happen to you," she insisted, talking into the void of the room that was her bedroom but was transformed. Dr. Holmes had insisted that the window blinds be drawn to allow the darkness to calm her, to promote rest. But that was not the type of darkness permeating the room. This darkness knew more than she, but withheld this knowledge, parsing it to her in sudden bursts of clarity and then stopping completely, receding back into obstinate, impenetrable silence. And how did she respond to this deeply knowing, deeply quiet force? By speaking in complete sentences all the questions that issued forth from within her.

Over time that was sometimes connected and sometimes not, the following questions were cast out from her: "How do you hurt someone you love and not see the hurt caused? Or see the hurt caused but continue the hurting? What part of me enjoyed hurting you, Rose? What did I think would come of it? What does that even mean, 'come of it'? When you can just die and nothing comes of it anymore and I am just left with what is."

She looked out across the haze of dusk-like darkness in the room to the portrait of her family on the opposing wall. The permanence of photographs was something she had always enjoyed, especially that picture with her two children's smiling faces, and her own and Mike's too. But these faces were indistinct now and even if they were not, she would not have experienced the same pleasure that it normally gave her because nothing was as it seemed, nothing was as stable and frozen in time as that or any photograph. And most of all, situations and people change of themselves, arcing through their own trajectory, touching and being touched by other unforeseen forces and sent imperceptibly in other directions, bit by bit until the original trajectory was all but scattered, indistinguishable.

Jen had never learned to forgive herself, for anything. The notion itself was outside of her mind's and spirit's grasp. If you lived by a simple set of rules you could advance through life without need of such nonsense. Control was the main thing above all else. If you screwed up, it was your own fault and you should be forced to *sleep in the bed you made*. The dangerousness of this notion of forgiveness went deeper, much deeper. If you allowed this fuzzy thinking to enter your thoughts, there was no end to it and no answers that would be satisfactory. That might be okay for those high minded folk, the big shots on the TV and in the news, but not for her and her family and set of friends. So you avoided these depths of feelings at all costs, lived conventionally and disavowed anything that broke with that convention. And if you succumbed to these depths of feelings, there was something wrong with you, it exposed a defect in your character. And when you saw a defect in yourself or another, you avoided it, did not speak of it, waited for it to pass and for the return of normalcy, and then forgot it had ever happened or existed.

Her words spoken into the darkness were sometimes audible and sometimes not. The words came through eviscerating shrieks and wails, or in the smallest whisper. Occasionally she would pull back some bit of insight from those experiences of the past, and the unforeseen consequences that would lead in increasingly diverse directions like the branches of a tree. But she would never consider forgiving herself, relinquishing herself from the enormous guilt that paralyzed her, that she would like to deny but had not the ability to do so.

Her children, downstairs, could hear her. This was as bad or worse than watching their father when he would stumble drunkenly through the house. They sat there now with their father, watching their TV shows. They tried to speak and act with a sense of normalcy but their world was in a free fall and all they could collectively think to do was hold on like a cat who digs its claws into the surface beneath them when its balance has been lost and pure terror is all that has replaced it. While Mike was out working and drinking with his buddies it was Jen who kept the house and children running. The children would not appreciate the effort involved in this until much later in their lives and even Mike was only dimly aware of it. But now that Jen was essentially incapacitated, the absence of her efforts were felt in a myriad of ways, from the decline in orderliness and cleanliness in the house to the breakdown of the daily schedule they followed individually and collectively.

But the worst fear, of course, was that she was going crazy, that she would continue acting and speaking in ways that scared her children and husband; that is if they were able to give words to what they were feeling, which they were not capable of for the most part. Instead, they shut down their emotional lives, substituting them with trying to remember what they would be doing and thinking if they were just doing and thinking about things in a normal way. What a relief it would be to not have to reflect on everything, and attempt to control their thoughts like cattle being shoved along narrow chutes, not even wanting to know where they were being led.

Jen let out a particularly harrowing scream which caused Tim to jump out of his seat.

"I need to see what's going on up there," he said and advanced to the staircase. He had a head of steam about him, and was feeling determined to get to the bottom of what was wrong and fixing it.

But before he reached the second step he found himself airborne. The sensation was not unpleasant and the next thing he knew he was rolling on the carpet in the open space of the living room, his landing on the floor so gradual that he hardly felt the impact and was in a state of wonderment as he rolled on the floor.

Mike had grabbed him under his arm pits and gently flung him away. There was no hostility in the gesture, just something he knew he needed to do. He looked at his two children, who he knew feared and loved him, but did not know him, and in some important fundamental ways never would and said, "No, you stay here, you two. This is something I need to take care of."

Mike mounted the steps, unsure of what awaited him. Certainly he knew his life would come apart if Jen was in as bad shape as she appeared to be. He was no doctor and could barely keep himself from going over the edge, and now Jen was cracking up or appeared to be. He entered their bedroom with its stale air and musty odor that had a charged, unfamiliar quality.

He took a seat next to Jen, who sensed he had entered the room but did not acknowledge him. The covers were drawn up to her chin and her eyes were open but lifeless. Mike rested his arms against the metal arms of the chair, or tried to. His hands came together and his thumbs tapped against each other absently. He felt like a child now, without a clue as to how to proceed, how to fix whatever was wrong with her.

"What's going on, hon?" he finally asked, the only thing he could think to say.

"We should have taken them in," She said, willing to share her thoughts with him, with anyone maybe. But her thoughts had taken a new direction, scouring a new source of pain, ravaging her like a wildfire swirling up from a different direction.

"Who's that?" Mike replied, not yet following the course of her thoughts.

"Don and Sara could have stayed with us. We were the closest family they had."

"That would have never worked." Mike said. "We've been through all that." But in fact they had talked very little about that possibility. The assumptions that had remained unspoken were about the clash that existed between Mike and Don, the lack of space in their house, and, to be completely blunt and honest, the burden the two would have caused. Of course you do not speak of these things and now that it was being brought up, Mike feared the direction the conversation was headed, questioned even more his ability to provide comfort to his wife.

"Why are you thinking of that now? Its been two years since we had to deal with that. And they're doing okay."

"We could have put bunk beds in the kids' rooms. How much more difficult would it have been with two more mouths to feed?"

Mike knew the answer was lots more, infinitely more, enough probably to tear apart the whole fabric of their lives. But he dared not say that now.

"Sure we could have, but we decided not to and it all worked out with Liz and Carlo taking them in."

"Look at us. Are we even a family anymore?" Jen said, still addressing Mike but addressing her own unwinding thoughts primarily. "Dan," she continued, referring to her younger brother, "moved hundreds of miles away because his company made him relocate. And now he's having his children that we never get to see. Frank and Jessie are still here but they'll never have kids. And we decide its too much bother to take care of Don and Sara. What's wrong with us? What kind of monsters are we? Back in Pittsburgh I have more family than I do where I live. What's left of us?"

"I'm not sure what you mean, hon." Mike responded sincerely. "We've got plenty of friends, people always ready to have a good time with us. We have a couple of good kids and another on the way. What more could you ask for?"

There was truth to his comments but Jen's mind was circling its prey, which could only be described as a separate part of herself. And as she responded she spoke not to what Mike said but to where the hunt led.

"Why did we treat her like that? Why was it so important that she think just like the rest of us?"

Again Mike was unable to provide a point of reference to these comments and asked, "Who? What are you talking about now?"

"We all treated her like a child, even though she was my older sister. It wasn't even what we said most of the time but the way we acted towards her." In a moment of clarity she saw things that were never there before: the absolute demand for conformity; the drunken revelry, one voice rising above another until the angle of repose was reached and anything defying it was blotted out with a wall of sound, both cunning and determined.

And then all but forgetting that Mike was there with her, she let out of a series of shrieks as loud and horrible as any that had issued forth from her. And between the shrieks she spat the words, "How could I have been so mean to her?"

The rewards of a simple life were supposed to be stability, pleasant emotions. This basic principle had been routed in the battle occurring inside Jen and she doubted she would ever know anything other than the turmoil that raged inside her. She became uncommunicative, and wept quietly. Mike sat there beside her not knowing what to do, not even knowing whether to place his hand upon Jen's that lay beside her body that seemed to have grown old even as it was preparing to bring new life into the world.

Mike was in the kitchen, looking through their personal phone directory. It was 8:00 PM so he dialed Dr. Holmes' home phone number. When Dr Holmes came to the phone, Mike explained Jen's symptoms as well as he could.

"Sounds like something we can deal with in the morning. Tomorrow being Saturday, I have hours half the day. We can get her in in the morning and I can give her something for her nerves."

"I don't think you understand doc; I'm afraid she's going to do something to herself. And with the baby on the way, I'm afraid of what might happen to it, too."

"Look Mike, I see these things all the time. Women getting hysterical. I'll give her some pills to take the edge off and that will settle her right down. She'll be back, good as new in no time."

Mike's forced congeniality had reached its limit as did his voice of reason, "Look doc, you're talking about my wife here. I think I know what's going on and she needs something and she needs something now. If I have to come over to your place and drag you over here that's what I'll do."

Husbands like this were also something that Dr. Holmes knew about and dealing with them was something not taught in med school. Instead he learned to resign himself to these situations.

"Okay, okay, Mike," Dr. Holmes said, "settle down. Let me get a few things together and I'll be right over."

Mike called Frank after Dr. Holmes had come and gone and Jen had calmed down. The visit had been short and officious and Mike had not liked it. He thought his rage towards the doctor would diminish when he arrived, but the manner in which he dealt with Jen was almost enough to send the doctor out of the house on an express route. But he administered a shot to Jen and within some short space of time she had fallen fast asleep. He also gave Mike some pills to give her in the morning and some prescriptions to fill. These, after all, were the things that Mike was looking for from the doctor, so who cares if he acted like this was "business as usual" in his dealings with Jen.

He called Frank on the phone and recounted to him as best he could the content of Jen's ravings. He conclude by saying, "I'm no doctor and our doctor's no doctor either. I can't figure out what to do or how to get her back on track."

"Doesn't sound much like Jen," Frank mused, sounding concerned. "Wonder what got into her."

"Beats me," Mike responded with a similar tone and set of emotions. "Maybe, the pregnancy's making her thoughts go crazy, turning her nerves into a knot." Mike had had his problems with Frank over the years, but he was happy now to have him to call, to have someone with whom he could share his thoughts and fears.

"Listen, Mike. No sense in me coming over tonight. From what you tell me Jen will be knocked out 'til morning at least. If I don't hear from you before then, I'll plan to drop by around noon and pay Jen a visit."

"That would be great Frank. We'd all appreciate that."

Frank poked his head into Jen's bedroom the next morning and saw that she was awake, not alert, but awake and apparently calm. They made eye contact, she from the bed and he at the door's threshold and she did not seem surprised to see him standing there.

"Hear you've had a rough time of it," Frank said as he settled himself into the same seat that Mike had occupied the night before.

"Yes, it's been a time," She responded with perfectly pitched ambivalence, not a passive ambivalence but what a tightrope walker must feel.

"All that's behind us now, you know," Frank offered after they sat in silence for some bit of time. He applied the information that Mike had given him and this placed him right in the middle of all that she had expressed and felt the night before. This was the only space for him to reside while in this room with Jen, and Jen whose attention had never left the framework of these thoughts, although they had been altered, smoothed down by the drugs administered the night before, allowed Frank to enter into them.

"If our new baby is a girl, I'm thinking of naming her Rose," Jen said dreamily.

Frank was startled by this idea and could not help but to jerk his head laterally as if he'd been struck by a glancing blow.

"There's no need to do that," Frank responded, maybe a little too assertively. The idea of this was distasteful to him, even morbid. "We all miss Rose, but do you want to think about what happened to her every time you look at your daughter?"

Jen started to cry again, but this time her tears were subdued. She had crossed over into something the night before that she did not yet understand but knew could not be undone, not totally. Her world would never again be so orderly, neat or simple as she imagined it had been.

"You've always trusted my judgment, Jen," Frank said. "Trust me on this. You would live to regret naming your daughter Rose. And don't worry about the way you are feeling now. You'll be good as new in no time."

Jen's gaze trailed off, became unfocused. She saw no other choice. Frank's lead was always the one she followed and she had no strength to consider moving off in any other direction now. She looked at him and gave him a little smile, the first she had expressed since all this had started. The smile spread across her face and he responded to it in kind and put his hand upon hers which gave her comfort, too.

And the demons receded, for now at least.

Chapter 15

She was back in bed again. She had expected her health to rebound after she delivered the baby but during the last two years since Norma was born, if anything, her health had deteriorated. Her purview was not so broad and she could be heard saying, "This last month I've just not been myself," with every turn of the page of the kitchen calendar that was tacked to the back of the pantry door.

This time Jen was having allergy problems, or at least that was the diagnosis she'd been given. Some combination of water and soaps was causing her hands to become irritated, scaly, and itchy. She lived with it for a while and then made an appointment with Dr. Holmes. He determined it was a mild dermatological problem and prescribed a lanolin salve for Jen to use 3 times a day. She applied it liberally to the affected parts of her body, but from the moment she applied it she perceived an uncomfortable sensation.

She continued to use the cream over the next few days. The discomfort increased, but the idea that it might be causing her harm did not register with her. Even as she saw the irritation on her arms steadily worsen, she continued to apply the medicine. The doctor had prescribed it and she assumed all she needed to do was wait it out and she would eventually turn the corner. It must be doing some good, she reasoned. It must be drawing out the infection, or whatever it was, which was why she was experiencing this temporary worsening condition.

Her hands and arms were beet red by the time she called the doctor again. When she was examined by the doctor, he questioned her about the red patches that had developed on her back, sides and groin area.

"How long has it been like this?"

"I suppose it started soon after I started applying the salve."

"Why didn't you come in right away?"

Jen recounted the conversation she and Mike had when the rash began to spread. They had decided to give the medicine a chance to work. Lots of things need to get worse before they get better, they had reasoned.

She spread her legs wider with some embarrassment, but less than what she might have expected to feel, to allow the doctor to see the extent of the problem. He listened to her story as he performed the exam and wondered how it was possible that people could be so stupid, or at least how their thinking could be so misguided. How could anyone believe that an ointment intended to sooth the skin must first burn and irritate it? How, he wondered, could ideas of this sort take root?

"The cream should have helped right away. It is meant to calm the swelling and irritation and should not result in the opposite effect." And then, completing the exam, he told her his diagnosis.

"You're lucky you came in when you did. If you'd have waited much longer you could have gone into anaphylactic shock. And if that happened you wouldn't have come into my office but would have had to go straight to the emergency room at the hospital. Medicines are meant to help you, but there are no guarantees that they will. And if they don't, you need to tell me and we'll find something else for you."

As she was being admonished, Jen surveyed the various angry reactions that rose off the skin across much of her body. The most severe of these sites formed clusters of little puss nodules. Their shape and size varied but still reminded her of the outcroppings of a beehive. She ran her finger over a section of them, wondering at their firmness, their foreignness, marveling at their strange beauty. She wondered if they were really of her body and from what source they had derived.

The message Dr. Holmes was imparting to her gave her a sense of deja vu, and she searched her mind unsuccessfully for the situation that had previously led in the same direction. There was something about the simple assurance that the medicine would help becoming paper thin, and the condition of her skin being proof of that, that was familiar. But her mind had not the dexterity to trace the pattern back to the source of this earlier experience.

"So, what now?" Jen responded absently, still searching for coherence through a filter, a haze, that was present in the room and in her mind, searching for that thing that she remembered but could not recall, as if the explanation would free her from this lethargy of thought. But until then, she would do whatever the doctor told her to do: take whatever medicines, apply whatever treatments, follow whatever regimens. She was never exactly disrespectful with Dr. Holmes in the past but she would take his comments and opinions with a certain skepticism. But that fight, that spirit, was something else she could not find, evaded her grasp.

I think we'll start you on a fairly high dose of penicillin and keep you on a steady diet of that for 2 weeks to knock this infection out of your system. I want you to pick up some Benedryl to soothe the rawness your skin is experiencing, too. I also want to prescribe something for your nerves. This seems to have gotten the better of you, Jen. And before you get back on your feet, I want you to get as much rest as possible for the next 2 weeks, even though I know you have a little one at home."

"That's fine. I'll do what I can. All I want is to get better." And with that Dr. Holmes completed the prescriptions, satisfied that Jen knew what he expected of her; he hoped that he had corrected her thinking on the topic of what she needed to do to take care of herself.

Back home, during this period of extended rest, she took all the drugs she was given that were intended to modulate both her body and mind. Her days spent in bed found her thoughts turned in on themselves, spinning like a top, dancing between the real and unreal without much of a detectable membrane to act as a filter. Even the normal demands of her life as a mother did not always gain ascendancy in the world that her mind had come to inhabit.

Tim had witnessed the slow disintegration of his family. He was now a sophomore in high school and 15 years old. He thought about it often but was never sure what it was he was seeing, what was different, what was wrong. But whatever it was, he was determined to figure it out, fix it, and return the family to the happiness that he had known, that he knew he had known but was gone now, missing.

He was changing the baby's diaper. During this recent spell he came home from school each day to find Norma in her crib, wanting, needing attention. His dad had told him that while his mother was in bed he would need to help out around the house, especially when Mike was at work. His dad had not needed to tell him this. He knew, as the oldest child, what was expected of him. His sister Anne, who was 13 was becoming more and more removed, absorbed in her life with her friends, and therefore not consciously aware of the changing dynamics of their household. What Mike did not realize was that long before this bout with the allergies, Tim had taken on the role of doting older brother. He was mesmerized by Norma's smile that lit up her face every time he entered a room that she occupied.

Everyday when Tim returned from school he looked in on Norma. They developed games that only they knew how to play and even if others learned the rules the games would not elicit the same level of joy from the participants. It was not long before he spent more time with her after school than he did with his friends. In her, he saw not only the curiosity and playfulness that he reasoned was probably a part of every baby, but also recognized something else, something that was tied to the resurgence of his own family, that he could bring about while helping Norma grow during this first part of her life.

He started drawing figures on a piece of paper from his notebook. He enjoyed drawing and was pretty good at capturing the likeness of his subject. He sat beside her, creating the members of their family and narrating the action that he was trying to draw into the scene. There were the two of them, a ubiquitous kite and glowing yellow sun, and just as he was about to fill in the scenery, she reached over for the paper, ripped it out of the book and did the best she could to crumble it into a ball.

"Norma doesn't like my picture," Tim said, and made a big, sad clown face which sent Norma rolling on the floor, all the while laughing hysterically, mirthfully. He finished the job of crumbling the paper and sent it flying into the air. He started to draw again: the same scene, the same narration... and the same results. He feigned even bigger distress, heartbreak, as she tugged the paper from the spiral notebook. He rolled on his back across the room stressing the agony she caused him by her rejection of his artwork. This went on and on. Each time he devised a new way to express his outsized emotional collapse. He imagined himself a jilted lover and began tearing out pieces of paper from his book, dabbing at his eyes before crumbling them up and letting them fly. Each time Norma responded on cue, having become a pliable audience. He began to sing the way he imagined an opera singer would, with great pathos, while flinging paper in every direction. With Norma bursting into fits of laughter, Tim with mounds of paper in both hands mounted a chair as he was delivering his operatic grand finale. At the moment of feigned rapture, as he was generously showering the floor with heaps of paper, his father walked through the doorway into the living room where they were, coming in unheard from the outside, returning from work.

Mike was not sure what situation he would be walking into and was not prepared for what he saw. He greeted the havoc with a dispassionate expression and demeanor.

"What's going on here?" Mike said, surveying debris, sensing the general chaos in the air. "I thought you were supposed to be here helping your mom while I was at work."

"We were just playing a little game," Tim said. He watched the sweep of his dad's gaze, saw what he saw, and added reflexively, wanting not to say it but saying it anyway, "Maybe things did get a little out of control."

Norma's hilarity was replaced by an expression of seriousness and, if not comprehension, then absorption of the scene playing out before her, as she watched the two men most important to her locked in some kind of inner battle, the effects of which would be imprinted upon her like few other experiences for the rest of her life.

"Looks to me like a cyclone just came through," Mike said, his voice charged with disbelief and displeasure with what he saw.

Tim had seen expressions of his father's anger and rage from his youngest years and they generally had the desired effect of intimidating him, shutting him down. And even though he was now aware of the early warning signs, it was different for him this time. He felt cheated, blamed for a wrong that did not exist. All the enjoyment that he had been experiencing with Norma was being flushed out of him and in its place was a stream of bile that he wanted no part of. As these emotions churned inside him he felt, from somewhere never before mined, his own rage boil up. But he was not very good at this: being tactical while feeling rage and aggression.

"Maybe that's what we need around here... a cyclone of fun ripping through this house. That's all we were doing, was having a little fun. Something we used to do a lot of around here." His voice was loud but constrained, like a bird's bleating when its young are being attacked by a superior foe and there is nothing else to do, even as all will be lost. His whole body convulsed, wanting to express his emotions, not only about the injustice he felt, but about how everything was different, changed for the worse. But each word, sentence, thought, veered wildly, far from the target he was seeking.

Mike did not expect to hear this tone – Tim's voice raised against him. His mind reflexively thought that he would have been bouncing off walls if he had spoken like this to his father. Or at least one of them would have, as he did until he stood up to his father at an age not much older than his own son's, matching him in battle that time, and from that time forward Mike never again had cause to do so. That was a hardscrabble life, one that you crawled your way out of any way you could.

That battle, the one he had gone through with his own father, was one he could understand. But there was something so distasteful about what he saw before him, and that something would remain unnameable to him.

"What exactly were you doing anyway?" Mike asked.

"Singing, laughing, drawing pictures and crumbling them up and then throwing them around the room. Acting silly and making Norma and me laugh, basically," Tim said with an anger totally at odds with the words that were spoken.

"Sorry, but I guess I'm not in the mood for that sort of *fun*." Mike said, with undisguised disgust, as the image of Tim acting the fool on the chair rose up again before him.

"What's wrong with doing those things, making people laugh, playing silly games?" But even as he spoke he was having to struggle against the judgment his father was placing upon him, a judgment he knew and understood all too well, whether it was deserved this time or not.

Mike could not formulate a response as his mind remaining unfocused. But he had a sense that the scene playing out before him was wrong, fundamentally wrong. There was also the feeling that whatever it was he was responding to, it was beyond his ability to control, and would continue to roll along on its path, whatever that was, without him being able to control its direction. His son, his only son, was unrecognizable to him. He had seen it from a very early age. Tim was too easily corralled. Although Mike would have been hot if Tim were rebellious, that is what he expected, unconsciously wanted. Every time he turned the screws on Tim he was waiting for him to buck the control, but it never happened. He just did what he was told and Mike found himself disappointed with that response. And now the rebelliousness arrived and he found the cause of it so deflating, small, sad.

The third game of the World Series had started a half hour before and he had been tracking the action on the radio on the way home. After getting home, Mike had planned to check in on Jen and then plant himself in front of the TV and enjoy a couple of beers and watch a few innings before putting dinner together. That is what upset him most about the scene that was playing out before him. How could his 15 year old son be home and be playing with his baby sister and not have the World Series on? It was unthinkable, offensive, weird.

"Sorry, but as I said, I'm not in the mood for this sort of fun," he said and motioned with his hand in the direction of the room where the paper lay crumbled and spewed about. "I've been working all day, something you haven't had the pleasure of experiencing yet. Try working the same shitty job for 15 years whether you like it or not. Try driving an hour each way in bumper to bumper traffic to get there and back. Might be hard for you to understand, but all I want right now is to sit in front of the TV and watch the World Series."

And then asking the question he could not resist asking, which was really at the bottom of his distaste with the tableau played out before him, he spoke again, this time with incredulity in his voice.

"Did you even know that game three was being played today?"

"Sure I knew. But I forgot." And at that moment Tim recognized the nature and degree of his own transgressions. And as they became clear to him, he felt a sense of shame. In years past he would have been on top of every play, the drama, the roller coaster ride of momentum characterizing the best of 7 series. But this year was different. He followed the action, but only from a distance. When he tried to figure out what caused this change, he was unable to do so.

Tim began cleaning up the mess. He cursed himself, knowing he had missed the opportunity to explain himself, explain why he was doing what he was doing with his sister. Instead, Tim's gaze drifted back to what had become his anchor in the storm. Although Norma's forehead remained scrunched up, an expression which had begun with the argument, Tim saw in it a cuteness that he had never seen in her before. She was cooing now, lost in the soundscape between baby sounds and normal speech. This was the short space in time when a child explores the aural world like a high wire trapeze artist, flinging her vocal chords across the panoply of sound recklessly and with abandon until one day, one day soon, when the demands of a single language shuts off all but the necessary subset of expressive utterances, and the others become like genes that fail to be expressed.

No, Tim, concluded to himself. This won't happen. She will not be limited in any way. I will, myself, make sure of it and dedicate myself to it. He continued to bathe in the beautiful sounds that Norma brought forth, that she brought forth without effort or forethought, the most enchanting sound that Tim had ever heard. He wanted to share this miracle, this symphony, with someone but his father was the only one there and was obviously not interested, had indirectly voiced his opinion on things of this nature. Tim was convinced at this moment that anyone who could not experience this purity was deficient in mind and spirit. The sense of purpose that he felt was made of a strong material, and he was flush with the renewed power that he had tapped with this discovery. He would bring them all along. He would save Norma from any bonds being placed upon her, but he would also bring them along, the others in his family. Bring them along and back to the glories they had known, had lived. And he was convinced now that if he did not do this thing it would not be done, that they all needed him to show them the way to their own salvation like he was learning about in his religion classes and absorbing like no one else in those classes.

Mike went over to the TV. The dial that turned the rotary channel selector had long since disappeared so he attached a pair of pliers to the knob jutting from the TV's casing instead. He clicked from network to network until he found the station that was carrying the game. He stood idly, dumbly waiting for an update on the score after which he would check in on Jen. He had been wanting to hear an update on the score since the time he had gotten out of the car and was growing impatient as the inning progressed and the camera did not pan to the scoreboard.

Jen heard voices down below. She had not moved from the bed for several hours and could not place the exact time when sleep had overtaken her and what hour of the day it was. For some time she had sensed activity, lively and festive, down below. The laughter and frivolity burst through the gauze of sleep surrounding her, only to vanish and be replaced by a descent back into her dreams. The laughter became the laughter of her dreams and she was back home again in Pittsburgh. They were kidding Rose about something, some dream of her own that she was expressing in an elaborate manner. But this time there was no animosity, no chafing in reaction to the way Rose was acting. Rose danced around the living room of their family home, grabbing, in turn, each member of her family, twirling herself and her partner. Jen heard the laughter from afar that became transformed so that it emanated from within the dream and then returned again to the other world, the one that, for her, lacked definition.

When she gained a greater degree of consciousness, and placed herself somewhat more clearly in the present, she sensed a change in the quality of the goings on down below and decided to investigate. She swung her body up and across the side of the bed, so that her feet landed on the floor and both hands steadied her sides while she remained seated. Her mind continued to turn as her body became stationary. She was aware of the pain from her sores dimly, rippling over her like the opening and closing of an accordion. She waited until her mind caught up with her body and then made the momentous effort to become mobile. Moving first one leg and then the other she became ambulatory, and made the motions of one wading through a swift current of water. Hands pressed against the wall until she reached the banister and then she allowed it to become her staff.

"What's going on?", she asked as plainly as she was able; and indeed it came off quite "matter of fact" she thought. She came down as Tim was cleaning up the paper strewn across the floor. It reminded her of Christmas after all the presents have been unwrapped. This jolted her mind back into the dreams from which she had just emerged. The festive happiness of that experience again enveloped her and she was lost momentarily to the current reality. Rose was happy in this dream, as she was so often really. And these drugs coursing through her clogged the self-recriminating reactions that had become the norm for her to remembrances of this kind. The guilt was absent, the penchant to be critical, absent. So she was able to float in and out of the dream and sense a family in the present tied to the one of the past, of her dreams, each complementing and enhancing the other.

Her husband loved her. She knew that and that was all that mattered. He would be there always, by her side, even as they waged the irrational skirmishes that somehow characterized their every day life. And she loved her children, two of whom looked up to her now from below, their eyes fixed on her, as hers were on them. What game, what fun were they in the midst of. This she could only wonder at, which is what she allowed her mind to contemplate in a way that made her feel like she was actually able to touch them, sense them with her mind.

If she no longer recognized all the effects the medications had on her, they were clear to her son and husband in a glaring, awful kind of way. The first rule always was: there can never be anything wrong, not really wrong. Because if there was, then the look inward would be all encompassing, searing, something no one was equal to; the mere act itself leading almost certainly to banishment from all they knew, all that gave structure and meaning. Jen continued to steady herself on the railing, unaware of the visage she projected, unaware too of her violation of the *first rule,* of which she, too, was a disciple.

You should rather take a swipe at me than talk of your feelings. That's no way to be. I could deal with you being in a gang, hanging out on street corners. We could fight our way through that. But how would you like me to respond to this? If I am some "it's okay" dad, who am I? Certainly not who I have always been. And that is not who I know how to be, can be, want to be. So I will ignore you and wait, wait for you to understand. But I know that will never happen because nothing can be explained, not so well that you can taste what another person knows and has suffered through, the things that have ground him down, made him what he is. It can not be done.

All I want is for us to be as we were. As I know we were. As I know we can be again.

But she was proof of something other than either of them could imagine. Her hair was unkempt, frizzed and undyed so that the graying roots and reddish length clashed and leapt over and around her head. Her pajamas had not been changed for days and exposed her flesh in an unseemly, embarrassing way. But she, herself, knew none of this, so immured in the first rule was she even now. The rule that posited illness, particularly mental illness, only in others, and those others resided at such a distance as to not be real at all.

We are such a happy family. Even in the darkest days we held together. Laughing and playing as one, dancing as Rose was just now. And she more than anyone knew how much she was loved. In all things we loved her because she was like her name, the most beautiful. The most, the most like we all were, wanted to be, were because she was there with us, is here with us even now.

We are a happy family

We are a family

We are

Chapter 16

One of Mike's old war buddies, Charlie Dent, died. He had moved out to Franklin Square, in Nassau County, which is where the funeral and burial were to be performed. They had kept in touch for a while but that diminished until the last couple of years when there was little more contact than the exchange of Christmas cards. But before he moved he had been a regular at the VFW and was well known to Mike and Jen's group of friends, many of whom were also in attendance.

Charlie had been a drinking buddy, and it shook Mike up when he heard he'd died. Charlie could have had it all, super smart and a job on Wall Street as a trader. But it never stayed good for him for long. He'd be okay for a while and then the drinking would take hold and there would be no end to it. Mike liked him, liked nothing better than to be out carousing with him, but Charlie also scared him; he saw too much of himself in him. Even though they lost touch for the most part, he would hear reports every so often. He bounced from one Wall Street firm to another for a while until no one would take a chance with him. Then Mike heard that his wife had finally had enough and walked out on him with the kids. He eventually lost the house, lost everything really including regular contact with most of his closest friends. His last known address had been some rooming house. Shortly before he died he'd lost one of his legs to drink.

The funeral was a low budget affair but the turn-out was strong. The priest providing the eulogy made vague references to the mistakes Charlie had made in his life but also brought attention to the many in attendance and stated how this attested to the many people Charlie had touched, even as he sometimes did not take the best care of himself. Everyone in attendance addressed his wife, Katie, as if she were the bereaved wife and she appeared willing to play the part, probably even feeling some of what one associates with that role.

There was no meal planned for after the burial and some old and current friends stood around after the casket had been laid in the ground, catching up on what was going on in their lives. An idea was hatched for some of them to meet at an Italian restaurant, Cardo's, which was close to where they were; it had recently reopened after being renovated. Some people were going to go over right away while others needed to go home first. Mike and Jen said they would be bringing their kids along because they were planning to take them out for dinner anyway and had nothing at home for them to eat.

Mike, Jen and their kids rushed to get ready, which in all likelihood made them take longer than normal to get out the door. Mike was probably the biggest impediment to the whole process, fuming and fussing at any delay, no matter how insignificant. The idea that the party had started already without him caused his frustration to ratchet up a notch with every minute that passed, because that was a minute when he would miss out on the fun and drinking.

When they finally arrived at the restaurant, they rushed out of the car and through the front door because their sense of being late and that they might be missing a good joke or two was still the filter of their experience, and the only relief would come when they had joined in on the festivities. But when they hit the inside, that changed immediately. Cardo's was no longer the casual restaurant they remembered. Instead, the owner was shooting for a whole different clientele that did not include them and that they chose not to be included into. The dining area retained its spaciousness but where there had been a friendly expansive atmosphere, now everything was hushed and *close*. The under lit rooms had walls with pastel colored frescoes and murals. Waiters, dressed like penguins, stood observant and silent.

None of this was to Mike's liking and he was not reluctant to show his displeasure. The maitre d' escorted them to their table where they were the last of their group to arrive. Their friends sat at one large, round table, somewhat removed from the main dining area and close to the doors by the kitchen, which the waiters hurled themselves against to pass from one room to the other.

"What happened to this joint?" Mike said as he was getting himself settled. The maitre d' was still in earshot when the comment issued forth, but he chose to ignore it as he would the entire party for as long as possible.

Seated at the table were Frank and Jessie and their good friends Marie and Bert Taglioni. Another three couples were also there, all people that they had a lot of history with. So the festive greeting they received allowed them to quickly dispel the displeasure they had experienced upon entering these surprising and unfamiliar surroundings. Mike and Jen had expected other kids to come along but they found that the other parents had made last minute arrangements that kept those children at home. Tim and Anne were not pleased, but there was nothing to be done about it. Anne remained sullen through the meal and Tim devoted himself to Norma, who was now 3 years-old. She brought along her coloring set and he knew they would wile away their time making marks and coloring on the pad they had brought.

"Hey Mike, did you need a police escort to find your way here?" Bert asked.

This set off peals of laughter from those "in the know", and quizzical expressions from the others. Without needing to be asked, Bert and Marie recounted the tale leading to the faked appendicitis and eventful ride to the VFW post which had happened five years before and had been incorporated into their mythic past. Recalling it established a sense of unity and purpose, which was principally to enjoy themselves and not let anything get in its way. It also started the derisive looks from those around them, the well heeled parties of 2's and 4's, seated at tables many rows deep. Tim became aware of the people around them and their awareness of the party of which he was a part, but he could not put into words the thoughts and feelings this caused him.

Mike could tell he was a couple drinks behind most of the others at the table and wasted no time catching up; Jen worked almost as rigorously in pursuit of the same goal.

The children were all but forgotten by the adults. They were expected to mind their business without being told to do so, even the youngest, and with Tim watching over Norma they pretty much complied with these expectations. But at one point during the meal, one of the men Tim had not met until that day looked over and said to him, "I bet you never knew what a good fighter your dad was in the ring."

This man, George Chapman, was different from the rest at their table. He looked as though he could have easily been sitting with his wife at one of the other tables, quietly enjoy their dinners like the others around them. But he wasn't, and did not seem bothered by his association with this group that continued to get drunker and proportionately louder with time. The amazing thing about George and his wife were that they were sitting here now with the rest of them, recounting their lives with the others at the table as if they were best friends, life long friends. So how could it be that Tim have never met them, never even heard their names mentioned before now.

George began recounting the Golden Glove battles his dad had waged before the war, leading up to the championship at Madison Square Garden.

"I was a camera man back then, Timmy," George said, his face growing beet red from the drink, but also from the strength of the remembrance. "Did a lot of work for the New York State Boxing Association. Your dad, he had one of the best left hooks in the business. Yes sir, one hell of a punch. The more I'd watch him fight the more I became aware of how he would lure his opponent in, waiting for him to drop his right. And then just at the right moment your dad would launch his left like it was coming up through his shoes. Well, at the championship I had a front row seat and I was taking my normal shots but I was waiting for him to let loose with that left. I saw it coming and was in perfect position. What a shot! I knew it was a winner as soon as I clicked it. And the punch did what it was supposed to do. His opponent crumbled to his knees and then was laid flat on the canvas. He didn't move again for a couple of minutes.

"Sad thing was, something happened in the developing of the film. I still don't know what. Maybe I was being too careful. But the pictures never came out, none of them. It still pains me when I think about it. Never had another chance either, with the war starting up soon after... But your old man, he was one hell of a fighter."

What followed was the only quiet space of time that would descend upon the table, as they all mulled over what was just said until the rawness of it's message died away.

"So, does your gang still get together?" Bea, one of the women at the table asked Jen, breaking the silence, "I can remember every

Friday and Saturday night there'd always be something going on with your crowd. You'd be off to someone's house or out to the VFW." She and her husband Kevin had been regulars at the VFW but had moved out onto Long Island when he got a promotion at the insurance company where he worked. She was a fun loving girl who clearly missed those days. Her hair was dyed a whitish color that gave high contrast to the heavy blue eye make up and brilliant red lipstick she had applied. Some would have seen a cheap quality in her but the innocence that still clung to their set was also cast upon her.

"We sure don't get out much," she said and struck an elbow into the soft middle of her husband Kevin. "Not with this lug coming home late every night and wanting nothing but his paper and a beer." Kevin, a good natured giant of a man, took the insult as he did all her insults, with a slow arching shrug of his shoulders.

"No, not really," Jen responded. "We still go down to the VFW on occasion but the parties in the houses are something we've gotten away from." She became lost in thought, as though seeing this change for the first time. "Can't say why exactly." Jen stopped again for a time before continuing. "It's a lot work preparing the food, getting the house cleaned up. It just got to be too much, I guess. We've all got a little extra money, too, most of us. So we'll go out to dinner more now then we ever did back then," she said, trying to present this as a balance to what she had just acknowledged had been lost over some unspecified span of time.

"Those were the best years of our lives. We'll never have fun like that again," Mike said wistfully, with a trace of sorrow in his voice. The sweat dripped off him, which was not uncommon. He would always be wearing just a tee shirt at home, even in the dead of winter. But here that was not an option; and the booze and the large piece of beef he was working his way through contributed to his condition.

Tim had been following the conversation closely and felt as though he had been punched in the stomach when his dad issued this last comment. He was not sure why at first but then realized how unimportant it made him feel he was in his father's eyes. And what he had said was true. He had seen it but never knew what he was looking at. His dad would rather be most anywhere than with his children. He provided for them and did not beat them, and that was good, but he wondered if he gave his father any pleasure of the kind either easily attained or hard fought for.

"Charlie sure looked good, didn't he?" Hank said out of the blue, related to nothing that had come before.

Hank's wife Ellen responded as if on cue, "Oh yes, very natural. Sometimes they don't look anything like themselves. Their faces can be all pulled and drawn and their color not right. But whoever got Charlie prepared, did a real fine job."

Ellen and Hank were good friends of Tim's parents and hearing them say these things was exactly in character, although he was not sure why. They were without malice but there was also little of substance that defined them. What it was they all stood for was something that Tim now searched for in vain.

The conversation picked up and the topic was Charlie and all the highs and lows they had gone through with him. Tim disengaged from the conversation and took in his surroundings. He had never used the word elegant but that was the one that came to him now, an elegance that was distant and that would remain forever apart from him he was sure, as it would for most of the others sitting at the table, those who were not born into it. He looked at the couples dressed smartly, laughing quietly. The only time they would be roused from their private conversation was when they would look towards him and their table when the raucous laughter broke through the enchanted quality of the evening that all the others seemed to share, and when they looked in his direction he turned his gaze away. The hardest thing for him to look out at was the families. They sat eating their meals, laughing politely and speaking to interested participants about topics which Tim would have loved to have known about. These were conversations he wished he could be fluent in but knew, knew with all his heart, he would never be able to engage in. He was there with the others, disconnected but none the less with them, more than he was with his own family and their friends, but he would never really be able to be with these others, not completely. It would be years before he would become acquainted with the term alienation, and decades would pass before he realized how thoroughly it defined the period of his life he was entering into.

Tim looked back at his mother. She seemed to be floating in front of him now. Her blue coat was draped back around her chair and the hat she had worn while walking through the dining room dangled from one of the coat sleeves. It was a woolen cap and had small, flat, plastic spheres attached around it so the light danced off them. She had not taken it off at first when she sat down. It was only after Mike asked her why she was still wearing her hat that she placed her hand upon her head and realized it was up there. They all had a big laugh over this and commented that Jen was up to one of her tricks again.

"And that Charlie sure liked to sing," Uncle Frank spoke up. "Get a few belts in him and he'd let loose with a fine Irish tenor."

Frank had recently joined a Barber Shop Quartet which had become the passion of his life. He was wearing part of one of the outfits that he and the boys sang in. His sports jacket consisted of red and white vertical stripes, his bow tie contained similarly patriotic splashes of red, white and blue.

What happened next took Tim totally by surprise, but not, apparently, anyone else at their table. Uncle Frank stood up and started a chorus of "When Irish Eyes are Smiling". Without skipping a beat, all the other adults at the table joined in. The comfortable quiet in the rest of the hall now became stunned silence. Tim wanted to escape but there was no escape. He no longer looked at anyone but could not erase the derisive looks, the looks of disbelief that would be uniformly cast towards them from throughout the dining hall which now seemed boundless in shape and dimension. If he could have found a way to set fire to the table cloths or curtains with the candles on the tables he would have done so. Out from the corner of his eyes he could see his uncle beckoning to the others throughout the room to join him and their table in song, but, of course, there were no takers.

How was this possible? Tim could not formulate a cohesive thought around what amounted to the competing rights and ethics at work here, but he knew the perspective he was swept into and was associated with was unredemptively wrong. And he knew he would suffer, was suffering, that this memory would be burned into him forever. He wondered if there would ever be a time when it was not all he thought about, wondered if it would ever not cripple him as it was crippling him now.

When the song ended, mercilessly another began. The maitre d', who had stayed on the sidelines with every nerve in his body clenched, moved forward to put an end to the sing-along when the second song began.

The maitre d' spoke with a Greek accent. He was dressed in a tuxedo that conformed perfectly to his trimly contoured body. On top of his head was a rug that gave him the appearance of having a full head of thick, curly hair. But his speech was short and clipped and had none of the smoothness that you would expect from his appearance and position. He projected the sense that he could not tolerate any misadventure, that any misstep in this carefully choreographed tableau would result in him getting his ass kicked by the boss and maybe losing his job.

"Please, please," he said while approaching the table, "we can't have any of this here."

Frank looked at the interlocutor as if he were speaking Greek. They all expressed surprised by this rebuke, but Frank most of all. How could anyone object to song, an offer to share in song?

'You mean you don't want us to sing?" Frank asked incredulously. "That's what we do when we get together."

"Not here," the maitre d' responded, not backing down. "We need to respect the rights of the people coming here to have a nice quiet dinner, those who don't want to be disturbed."

"So we are disturbing your fine patrons," Mike chimed in, entering the fray. And then in a more menacing tone, "Wouldn't want to do that now would we?"

"No sir. We wouldn't. So I must ask you to not start this up again, in consideration of the others around you."

"We used to come in here and sing all the time, before this place got all gussied up. Now I suppose it is too fine for us and our ways," Mike said, still uncertain himself where he wanted to go with this conflict.

"Yes sir. If that is how you look at it, I'm sorry. But I am sure there are many establishments that would not be offended by behavior of this kind... So if you excuse me, I have other business I must attend to."

After he left they all started laughing like children, like they had put one over on someone. They remained unfazed by the ostracism directed at their party by the rest of the diners. The situation was past, as was the possibility for any real confrontation.

"People just don't know how to enjoy themselves anymore," Frank said

"That's so," Mike responded and this conviction was echoed by the others and this shared belief held them strong together.

This would no doubt become another chapter to add to the canon of their combined experience. But Tim realized he would never view it the way that the narrative of the group would mold it. He had stepped outside and doubted he would ever fit properly inside the convention of their experience again. This was the muse guiding their generation and class, and it had served them through the tragedies of the Depression and World War II and so perhaps deserved to not be cast off with indifference. But it was old and increasingly irrelevant, increasingly wrong. They laughed at and were immune to the criticism that the wider world placed upon them because they never cared a great deal for the wider world, as it likewise did not care terribly much for them. But the wider world beckoned Tim. He found he could not delight in their stories, their jokes and bluffs, and their sense of right and wrong any longer.

Chapter 17

Shortly after Tim turned 17 he walked into a photography studio that did business out of a store front on Jamaica Avenue, near to where he lived. The reason for the visit was a "Help Wanted" sign in the window. The photographer was an older man who wanted someone to help out around the office with minor tasks but mostly someone who was available on weekends to help with carting his equipment around to the various functions, mostly weddings and anniversary parties, for which he was hired to take pictures.

Tim and Mr. Mitchell hit it off instantly, although their styles differed in many ways. Mr. Mitchell was a big, gregarious man whose personality accounted for landing a great many of his jobs. He listened intently to the desires and wishes of the people hiring him but once the amount of money to be spent was determined, he plugged the job into a predefined format of pictures that were more or less the same for everyone in the same price range. The wedding shots would invariable include the bride and groom in the back seat of the car looking out the rear window, their first dance, each feeding the other the first pieces of wedding cake, and the like. These were tried and true and rarely brought complaint, although it was doubtful that the subjects saw much of themselves in any of these shots at the time or when they would be reviewed years later. Mr. Mitchell would engage with the party revelers and may even tip a glass or two if asked to do so. But he was always very conscientious and made sure the job got done with a high degree of skill and professionalism.

Within a short amount of time Tim became an able assistant. He quietly observed the process Mr. Mitchell used to select his shots and began to study and become knowledgeable of the technical aspects of photography. When it was time to load everything up for a shoot at a wedding or anniversary party, he never experienced it as routine, but instead enjoyed the excitement and looked forward to the pageantry, the sense that something important was about to take place. It was his opportunity to observe families and groupings of people generally on their best behavior, who had weathered all the storms to get to this point and now would savor the brief period of joyous celebration that they had worked so hard to attain.

Tim continued to work at this job through his last year of high school and also when he started taking courses at a local community college. It was 1967 and there was wide spread discontent on all the campuses in the New York area. Much of what he heard being protested about he agreed with, but he could not relate to the venom, the absolute certainty the protesters felt about every issue their minds jumped to. Learning was also something that took a back seat to over-heated protests. He tried to feel a part of the movement and started seeing a girl who was heavily involved. He tried to adopt her point of view on these related matters but realized there was no future in this relationship for him when she tried to explain to him how privileged he was, as a white male, and that he should be willing to step aside and let others have what was his, particularly in regard to jobs and opportunities. How he had led a privileged life or was expected to give up what he had, or she thought he had, was something that escaped him and he decided to disengage from most of what he saw going on and filter what was being said from a distance.

He stumbled through two semesters of college and then reached a decision that he would stick with the photography. Mr. Mitchell saw that Tim had a future in this business if he wanted it and made an offer to take him on full time and, at some point in the future, possibly sell the business to him. Within a year or two Tim was working his own accounts and developing his own style. He had a special talent for entering a situation and recognizing relationships to take advantage of and those to stay away from, as if he could see lines of energy and the type of charge associated with them. He instinctively trusted his decisions and was seemingly always in the right place at the right time for the picture that called out to be taken.

After he developed the pictures, he would pore over them, engrossed in their placement in the photo album, realizing there was a power in what he was doing if he did his job properly. While he was able to snap the pictures with casual assurance, the final placement was a much more pain staking affair. He would also crop and recrop the pictures, as though accepting the raw material of the pictures' content but never being quite sure of their final alignment. But invariably he came through this difficult decision making process with the right sequence and spacing; the one he arrived at appearing the only one that could have been chosen, different than any before or that which were still to come – so obvious was the choice once it was uncovered.

Business was brisk and getting brisker. Mr Mitchell began receiving calls from clients who were of a *certain quality*, a quality that he had rarely dealt with in the past. And these clients asked specifically for the young man who had done such a marvelous job for Mr. and Mrs. so and so. Mr. Mitchell was not an overly proud man and was given no cause to resent his former apprentice who had quickly eclipsed his own skills. Tim continued to act deferentially towards his boss and seemed scarcely aware of how he had turned the business upside down in a few short years. The jobs that Tim brought in required more and better of everything: cameras, lights, facades. Tim would preview the site where they would be shooting a big event, talk to his patrons, and return with a list of props and equipment he felt he needed.

This was one area where Tim demonstrated a lack of something: maturity, maybe, or sense of reality, of proportion. If there would ever be any friction between Tim and his boss, this is when it would occur. One time he met a young couple whose wedding he was to shoot. Their parents were wealthy but they, themselves, were very much of the time, especially the woman who was about to be wed. She was young, in her early 20s and had innocence and simplicity stamped indelibly on her and was most observable in her red, wavy hair that might have been described as frizzy except that it had a quality of softness that would render this description totally wrong.

The scene was some Bollywood-type reception coliseum. Gargoyles spouted liquid out of every joint and orifice in their morbidly formed bodies. Tim was afraid the heavily framed columns surrounding the building would crush this young couple before they had a chance to begin their lives together.

Tim came back from these investigations to tell Mr. Mitchell that he wanted to purchase several bolts of orange and gold cloth that he would drape all around the reception hall. Numerous small fans would also need to be positioned around the room to enhance the flowing design of the sets. This, he explained, would free the couple's spirit in the midst of so much linear non-movement. Without props such as these Tim feared for the couple, wondering if they would make it to the finish line of their wedding day. This was one of the few cases where Mr Mitchell put his foot down, explaining it was out of the question and that Tim would need to find some other, less costly and intrusive way to protect his charges.

On this day Tim was packing his equipment for another event that he would be shooting. But it was different than any he'd done before because it was an event that his own family was having. His parents were having their 25th wedding anniversary and they had rented a big room in a building intended for catering parties.

Although Tim worked close to his parent's home, he spent relatively little time with them, just as much as would be deemed acceptable to him and them. He was no longer a child but did not know if he had been elevated to the role of drinking buddy, nor was he sure he wanted to be. He explained his lack of involvement with them on his work schedule, which indeed took up most of his time. His busiest time was the weekends and he would spend long hours at the shop during the week as well. He had taken an apartment in Astoria, a section of Queens more built up than where he grew up and about a half hour's drive from his parents' house. The apartment was the upstairs portion of a row house with the landlord living in the bottom section. He had shared it with an acquaintance at first but that did not work out. Even though the rent was steep for him, he preferred having his own place and found some way to make the payments.

He was doing the shoot for free, explaining to his parents that this would be his present to them. They were pleased by this news and thanked him for offering to do this; it was something they would not have done for themselves.

The party was to be held in a banquet hall named The

Community Gardens, near where his parent lived. The VFW hall, that had been what amounted to their spiritual center for most of their adult years, was deemed too drab and shabby for this event. The Community Gardens was also fading in comparison to what it had once been. This was a place with a storied past but was the victim of the neighborhood around it, which was in decline. Even as they tried to maintain the quality of their image and facade, store fronts around them had given way to transient businesses and that was apparent at a glance; the movie house down the street, which had once been a glamorous place, a meeting place, now showed nothing but X rated movies which were announced with lurid titles on the marque preceded and followed by streams of Xs. All the money was moving out of the neighborhood, out towards Long Island mostly; white flight was in full throttle.

The guests arrived and entered the building; the doorman and valet there to greet them, just as they'd always been. People who hadn't seen each other for years embraced and launched into the stories that defined their lives together; none of them having the least problem reestablishing themselves within those memories, and the times when those events took place. Even the children of their best friends and family that Tim had grown up with got into the act and allowed themselves to be swept into the festive mood and spirit of the celebration.

Tim tried to work the crowd as he worked every event he shot. Even more than normal he tried to shield himself with his camera from direct human contact, but he was unable to stop the images he perceived through the view finder from penetrating deeply into him.

He thought he was done with them, had moved beyond them. The prejudice and small mindedness had become the dominant way he perceived his parents and their set and he was determined to chart his his own course and embark in another direction. As he walked around the room, some part of his attention was devoted to his cousins Don and Sara, who said they were coming but had not arrived yet. The chance they would come was slim. They would still get invited to some affairs but then not show up and this became something of a joke to the rest of the family, a joke evoking more pain than laughter. He had all but lost touch with Don over the last several years. Their diminished contact and involvement in each other's lives could be traced to the night he spent visiting Don just before Tim started high school. The time they spent together after that became increasingly uncomfortable for Tim as he realized the paths of their lives were leading in different directions and he suspected that Don was feeling this as well. He felt some guilt for the way their relationship had disintegrated, losing the core value that it had once possessed for both of them.

The images passed before him and he clicked away. The heavily brocaded women wore loose fitting garments that no longer attempted to hide the effects of time and lack of fitness. But they seemed no less fit or energetic as they talked with other women and the men in their small groupings. The men, universally overweight, mixed as well, happy, genuinely happy to be a part of, and caught up in, this event. All had on fine suits and ties, their hair shimmering and whipped into place. Tim spotted his dad with one such group of men. Mike was assuming his boxing stance and was reenacting some feat of his former glory. Tim had seen this little stutter step hundreds of time and he observed it again now. He knew his dad's shoulders were riddled with arthritis and he couldn't really execute the moves that he was approximating now... or could he, he wondered?

Tim caught snippets of the conversation as well, as he passed through the room. Although, these people were not old, most around 50, they were already planning their retirement, their escape. The 20 or 25 years of service required for retirement from government jobs was within reach of most of them and almost all were looking forward to moving to some other locale; many acting as if there was something wrong with you if you were not thinking of moving away. Maybe it was further out on Long Island or for the most adventurous the southwest, Arizona or New Mexico. But the destination of choice, the clear favorite, was Florida. What awaited all these people was unclear but the excitement they expressed at the prospect of moving to the warm south was palpable.

In the midst of his observations, Tim turned and saw that Don and Sara had indeed arrived. They were greeted by Tim's mother, who more than anyone seemed freed from the past misdeeds done to Don and Sara and was able to greet them with nearly unfiltered happiness when they showed up at an event like they were doing now. She gently grabbed one and then the other cousin, placing herself in the middle and entwining one arm with each of them and then spirited them away. Tim could see them laughing, as they strode to another grouping, another introduction or maybe even a reunion of sorts. If he had been more attentive to his task he would have made his way over to them and snapped what would have been a great picture. Instead his mind ran over the catalog of what they might be talking about. But sadly he had no idea what was the source of such mirth.

Don had let his hair grow. It was parted in the middle and fell to both sides of his head and had a loose waviness to it. He had not grown much since his early teens and Tim was several inches taller than him now. But there was a solidity to him that suggested he would be the last object, certainly the last human, standing if a tornado ever swept through. His sister stayed by his side where she seemed most comfortable. Her demeanor was muted, but she seemed happy to be here, shaking peoples' hands and exchanging hugs even though she was, without a doubt, unsure where some of these people fit into her life.

It was some time before Tim and Don made eye contact and it was not until the meal was served that they were able to sit down and talk to each other. They were seated with Sara and Anne and four other people around their age, the early 20s, who were friends of the family.

"So what have you been up to?" Don asked Tim.

"I started working for a photographer in High School and been with him ever since. It's in the old neighborhood. Not far from here on the corner of Jamaica Ave and 212th Street."

"I remember you had that job but didn't realize you'd stayed with it. Always figured you for a college boy but this sounds like a pretty good gig," Don responded.

"I like it okay. We do mostly weddings, anniversaries and family shots. That sort of thing. Have to say that it takes up most of my time. Especially on the weekends."

"That's too bad."

"I suppose. But you get used to it."

"I think it's pretty cool that we have a photographer in the family, though," Don said, with something like pride in the tone of his voice.

Tim thought about how little he expressed concerning his work but was used to holding in what he was feeling, and was therefore hardly aware of any effect caused by not expressing himself to his satisfaction. The fact that Don was appreciative made him feel good though, feel accepted.

"How about you, Don. What have you been up to?"

"Some different things," Don began. "You know I work on cars. Well, a couple of years ago my buddy and I fixed up an old Chevy Nova and drove it out west." Tim thought about the Chevy Nova that Don had coveted all those years ago and wondered how this one compared with that.

"We ended up finding work in a couple of places and stayed out there for the better part of a year. Mostly we hung out around San Francisco. Haight Ashbury... peace and love and all that. It was a hell of a ride and a lot of fun. But it's not all it's cracked up to be and I'm glad to be back home again."

Everyone's ears at the table perked up at the news of his travels and Don became the center of attention. The others at the table peppered him with questions and he was happy to put on display his ample story telling talents. The drinks had been flowing and now he fueled the mystery that the alcohol had provided with tales of the rugged terrain and the treks he had taken across it. But this did not compare with the outlandish characters and lifestyles he'd come in contact with and who peopled his tales.

Only Tim seemed distant, removed from the recounting of Don's exploits. Tim considered how his own life story paled in comparison to his cousin's. Don, perhaps sensing this, tried to bring the conversation back around again in Tim's direction.

"Being on the road is great. But you've got things around here just as great as anything I saw out west. Why, just up the street practically is the Belmont Race Track. Home of one of the Triple Crown races. A national landmark. You go there much, Tim?"

Tim felt blind-sided by this. His only contact with the track was the few times he'd gotten on the bus when Belmont was letting out. Scores of men would be riding, mostly fidgeting around and talking to themselves about the bets that nearly hit big. Other than that he was hardly aware of its existence, never considered spending his time there.

"Actually Don, I've never stepped inside Belmont. Don't even know where the entrance is."

Don showed a mixture of feelings too numerous and intertwined to accurately tally, and it was cause enough to cut through the pleasantries and restraint that had characterized the conversation to this point. They were sitting next to each other and Don wrapped his meaty arm around Tim and with feeling said, "We've got to get you out there. When you have something in your own back yard that the rest of the country talks about and falls over themselves about, you've got to make it part of who you are. It is a part of who you are!"

Tim said nothing. The words had their desired effect though, and he felt as if Don was trying to administer some sort of life saving technique to him. He looked at Don and stammered his response, "Yeah, sure, yeah. I'd like that... We should definitely plan to do that... As soon as possible."

As the meal was finishing Tim got up and began taking pictures of people at all the tables. As he was doing so he found himself lowering the camera and interacting more with those he was photographing than he had before, either at this party or at any party. Instead of merely chronicling the joy of the event, as he was always intent on doing, he pushed himself into the action and tried to be responsible for promoting its life, engendering it. This was the secret that Mr. Mitchell knew: that the finished product is not the only value you provide; there is also the living of the event itself, the giving of oneself to it. And in their own ways this was

Don's secret and his own mother's and father's too, warts and all.

The singing began. Jen's younger brother, Dan, had finally gotten a transfer and was back living among them again. He got the ball rolling as he always did. With his head bobbing and hands clapping to set up the beat, he broke into a chorus of "Fly Me to the Moon". Tim was consumed by the visceral feelings that roared through him every time the singing occurred, regardless of the situation. It spun him to the periphery of the hall and he ended up standing next to a couple of servers, one around his age and the other was about the age of his parents. After a few moments he offered an apology to them and they both looked at him liked he was cracked.

"No need to apologize. This is great. We love to see and hear people enjoying themselves," the older of the two answered, and the younger one readily assented to this point of view.

Tim felt chastened again, and his mind was sent reeling, unable to find stability because he felt as though all the questions of his life were rising up before him. He stood there silently as one song followed another and then sensed Don had come up beside him. They stood that way in silence and when the song ended Don again wrapped his arm around Tim's back and let his hand rest upon Tim's shoulder. After standing this way for a brief span of time Don said,

"Wasn't it great growing up among the old songs."

All the questions that had been buzzing around Tim's head were now obliterated. But it did not leave him as unstable as he had been just moments before.

Tim laughed, realizing that experience was just experience in the flow of experience, and all of it was mutable. Their prejudice was horrible, detestable. And their disregard for others could be offensive, unpardonable. But here they were, singing together, glorifying in the songs. Did they wonder how many more times they would be brought together in this unity, this unity that had been tested and had gotten them through catastrophes as great as any the world had ever served up, and would soon be flinging them in different directions, to the far corners of America. Maybe, maybe not. But there was a profound trust they had in each other, a trust that Tim decided he would honor, as well as he was able.

Made in the USA
Charleston, SC
17 February 2012